ZoD WaLLoP

ZoD WaLLoP

WiLLiaM BRoWNiNG SPeNCeR

St. Martin's Press
New York

This is a work of fiction. Names, characters, places, and incidents either are the product of the author's imagination or are used fictitiously. Any resemblance to events or persons, living or dead, is entirely coincidental.

Design by Junie Lee

Library of Congress Cataloging-in-Publication Data

Spencer, William Browning.
   Zod Wallop / William Browning Spencer.
     p.   cm.
   ISBN 0-312-13629-3
    1. Children's stories—Authorship—Fiction. 2. Authors and readers —Fiction. 3. Books and reading—Fiction. I. Title.
PS3569.P458Z63   1995
813'.54—dc20   95-32433
                                            CIP

First Edition: November 1995

10 9 8 7 6 5 4 3 2 1

This book is dedicated to my sister, Susan,
all the children lost and found,
and the writers of the books that chronicle the
journey.

ZoD WaLLoP

CHaPTeR oNe

❧ ❧ ❧ ❧ ❧ ❧ ❧ ❧ ❧ ❧ ❧ ❧

THE WEDDING WAS held outdoors. An April sky darkened and gusts of wind, like large, unruly hounds, knocked over folding chairs and made off with hats and handkerchiefs. A bright yellow hat went sailing over the lake, cheered on by two small children.

Ada Story said to her husband, "I told Raymond this was not the season for an outdoor wedding."

Her husband, who was watching a black cloud race toward him as though it had singled him out and intended some mischief to his new summer suit, replied: "I don't know how you've lived this long and missed it, Ada. Our Raymond isn't interested in traveling the highway of our advice." Their son did march to his own drum, particularly when he was refusing to take his medication.

Mrs. Story sniffed and lifted her face to the darkening heavens. *I hope they hold off,* she thought.

In case her own mind might misinterpret her thoughts,

she added, *The rain clouds, I mean. I hope the rain holds off.*

All the chairs were filled with the wedding guests now, and there was, really, something exciting in the prospect of so much finery exposed to the elements. The riskiness of life, of all human ventures, was underlined by the first large raindrops and the growl of approaching thunder. The minister's robes billowed in the winds, and the coming storm seemed intent on editing him, first snatching one piece of paper, then another, and launching them into the air. Reverend Gates displayed considerable dexterity as he darted after his text, and the crowd burst into a flurry of applause when he executed a twisting leap and fetched a loose page that seemed already lost to the lake. No outfielder snagging a bleacher-bound fly ball could have displayed greater style, and since the crowd had no way of knowing that the retrieved paper contained a rather tedious rehash of St. Paul's thoughts on duty, their enthusiasm was unrestrained.

The Reverend Gates, having regained command of his notes, was giving them the once-over through gold-rimmed spectacles, when a stirring of voices caused him to look up.

A fat man in a tuxedo, perilously perched on a bicycle and pedaling with frantic enterprise, had crested a green hill and was now racing toward the gathering. His speed was disconcerting, but what truly troubled the Reverend Gates was the man's appearance. He had two heads.

The minister's rational mind harumphed loudly, but as the cyclist drew rapidly nearer, his two-headedness seemed more undeniable.

In the next instant, Reverend Gates realized that he was looking at a man—now so close that his blue eyes and explosion of brown mustache identified him as the groom, Raymond Story—and a monkey. The monkey, a small, soot-black, frightened mammal, was clutching Raymond's neck and chattering wildly in the time-honored tradition of a passenger attempting to exert some control over his destiny.

Raymond Story cycled down the aisle between the folding chairs and stopped. He dismounted, frowned, and approached Reverend Gates.

"I've brought a monkey," Raymond said, in a matter-of-fact tone that the minister found comforting—for no good reason, really. Raymond looked around, turning in a slow circle, and said, "They can't influence a monkey."

The Reverend Gates had known Raymond since the day of Raymond's birth. The reverend was not, therefore, as unsettled as a stranger might have been under similar circumstances.

"Your mother's arranged a lovely ceremony," Reverend Gates said. "All we seem to lack, indeed, is the . . . ah . . . bride." *I'm not,* the reverend thought, *marrying you to any monkey.*

But the monkey was not Raymond's intended. The monkey's role was instantly revealed, as Raymond turned to the animal crouching on his shoulder and said, "Have you got the ring?"

The monkey, grinning as though savoring a bawdy joke, opened a long-fingered hand to reveal a large, ornately engraved ring.

"All right. Hang on to it."

The monkey promptly put the ring in its mouth.

A large white van rose up over the hill and bore down on the crowd. Reverend Gates felt his arm clutched tightly and Raymond's voice boomed in his ear. "Allan has not failed me. We'll want a short ceremony, Reverend."

The van spun sideways and lurched to a stop, revealing a

blue insignia and the words HARWOOD PSYCHIATRIC emblazoned on its side. The vehicle rested placidly on the grass, and then it began to rock, the sliding door slid open, a ramp lowered to the ground, and someone in a wheelchair, flanked by a half dozen milling shapes, emerged.

"My Queen!" Raymond bellowed, causing the reverend to jump. The sky exploded; the world dimmed under sheets of gray, implacable rain. Umbrellas bloomed.

"Oh dear," Ada said, as she huddled under her husband's umbrella. "Wouldn't you know it."

She felt her husband's arm encircle her waist and draw her closer. "It's only weather," he said.

Reverend Gates had ceased congratulating himself on his calm. His own umbrella had been wrenched from his hand by the brutish gale. One of the wedding guests offered him an umbrella. *I'm as wet as I am going to get,* Reverend Gates thought, and he dismissed the offer with a wave of his hand. His notes were a sodden lump. His white hair, generally a fine, regal mist, was plastered to his skull. He wondered if he looked as bad as the monkey, which had been transformed into a sort of gigantic sodden spider.

The reverend leaned forward, clutching his Bible, squinting through the deluge. Dim figures were coming down the aisle between the twin fields of umbrellas. A giant in a billowing raincoat emerged from the shadowy curtain of rain. He was pushing a wheelchair that contained a gray, hooded figure. A lovely girl, barefoot and wearing a white, one-piece bathing suit, walked beside the wheelchair, one hand casually resting on the occupant's cloaked shoulder. She wore a white terry cloth headband into which bright yellow daisies had been tucked. The effect was oddly elegant. She smiled, pushed a strand of black hair from her cheek, and looked up at the minister who, disconcerted by the candor of her gaze, retreated into austerity, motioning them to move forward quickly.

"My beloved approaches," Raymond said. "Like the sun."

Reverend Gates glanced at Raymond, whose round face was slick with rain. Raindrops danced on the young man's rain-glued hair, creating a silver halo. His eyes seemed unusually blue and bright. God, Reverend Gates thought (and not for the first time), had hugged this boy too tightly.

The three approaching figures halted in front of the minister, who was aware that other occupants of the van moved on the periphery of his vision. The minister leaned forward, compelled to touch this extraordinary girl's arm, and said, "My dear—"

Before he could continue, she giggled and said, "Not me, silly. This is Emily's show." The girl patted the bundled figure in the wheelchair, whose head was bobbing rhythmically.

"My beloved," Raymond said, reaching past the minister and pushing the raincoat's hood back. "Emily Engel."

The bride regarded the heavens with her left eye while her right eye studied the minister's forehead. Her face was pale, round, immobile, and oddly flattened, the face of a fat child pressed up against a windowpane. Her hair was a snarl of brown curls and the daisies in it seemed like a cheerful act of vandalism. The bride's head bobbed constantly, her mouth was open, and she was drooling slightly.

The rain seemed to abate, as though pausing with the minister's held breath, and then the storm lost all sense of decorum and roared. An angry sea fell from the sky.

Perhaps it was this urgency of the elements that allowed

the Reverend Gates to perform the ceremony. The drumming deluge did not allow for cool reflection.

They raced through the ritual. "Do you, Emily Engel," the minister intoned, "take this man, Raymond Story, to be . . ."

"Gaaaaaaa," the bride said. Miraculously, the monkey had not swallowed the ring and produced it with a courtly, old-world flourish.

"You may kiss the bride!" the minister shouted through a hole in the thunder, and Raymond reached down, wrested his bride from her wheeled chair, lifted her in his arms, and shouted, "Allan! Behind you! They come!"

The Reverend Gates peered through the writhing sheets of rain. A low, black limousine had pulled sideways to the van and several dark figures in raincoats were emerging. The rain seemed suddenly colder.

"Raymond," the reverend said, "I think—"

"Good friar," Raymond shouted, cradling his bride in his arms, "you've done well. What God has joined no man will sunder."

Two of the men from the limousine had reached the giant and were struggling with him. He hurled one of them into the crowd.

"Oh dear," Ada Story said to her husband. "I guess Raymond and his friends didn't really have permission."

Her husband patted her hand. "Oh, probably not," he said.

The Reverend Gates watched as several more dark figures fell upon the giant, dragging him to the ground. Then the bridesmaid—and the reverend could not help noticing that the rain had invested her bathing suit with translucent properties—shouted a rallying shout that brought her companions pouring from the sidelines.

A brawl, the reverend thought. *I have married a half-wit and a madman and it has ended in a brawl.*

He prayed he had done the right thing.

His prayer was interrupted by the appearance of a large bald man whose raincoat flapped open to reveal a white uniform.

"You ain't been taking your medication," the man said.

The Reverend Gates, momentarily confused—for he did not take medication—was on the point of responding, when he realized that the man was speaking to Raymond.

"You gone right off your head, Ray-boy," the man said. "You tore it this time, and you are going down in the Deep One."

The man brandished a large hypodermic needle.

"Here now!" the reverend shouted.

Raymond Story, clutching his bundled bride, stepped back. "Blackguard," Raymond bellowed, "your master will taste the bitter fruit of our joy this day!"

"Right around the bend," the man shouted, lurching forward. "Right over the hill and into the trees!"

The monkey screamed, leaped through the air, and embraced the bald man's head. The reverend watched as the monkey bit down on the big man's nose. Those large, yellow teeth haunted the minister's dreams for weeks, and it was a great wonder to him how an event occupying no more than a second could etch itself so perfectly on his memory. The reverend's conclusion was that the bald man's scream—a high-pitched, animal howl—worked as a kind of psychic cement, gluing the moment to the faculties of recall.

The big man's arms flailed the air, and the monkey added its own hysterical shrieks to the fray. The man stumbled backward, slipped on the wet grass, and fell, knocking the wheelchair over. The monkey jumped away and raced off toward the trees.

Raymond, clasping his bride in his arms, turned and raced after the monkey. He disappeared into the rain, a great flapping, flamboyant boy who, on his eleventh birthday, had drowned in a swimming pool and whose return to this world was tragically incomplete.

"God bless you!" the Reverend shouted after him. "God bless you Raymond and Emily. God bless the both of you."

The rain held its breath again. Two little girls in matching blue dresses ran after the couple. The girls stopped when it became clear that they would never close the distance. They stood on a green hill, leaping in the air with excitement, giggling and shrieking, and they threw their handfuls of birdseed in the wake of the newlyweds.

CHaPTeR TWo

❖ ❖ ❖ ❖ ❖ ❖ ❖ ❖ ❖ ❖ ❖ ❖

HARRY GAINESBOROUGH WOKE around noon when the phone began to cry. The phone bawled like a hungry baby at midnight. This was only startling to strangers. Three years ago a fan of Harry's children's book, *Bocky and the Moon Weasels*, had sent Harry a telephone with a note that read: "Here is a telephone from the planet Spem." On Spem, a phone is always startled when it is called up, and so bursts into tears. The fan, an engineer, had rigged this phone to do just that, its ring an infant's bellow. Harry had originally been enchanted, had later found it irritating and would, no doubt, have junked it had tragedy not struck and rendered him indifferent to everything.

Harry lifted the receiver. "Yeah?" he said.

"Lord Gainesborough!" the voice shouted. "This is Raymond Story. Don't give up! We are on our way. I've got to free Lord Allan from the dungeon, and that will delay us some, but we are definitely on our way. And have I got a surprise for you. Boy! Uh-oh.''

The phone clicked, the buzz of a dial tone returned, and Harry replaced the receiver.

It began crying again, and Harry snatched it up and shouted, "Keep away from me! I've got a gun!''

A woman's voice said, "Harry?''

"Who's this?''

"This is your agent, Harry. Remember me? Helen Kurtis.''

"Oh. Helen. Hey.''

"Yeah, me. Well, how you doing, Harry?''

"Oh, I'm okay.''

"I bet you are. I bet you are jogging five miles a day and taking vitamins and boffing the college girls down at Elgin's and writing—just writing your ass off up there in the woods.''

Harry didn't say anything.

"Hey, you still on the line?'' Helen hollered. "Look Harry, I'm coming to visit you. I'm taking my life in my hands and driving down to that hell-and-gone briar patch you're holed up in. I should be there tomorrow evening, so look decent. You don't have to dress up, but I don't want you answering the door in your underwear. Let my own example inspire you. I'm an old, fat woman who's going bald and God, for his own good reasons, has given me bad teeth and a spine that's nothing but a rope of pain, but I put on the business suit, the makeup, the perfume—I get up and go out into the shit storm.''

"Maybe you could save all this for when you get here,'' Harry said.

A small, hurt silence, and then: "Sure. Okay. Oh, and Harry?''

"Yeah."

"They want to make a movie of *Zod Wallop.*"

"No."

"We'll talk about it," Helen said. "It doesn't hurt to talk about it. I'll see you." She hung up.

Harry walked outside. He was still in his underwear, but he had a little over a day to get dressed.

The sun-glared surface of the pond made Harry's head ache. He had started drinking again about two months ago, and he hadn't gotten around to stopping yet. If Thoreau had been a drinker, *Walden* would have been a different book. ("Damn birds shrieking like hyenas this morning; I have nailed boards to the windows to keep the sunlight out.")

The phone began crying again, but Harry moved away from it, walked to the edge of the porch, and pressed his face up against the screen. *You old fraud,* he thought. It was a sentence that sailed in and out of his mind and had no precise meaning. It was the sentence of his discontent, his self-disgust.

He had come to this small North Carolina town to teach children's literature at Elgin College, and he had come with some vague notion that it would be a way to re-establish contact with his fellow humans. Lord knows he didn't need the money. Two years after its publication, *Zod Wallop* was still on the *New York Times'* best-seller list, and the other books were doing almost as well.

"Life goes on," Jeanne had said, and Harry agreed with that. Harry hated self-pity. In his book, *The Sneeze That Destroyed New Jersey,* a little boy becomes bloated with self-pity, growing so large that he attracts the attention of aliens who use self-pity to power their spaceships.

Although Harry and Jeanne were no longer married,

they still talked, and he had called her on the first day of classes and said, "I was wrong. They want me to talk about my books, and I can't do that."

"Maybe it will get better," Jeanne said, her voice coming through the wire from upstate New York without much hope that it would, neither of them owning enough of hope to feed a winter sparrow.

Harry said, "I don't even write children's books, Jeanne. You know that."

She said nothing.

"I write Amy books," Harry said. "That's all I write . . . wrote. Amy books."

Harry had stayed at the cabin. He'd already rented it, signed a year's lease. It was as good a place as any.

Harry watched a lizard run quickly across a weathered railing, pause, do a few staccato push-ups like a jogger at a red light, and race on.

Busy, busy, Harry thought. He went back inside and dressed, donning a camouflage T-shirt, baggy gray slacks, and tennis shoes. He sat on his rumpled bed and regarded the room from a visitor's viewpoint. Various slivers of pizza, melting into the wooden floor like irradiated slugs, would have to go. The hordes of empty beer cans would have to be disposed of. The pot of soup that had caught fire and apparently exploded—there should be some sort of warning on really volatile soups—would have to be tossed. There would have to be a general marshaling of renegade laundry. A shorted-out floor lamp that lay on the kitchen table in preparation for surgery would have to be repaired or dumped in a closet.

All that stuff was easy. But what if the room had acquired an inherent lunatic character that mere "straightening up" would fail to address? Would Helen find the bulletin board covered with photos of Amy a bad sign? Perhaps he should take the photos down, or at least the one of Amy in a bathing suit. Would Helen attach some special significance to the bloodstain on the throw rug (which was nothing more dramatic than a fall, a broken glass, a few stitches at the local emergency room)? Would she stare unblinking at the empty shelf and ask, "Where are your books, Harry? Didn't you bring them?"

And would he, Harry Gainesborough, crack like the last witness in an old "Perry Mason" and blurt it out: "All those damned books are at the bottom of the pond! I was drunk, okay? There was a full moon. I rowed out to the middle of the pond and heaved the whole goddamn lot of them over the side, and I was sobbing my eyes out while I did it, like a TV evangelist up on a morals charge. It was just one of those melodramatic gestures drunks make, and I'm going to have my publisher send me copies of all my books again. I'm going to stop drinking. I was just off balance when I got here. I'm all right now."

Harry wanted Helen to approve of his mental health. She was a good friend, but four years ago she had overreacted and single-handedly wrestled him into Harwood Psychiatric. No doubt the experience had been a bracing one and good for him, but he did not wish to repeat it.

Harry slapped his thighs. "Gotta get moving," he said, standing up. He began walking around the room, stooping to pick up vagrant socks and T-shirts.

Harry was unaware that he had just spoken the second

line of his children's book, *Zod Wallop,* a book that the reviewer at the *New York Times* had called an instant classic.

This is how *Zod Wallop* begins:

Rock yawned. "Gotta get moving," Rock said. A couple of hundred million years went by. A rock is always slow to take action. A rock watches an oak grow from a sapling to a towering tree, and it's a flash and a dazzle in the mind of a rock. *What was that?* Rock thinks. Or maybe, *Huh?*

CHaPTeR THRee

THE GIANT'S NAME was Paul Allan but nobody called him Paul, because he did not like the name and would react violently.

"It's your fucking name, you should get used to it," the orderly named Baker told him.

"You should get used to me hitting you," Allan said.

Allan had been in and out of Harwood Psychiatric since he was thirteen. He had a problem with violence. He was now twenty-three years old.

His mother, Mrs. Gabriel Allan-Tate, came to visit him the day after Raymond Story's wedding.

"I'm afraid he can't see visitors right now. He's in the quiet room," the nurse told her.

"You are new here," Mrs. Allan-Tate told the nurse. "No one has told you that I can see my son whenever I wish. The oversight is theirs, not yours. Just get Dr. Lavin on the phone and tell him Gabriel is here to see her son."

"I'm sorry. Dr. Lavin gave specific instructions that he not—"

"Really," Mrs. Allan-Tate said. She grabbed the phone, deftly punched four digits, and waited. She tapped the desktop with a long fingernail while the phone rang. "Theo," she shouted into the receiver, "This is Gabriel. I'm here to see my son. Shake the lead out of your ass and get down here. Yes." She replaced the receiver. Her breathing was labored, and she took an inhaler from her purse and brought it to her lips.

The nurse, who was indeed new, studied this small, elegant woman with the high white forehead and dark, flashing eyes. Mrs. Gabriel Allan-Tate replaced the inhaler, smiled at the girl, and leaned forward. "I'm a rich patron of the mental-health professions," she said, and suddenly she giggled, as a child might, and put a hand to her lips.

Dr. Theodore Lavin came bustling through the swinging doors. He would have had to run to reach the lobby this quickly. He was an overweight, red-faced man, presently wheezing from his exertions.

"Gabriel," he gushed, rushing forward, arms outstretched. "It's so good to see you."

"Don't actually hug me," Mrs. Allan-Tate said, and Harwood Psychiatric's director came to an abrupt halt.

Well, well, the nurse thought, as she watched her boss struggle to regain his composure. The tone of Mrs. Gabriel Allan-Tate's voice suggested that she was every bit as capable of violence as her troubled son.

When the door to her son's room closed behind her, Gabriel Allan-Tate stood in the middle of the room and screamed, throwing her head back and emitting a series of shrieks as though auditioning for a horror film.

She stopped abruptly, smiled demurely at her son who sat on the bed regarding her with a steady gaze, and said, "Excuse me, Allan. But quiet rooms just bring the lunatic out in me."

"That's a pretty good joke," her son said, although he did not smile.

Gabriel Allan-Tate sighed, her shoulders sagged, and she came over and sat beside her son on the bed. He stiffened a little when she patted his knee.

"I don't wish to blame you for this incident, Allan. I wish to file it under high spirits, a lark. I'm told that your companion, this Raymond Story, is a very convincing lunatic. But I believe you could say I have had my fill of your pathological behavior. I will do my duty as a mother, of course, but I will not empathize or attempt to follow whatever convoluted logic you might offer for stealing a van and jeopardizing the lives of your fellow patients. Since your father's death, I don't have the energy I once had, so you will just have to excuse me."

"It would be a waste of time, anyway," Allan said. Allan's voice was flat and seemed to shift around inside his chest, like a bored tour guide in a cathedral. Allan was a half-inch under seven feet tall, and he sat straight-backed on the bed, hands on his knees. He was wearing black jeans and a T-shirt that said THE UNIVERSITY OF LIFE and had a cartoon picture of a tennis-shoed foot about to step on a dog turd.

"A waste of time," his mother said, nodding her head slowly. "I don't know how you can say that. I have found all my dealings with police and mental-health professionals wildly enriching. I have learned such a lot about the ways the human brain malfunctions. And it has been especially enlightening to have strangers tell me that my son's terrible behavior is all my fault. I might have gone through life foolishly assuming that I was a good mother, utterly oblivious to my monstrous nature. I thank God daily for the insight these people—who have never even met me—have so generously offered."

This speech seemed to cheer Gabriel up, and she leaned forward and kissed her son on the cheek.

Her voice turned gratingly bright. "Where is your friend? Where is little Raymond?"

Allan shook his head from side to side.

His mother stood up. She touched the back of her son's neck, and his eyes widened, as though her finger were the cold muzzle of a gun.

Gabriel continued, "Dr. Lavin is afraid this Raymond Story will do himself harm if he isn't found. And that poor, helpless girl. My God, my stomach turns when I think of her fate. The minister who participated in that travesty of a wedding should be—what's the word?—disbarred, excommunicated, something. Do you suppose this Story will attempt sexual intercourse with that poor, crippled, mindless child? There are limits to where my imagination will go, and I draw the line there. But it is hard not to think—"

Her son interrupted. "Mother," he said, "it's not like that at all. You've got it all wrong."

"I'm sure I do," she said. "Just tell me where they are, Allan, and Dr. Lavin can bring them back here, and they can explain everything."

"I can't do that," Allan said.

"Why not?"

"They'll kill her," Allan said, lowering his voice.

Without another word, Mrs. Gabriel Allan-Tate walked to the door. Standing on tiptoe, she knocked on the small, wire mesh window, waited, and, when the door was opened, turned back to her son.

"Allan," she said, "I told you I was not listening to crazy talk, and I am not. I will visit again when you are more lucid. I might remind you that the only one I know who wants to kill anyone is you. I am sorry to have to be so confrontational, but I want you to reflect on that. It is your own violence that you fear. Dr. Lavin suggested I never bring the subject up, but I am convinced he is wrong. You need an awakening. I suggest you stop worrying about your precious friends and concentrate on your own problems. I suggest you think about how you tried to kill me, your own mother. Twice you tried to kill me, Allan. That's what you should be thinking about."

And she left before he could reply, although he had no intention of replying.

And what, he wondered, *did she mean by twice?* He had tried to kill her once, yes, and he regretted that, was sincerely sorry because he *did* love her—every bit as much as he hated her. But *twice?*

Allan closed his eyes tight and thought. It came to him immediately. How could he forget? She talked about it all the time. He had tried to kill her when he was born.

Later that afternoon, the orderly named Baker unlocked the door to the quiet room.

"Hey asshole," Baker hollered, "Time to stop counting your farts, time to move!" Baker's bandaged nose gave his voice a muffled-megaphone quality that Allan found comic.

Allan smiled. "You got sinus problems?" he asked.

"Your pal Ray-boy is gonna have finding-his-balls problems," Baker said. There were dark circles under Baker's eyes, which contributed to the gloomy-clown look.

Back in his room, Allan lay on his bed and studied the ceiling. He remembered that he was in love, and he got up and went into the dayroom to see if he could find her. Hank and Jason, both of whom had been on the van when Allan commandeered it and drove it to the wedding, waved to Allan from the sofa. They were holding hands—furtively, since such displays of affection were frowned on by the staff and could result in the instant revoking of privileges like television watching.

Hank and Jason weren't queer—that had been Allan's first thought—they were just dim-witted and fond of each other. Hank had small, raisinlike eyes in a round face, and when he laughed his body got away from him, arms flapped, his shoulders jumped, his nose was inclined to run. Jason was a thin, acne-scarred boy who didn't talk much. His pants were always sliding down so that you could see the crack in his ass, and when he did talk he'd say things like "Have a good day," or "Fine, thanks," kind of nothing sentences, other people's cast-off words that he'd picked up.

Allan waved back at them. Rene wasn't in the room, so Allan walked back down the hall and pushed the door open on the courtyard, and walked out into the late afternoon sunlight and Rene was sitting there, next to the stone gargoyle, on the edge of the goldfish pond. Yesterday's bathing suit was replaced by pale blue overalls and a yellow tank top.

She looked like she had swallowed the sun, and now light was pouring out of her skin. Most of the trees in the courtyard were leaning toward her.

Allan felt dizzy and oddly angry, which always confused

him. He didn't want to hurt Rene, but sometimes it seemed that the thing he hated hid inside her.

She looked at him and smiled and waved a hand that held a cigarette. He didn't smile back, but he walked over to her and said, "Hi, Rene."

"No," she said, "I'm not high. This is just a regular cigarette." She laughed. Allan thought of reaching out and touching the tattoo on her upper right arm. It was a red and blue tattoo of a rainbow in the clouds and when he'd asked about it, she'd said, "Cause of my name." He'd felt stupid because he didn't get it. "Gold," she had said. "You know, Rene *Gold.*" And she could tell he still didn't get it so she had said, "Like the pot of *gold* at the end of the rainbow," stretching the word *gold* out. Allan had nodded then.

She was smiling today, her mouth displaying small, white perfect teeth. She leaned forward and touched Allan's arm. She grew serious.

"I saw a Ralewing last night," she said.

Allan stared back at her, not saying anything. His heart was beating fast.

"I woke up and there it was, on the ceiling," Rene said. "At first I thought it was a shadow, but then it started flying around the room, real slow, and I could see two little pins of red light—those were its eyes—and I got scared. I thought it would land on my face." She stopped speaking, her eyes wide.

Allan didn't like to think of waking in the night with a Ralewing in his room. A Ralewing looked a little like a sting ray, except that it had a head like a snake on a long stalked appendage and could travel the air as easily as it traveled the underground waters of Mal Ganvern. Ralewings ate the faces from people, stole infants, and vomited a volatile fluid that burst into flames. Ralewings were the creatures of Lord Draining, king of the Less-Than.

All this Allan knew from having read *Zod Wallop* every night since Raymond Story had given him the book, but he knew something else, knew it because Raymond had told him. He knew what the Ralewing was looking for. It was looking for the author of *Zod Wallop;* it was looking for Harry Gainesborough, who, Raymond said, had tried to hide in Harwood Psychiatric four years ago but had been discovered by the powers that wanted to destroy him and had fled.

Rene was squeezing Allan's arm. "It finally went away. It slid under the door, like smoke. But I couldn't go back to sleep. I had to pee, but I couldn't even get out of bed."

"It's okay," Allan said. "Raymond is going to come and get us."

"He better hurry," Rene said. "Before I woke and saw the Ralewing, I was dreaming. I dreamed that the Cold One was coming."

"Don't even think about it," Allan told her. "It won't happen." The Cold One was one of the end-of-the-world creatures created when the two Vile Contenders clashed at the Ocean of Responsibility.

"Sure, just pretend it away," Rene said. "That's what everybody does. Until it's too late."

"It won't be too late," Allan said. "Don't worry."

But Allan was worried.

Dinner was announced, and they marched down to the cafeteria where they were fed gravy-flavored sponges that were supposed to be Salisbury steaks. After dinner, Allan went to his room. He took *Zod Wallop* from under his mattress and studied the cover. The man who had written the book had also painted the pictures. The cover was a painting of a vast mountain range, shrouded in clouds. The sky was green. A long, pale yellow ribbon of road ran across a deserted plain. In the foreground, occupying the lower third of the painting, a single figure, a little girl, faced the mountains. Only the back of her head and shoulders were visible. Her hair was brown, long and gleaming, as though it had been washed and combed for hours. There was a red bow in her hair, near her left ear. She held a doll, which peered over her shoulder, smiling at the reader. The painting looked like a luminous photograph, and the doll's blind gaze was unsettling. The doll appeared to be made out of granite that was cracking. The doll was a cherubic male infant, smiling sweetly. But one of the eyes was shattered, and a blotch of pale green lichen bloomed on the doll's cheek. The doll's small fist clutched a withered rose.

Allan intended to read a few pages. The book frightened him, but Raymond said it was important to know the story by heart, to be prepared, and so Allan tried to read it, skipping only those parts that were just too awful—like when Henry Bottle fights the Midnight Machine—but the minute he lay back against the pillow, he fell asleep. He slept on his back, clutching *Zod Wallop,* and he awoke with a sense that the book had grown oddly heavy, making it difficult to breathe.

Allan opened his eyes to stare directly into another pair of eyes, and the effect was unpleasant, like waking to find you are on the edge of a cliff, although here, instead of falling into space, one might topple into another person's consciousness and be lost.

Allan did not panic, however, for he instantly recognized an unmistakable odor of wet hair and rotted fruit that belonged to Arbus. If you fell into Arbus's consciousness, you could climb out easily enough. Lord Arbus was Raymond's monkey.

"Arbus," Allan said. "What are you doing here?" Allan reached over to the nightstand and turned the lamp on. He saw that the door to his room was open. "Is Raymond here?" he asked.

The monkey grinned and offered Allan a crumpled ball of paper. Allan smoothed the piece of paper on his knee. It was a single sheet of ruled paper, the sort of off-white, porous stuff upon which schoolkids laboriously practice block letters.

A more studied hand had employed this piece of paper to write: "Lord Allan—Upon reading this piece of paper, find Lady Rene Gold and hasten to the courtyard where means of escape await you. Bring the book with you. And may Blodkin smile upon this enterprise. R."

Allan dressed quickly, started to leave the room, remembered the book and retrieved it. He stuffed it down the back of his pants and left the room.

In the hall, Arbus uttered a small, high-pitched trill, no doubt inspired by nervousness, and Allan put a finger to his lips and said, "Shhhhhhhhhhsh."

When Allan tapped softly on Rene's door, she opened it immediately, causing Allan to jump back and eliciting a small squeak from Arbus.

"Arbus. Allan." Rene said. She was still dressed in the overalls and yellow tank top, and she held a blue backpack in her left hand.

"I'm ready," she said, slipping out into the hall and pulling her door closed behind her.

Allan would have liked to ask her how she had known to be ready and for what, but he decided to save the questions for later.

They crept down the hall and into the courtyard.

Harwood Psychiatric was not a high-security institution. It was an expensive, private asylum, and most of those within its walls had no intention of fleeing. This was their refuge, in fact, from the larger, hostile world. But in recent years, a growing adolescent population had required Harwood to acknowledge some security measures. Young men and women had been placed in Harwood by exasperated parents, and these kids were inclined to bolt if the opportunity presented itself. So Harwood had acquired additional security guards, electronically locked doors, and the gray walls surrounding the courtyard had been raised. Those trees abutting the walls had been removed.

A full moon hovered overhead, so bright that the grass looked as though it had been spray-painted silver. Arbus darted across the grass, past the gurgling fountain, and Allan and Rene followed.

"All right!" Rene said. "All right, Raymond!"

Allan and Rene watched Arbus scramble up a swinging ladder made of rope and wooden slats. The monkey reached the top and turned, squatting on the wall. It spread its arms and grinned, as though expecting applause.

"You first," Allan said, but he needn't have bothered. Rene had slipped the backpack on and was briskly negotiating the ladder, an athletic girl whose retreating buttocks, despite being shrouded in shapeless overalls, filled Allan's heart with the full meaning and exhilaration of the word *escape.*

A voice behind Allan shouted, "Stop!"

Allan saw Baker running across the grass. Allan turned,

grabbed the first rung of the dancing ladder, and hauled himself up.

Negotiating the ladder was a shaky business. Rungs were not necessarily where feet could find them, but Allan floundered his way to the top and prepared to haul himself up when a hand suddenly hooked his foot.

Allan looked down to see the orderly, whose bandaged face was sweaty with determination. Allan kicked out, but in so doing lost his balance and leaned back into the terrible hollow of empty space, the moon falling toward him, his ears filling with his own shout of terror.

Allan hit the ground on his back, a whump of suddenness as though a circuit had been banged shut on the engines of gravity. He couldn't move.

He saw Baker towering over him. The orderly was grinning, arms folded across his chest. His bandaged nose lent an outlaw aspect to his demeanor. He was saying something, but Allan couldn't make it out.

And then, a trick of the shadows, Allan saw a yellow toothy smile floating in the dark foliage of the tree behind Baker, saw the smile drift forward, as though propelled by a gentle breeze, and saw the simian features of Arbus take shape behind the large, piano-key grin.

Baker must have sensed the approach of those teeth. Perhaps his nose signaled some telepathic warning to his brain. Whatever. It was too late. He began to turn just as Arbus craned forward, hooted mightily, and struck.

Baker screamed, and Allan, in the one brief instant before he rolled over, righted himself, and scrambled up the ladder and over the wall, saw Baker execute a rapid pirouette that spun the monkey from him and removed, in accordance with the laws of physics, a substantial portion of his ear.

Raymond was waiting for Allan on the other side and hugged him.

"Lord Allan," Raymond said. "I trust you are unharmed."

Arbus, also unharmed, leapt from the top of the wall to join them.

"We had best be on our way," Raymond said.

Allan followed Raymond to the car, where Emily and Rene awaited them.

It was only after they were out on the interstate, the night air dispelling confusion, that Allan realized, with a start of dismay, that he had lost the book. It must have been jolted out of his pants when he fell.

"I've lost *Zod Wallop!*" Allan blurted, and Raymond, who had been concentrating on his driving (with the assistance of Arbus who perched on his shoulder) involuntarily swerved, eliciting a horn blast from a car in the neighboring lane.

No one said anything for some time, and then Raymond, his voice devoid of its usual enthusiasm, said, "Bad luck, Allan. I think we'd better drive straight through."

The car accelerated, bound southward into the night. It flew by diesel trucks outlined in points of light, and Emily Engel, Raymond's new bride, slipped down in her seat and tilted sideways. "Heeeeeg," she said, announcing her displeasure, and Rene leaned over from the backseat and tugged Emily back into a sitting position.

"Hey Emily," Rene said.

"Faaaaaaaa," Emily said.

CHaPTeR FouR

꙳ ꙳ ꙳ ꙳ ꙳ ꙳ ꙳ ꙳ ꙳ ꙳ ꙳ ꙳

"I DON'T KNOW," Helen said. "I am basically a city person."

Harry offered her his hand. "Come on. Nothing to it."

Harry helped his agent into the boat. "Sit there," he said. "Okay, we are off."

Helen Kurtis, a woman known in Manhattan for the ferocity of her demeanor, a woman who might have inspired the oft-quoted analogy that an agent is to a publisher as a knife is to a throat—Helen Kurtis was remarkably subdued as she perched on the rowboat's plank seat. Her imposing bulk, generally swathed in primary colors and garnished with gold belts, earrings, and bracelets, was housed in khaki slacks, a green, short-sleeve blouse obscured by an orange life jacket, and a large straw hat. Yellow-framed sunglasses completed her costume.

"Everybody should go fishing at least once," Harry said. "It would be wrong to let the opportunity pass. You've come all this way to visit me. What kind of a host would I be if I didn't make an attempt to fill this gap in your education?"

"You have a mean streak that I was unaware of, Harry Gainesborough," Helen said. She looked around her as Harry rowed out to the middle of the pond.

"If I were really cruel, I'd let you hook your own earthworms. I'm taking into account your delicate feminine sensibilities." It was almost noon, and the sun had boiled the color from the sky. Dragonflies zigzagged over the brown palm of water.

Harry stopped rowing and tossed the anchor overboard. He dug a worm out of the coffee can and expertly threaded it on the hook. He stood up and cast into the water. The bobber landed with a soft splash, and he handed the rod to Helen. "You keep your eye on the bobber," he said. "It goes under, you yank."

"All right." Helen Kurtis held the fishing rod as though it were a broom, and Harry suspected that she was indifferent to his instructions, did not, indeed, wish to snare any fish.

Proof of this was immediately furnished. She leaned forward and began talking about the proposed Hollywood deal for *Zod Wallop*.

"The option is very generous, and that's money you can just walk away with. Most options come to nothing, you know. You'd still have the money. Also, they are willing to give you a percentage of gross—we are not talking monkey points here. That's rare. They just don't give that to a writer."

Harry let her talk. He knew there was no sense in trying to interrupt her. She was forgetting she was on a boat now; she was in her element, the country of the deal.

Harry smiled. He was glad she had come. He had forgotten how much he missed her. She'd arrived late the night before, laden with groceries, and smoked the better part of a pack of cigarettes while bustling around his kitchen preparing an omelette. "I'm the host here," he had protested, and she had responded, "Well, you can't cook, and I'm hungry so I guess you'll have to confine your hosting to good conversation." She had watched him drink a beer with a narrowing of eye and a stiffening of her square jaw, but she had said nothing.

Harry had managed to clean up before she came. He had taken the photos of Amy down but then, defiantly and at the last minute, he had put them back up—minus the bathing suit picture (his courage had failed there). Helen hadn't said anything about the pictures, although she had seen them, of course. She didn't miss much.

In the morning, Harry had driven her into town and they had eaten breakfast at Kenny's Kitchen. Helen had enjoyed the experience immensely, but Harry had found her enjoyment annoying, containing, as it did, a lot of civilized eyebrow raising and commentary. "I've heard of grits," she had said, playing with her food. "I shouldn't be surprised if they are a great aid to digestion."

Back at the cabin, the phone had cried, and Harry had answered it, recognized the voice of Raymond Story on the other end, and hung up immediately.

"Who was that?" Helen had asked.

"That was Raymond Story," Harry said. "He is a young man who suffers from schizophrenia, but before you offer any sympathy, let me add that he is an extremely irritating and offensive human being, mentally ill or not. Dr. Moore told me that it is not uncommon for schizophrenics to create elaborate scenarios, and unfortunately Story's scenario includes me. In a way, dear Helen, you are responsible. I met Story while at Harwood. He sees, in the drowning of my daughter and in his own near drowning when he was a child, some sort of bond. It's unpleasantly weird, and has to do with *Zod Wallop* which he seems incapable of regarding as fiction. Anyway, let's not talk about it."

Helen frowned. "Is he dangerous?"

"Oh, he's completely harmless. He's just a nuisance." Harry frowned. "A very resourceful nuisance. I have no idea how he managed to get my phone number."

To escape another telephone call, Harry had decided to take Helen fishing. Ostensibly, that is what they were now doing, although when Helen's bobber suddenly submerged in the middle of her lengthy discussion of film contracts, she reacted by throwing the fishing rod overboard.

The next half hour was spent in rowing after the bobber, which occasionally surfaced. Harry finally snatched the bobber out of the water along with a three-inch bluegill. The fish was released, and, by reeling the line hand over hand, the fishing rod, filmed with black muck, was retrieved.

"So this is fishing," Helen said.

Harry glared at her. "No, this is not fishing. And no, *Zod Wallop* is not for sale to Hollywood. I'll tell you something, Helen. I regret publishing *Zod Wallop*. That book's a zombie. Or at least it's a lie. I shouldn't have done it."

"It's a beautiful book," Helen said.

"And that's the lie." Harry said. "I had no business turning it into a beautiful book."

Helen took her sunglasses off and studied Harry.

"Harry," she said, "I know that Amy's death shattered your life. I know that. I've never had children, so I won't try to imagine the extent of your loss. I was married to the same man for forty-two years, and when Abe died, I didn't know how I was going to go on. You remember how it was. I'd call you up, and I couldn't remember why I'd called."

Harry nodded. Abe Kurtis had been a bright-eyed, stocky little man who had worshiped his wife and when he died of a heart attack, suddenly and with no prior history, Helen had been devastated.

Helen said, "I kept on going to the office. I had this feeling that my clients, their lives, their well-being, shouldn't have to suffer in this tragedy. I was going to protect them. So work, I guess, is what got me through that time. It helped me avoid self-pity."

"Well—" Harry began.

Helen reached out and touched his knee, silencing him. "You've written seven children's books, every one of them better than the last. *Zod Wallop* is some sort of gift the muse gave you, Harry. It's a kind of wonderful, extraordinary act of grace. It may be a painful book, personally. But it is a great book, and you should accept that—with pride and humility. Maybe I should emphasize the humility. Ask yourself: *Why me? Why was I given this gift?*"

Helen hurriedly put her sunglasses back on, hunted up her cigarettes, tapped one out of the pack, and lit it. She blew smoke at Harry. "You there?"

Harry's voice came from a distance, traveled all the way from Dr. Moore's office at Harwood Psychiatric. Harry said, "I never told you this, Helen, but when I first wrote *Zod Wallop,* the Less-Than triumphed. The Midnight Machine killed Henry Bottle. Lydia died too—when the River of Stone flooded the castle."

Helen Kurtis found that her mouth was open. She closed it and smoke drifted from her nostrils.

Harry Gainesborough sat in Dr. Moore's office. Dr. Moore looked like a kindly farmer, silver hair falling across his forehead, gray eyes squinted from a long assessment of droughts and floods. He folded his hands and gave Harry a long look. "I know. I know what I'm asking."

"I don't think you do, Doctor. I am not about to write any more children's books. It's not what I would call therapy. Splinters under my fingernails would be more profitable. I wrote those books to make Amy laugh . . . " Here his voice broke. Damn it! He stopped, collected himself, continued: "Look Doctor, your suggestion that I 'get on with my work,' might make sense if I were a carpenter or a doctor or something, but I'm not. Don't give me that crap about not wasting a gift. I don't want to make other people's children laugh. I resent those other children's lives, frankly." Harry paused. "That's a little strong, isn't it?" He sat in silence. Finally he said, "But that's about the size of it. I think about it, and it's ugly but true. Let the little bastards get their sweetness and light elsewhere."

Dr. Moore nodded slowly. "Exactly my thought," he said. "I wasn't asking you to write a happy-ever-after fable. But you are an artist, Harry, and art might still be your salvation. Write something dark, if that's what's required. Don't worry about what is expected of you. Don't look over your shoulder. Don't bother being a good boy. Get it out. Purge yourself through your gifts, your paintings, your writing. Kill all the children, if you must."

"Kill all the children," Harry said.

"What's that?" Helen said.

"Sorry," Harry said. "I've been out in the sun too long today. I'm sorry, Helen. Unless you are determined to catch some fish, I say we retreat to air-conditioning and iced tea. What do you say?"

Helen smiled. "Oh, you know how I live to fish. But you could twist my arm."

Harry rowed back to the dock and helped Helen out of the boat.

"That was fun, right?" Harry said.

Helen was looking past Harry. "Looks like you have company."

Harry turned, and they both watched a large brown car rattle its way up the dirt road. The car was moving fast, churning clouds of dust, fishtailing as it negotiated the curves.

The car stopped in front of the cabin, the back door on the passenger side banged open, and a pretty girl in blue overalls stepped out.

"Who's that?" Helen asked.

"No one I know," Harry said.

The driver's side door opened, and a large rumpled figure appeared.

"I know that one," Harry said, his voice grim. "That's the lunatic I was telling you about."

CHaPTeR FiVe

❧ ❧ ❧ ❧ ❧ ❧ ❧ ❧ ❧ ❧ ❧ ❧ ❧

HARRY FOUND HIMSELF being embraced before he could prevent it.

"Thank God we are not too late!" Raymond shouted.

"Let go of me!" Harry shouted back.

Raymond instantly dropped his arms and fell to his knees. He stared at the ground. "I'm sorry, I'm sorry, I'm sorry," he muttered. "I forgot my place."

"Does Dr. Moore know you are here?" Harry asked. Harry's first thought—presciently accurate—was that Raymond and his companions had escaped from the institution.

Raymond looked up. "Dr. Moore's dead, my Lord. They say it was cancer, but they could say anything, of course."

"Dead?" Harry said. "That can't be, Raymond. I only talked to him—" *God*, thought Harry, *it's been two years at least since that last time.*

Raymond Story stood up, brushed dirt from his knees,

and smiled. "I've brought a few good men—well, and women—and a monkey. We are a small band, but I don't think you can fault our loyalty."

"Raymond," Harry said, "you've stopped taking your medication, haven't you?"

Raymond pointed to a large young man who slouched against the car's fender. "That's Lord Allan. You won't find a more stalwart lad in the kingdom. And next to him is Lady Rene Gold. Do not be fooled by the softness of her demeanor; she is a warrior with a fierce, proud heart. The monkey is named Arbus, of course."

"Of course," Harry said. Any monkey Raymond owned would have to be named Arbus after the one in *Zod Wallop*.

The massive young man leaning against the car folded his arms and glared at Harry. He was handsome, with dark black hair and eyes, but the planes of his face seemed sculpted by some reckless, troubled artist. His eyebrows ran along a ridge of bone that kept his eyes in shadow. Harry realized that he had seen this young man at Harwood, although they had never been in group together. A violent young man, Harry remembered, always being reprimanded for some altercation with another patient.

The girl next to the young man was undeniably lovely, and when she smiled and waved at Harry, he found himself smiling back, despite his resolve to get rid of Raymond and his companions as quickly as possible. And Harry seemed to recall her, too, and even remembered that she was the subject of a number of ardent love poems penned by Harwood's young male contingent—and at least one suicide note (whose author decided to eat a quart of ice cream in lieu of killing himself).

"—my bride!" Raymond was saying. "I want you to meet my bride."

Raymond Story, in his manic phase, was a compelling personality, and Harry found himself led to the car's passenger side. At Raymond's urging, Harry peered into the car's window.

"Emily, my love," Raymond said, "Meet Lord Gainesborough."

The girl had slid down flat on the seat, her face pressed against the seat's back. Her features were distorted, the right eye squeezed shut. By tilting his head slightly, Harry made out a china-doll face, oddly smoothed and abstract. The girl's mouth was open, and the only sign of life was the slight trembling motion of a pink tongue.

"Ah, hello," Harry said.

The girl did not respond.

"She's beautiful, isn't she?" Raymond said.

Harry was unable to speak.

"You recognize her, of course," Raymond said.

"No, Raymond." He really couldn't recall her from Harwood, although she might have been there, one of the muffled wheelchair crowd in the rec room.

"She's the Frozen Princess!" Raymond shouted. He clutched Harry's shoulder. "Emily is the Frozen Princess, of course! I knew that the minute I saw her. And I've married her, my Lord! You know what this means, of course. It means it's all beginning now. The die is cast. There's no turning back. Oh, and bad news. We've lost the Dark Book. I'm afraid there's a very good chance our enemies are in possession of it. We'll have to move fast."

* * *

Harry, feeling that events might get away from him if he did not act decisively and soon, turned to see his agent approaching him. She was holding the monkey in her arms and smiling.

"Isn't he dear?" she said.

"Helen," Harry said, "Don't encourage these people."

"That's Arbus," Raymond said. "Don't worry, he's very sweet-tempered." Raymond turned back to Harry. "Arbus's had a rough life. Chained for two years next to a sullen cockatoo in a dirty little pet store. I only recently bought him out of bondage, and his gratitude has been touching. He has a hatred of jailers though, I can tell you that."

Harry interrupted, putting a hand on Raymond's shoulder.

"Raymond," Harry said. "I'm going to call your mother."

Raymond took a step backward and narrowed his eyes. "That's not a good idea," he said.

"I'm sure she's worried about you," Harry said.

"That can't be helped. Her worrying is part of the natural order. We have very little time, my Lord, and my mother, whose claim on my heart is absolute, devours time. We do not have the leisure to consult her."

"Nonetheless," said Harry, who remembered Ada Story favorably from his Harwood experience, "your mother deserves to know where you are. I think we can spare her a phone call. What is that number?"

Raymond shook his head and stared at his feet. "No," he said. "It's out of the question."

"Raymond," Harry said, "I *order* you to give me that number."

Raymond shuddered and pressed the palms of his hands

flat against his thighs. He mumbled the telephone number and Harry made him repeat it.

"Thank you, Raymond," Harry said.

Ada Story and her husband were watching television when the call came. Ada always felt guilty when watching television, for it was a pastime denied her when her son was living at home. Raymond hated television and said that it made a person's soul thinner. The doctors had advised Ada not to indulge her son's delusions, but then, the doctors did not live with Raymond. His delusions were powerful. How powerful, the doctors would never know.

She would be watching television and Raymond would come into the room. The moment he saw the television, he would lurch backward as though struck by an invisible fist. He would stumble like an extra in a cheap zombie film, drop his vast bulk onto the couch, roll his eyes, gag. All the color would go out of his face. Once, spectacularly, he had sneezed blood.

Television had become, for Ada Story, a furtive vice, and she felt a guilty inevitability when the phone call proved to be about her son.

"Oh yes, of course I remember you," she said. How could she forget Harry Gainesborough and that book he had written? She even had, well, a sort of artifact. . . .

He was a nice man, Harry Gainesborough, but sad and remote, insulated in his politeness, like someone with a terminal illness, someone whose attention was elsewhere.

"Your son is here," Harry was saying. *Where was here?* She meant to ask, but heard herself ask instead: "Are you all right?" He was such a sad man.

"I'm fine. It's your son I'm worried about. He and some of his friends have shown up on my doorstep. He says he is married."

"He is."

"Oh? Well. In any event, he appears to be in an excited condition—rather like the time he set the Christmas tree on fire at Harwood, and well, let's just say I'm not a professional, and I think what is wanted here is a professional."

"Oh, dear," Ada said. "Where are you?"

Harry began to tell her.

"North Carolina," Ada said. "Wait. I'm no good at out-of-state directions. I'm only for local. John does all the out-of-state. Wait. John! Come here, John. I'm putting my husband on the line, Mr. Gainesborough."

John Story took the phone. "All right," he said. "Give me the coordinates, and we'll fetch the boy."

After the phone call, Harry sat in the chair looking out the window. Dusk had arrived, the sky was luminous, like light behind smoked glass. A net of fireflies blinked in the tree branches. Harry could see Raymond, flanked by the pretty girl and the giant. Raymond was pointing at the fireflies.

Harry turned to his agent. "See that?" he said.

She looked out the window.

"Raymond is telling his friends that the fireflies are the Ember People," Harry said. Harry felt very tired.

Helen put her hand on Harry's shoulder and said, "Every time a boy and girl exchange their first breathless kiss, an Ember child comes into being in a burst of light."

"Yep," Harry said. "The Ember People. It is in their interest, as a race, to encourage human love. A whole tribe of cupids. In the original story, their fate was just a little different. An Ember child would burst into flame when a human boy and girl kissed for the first time. Human passion murdered the Ember folk. Quite a different perspective, wouldn't you say?"

"What became of that first *Zod Wallop?*"

"Raymond burned it."

Harry and Helen stared out the window, watching Raymond Story's arms stretch toward the heavens, encompassing the world of wonder and fantastic portents.

"It looks like we are stuck with them for the night," Harry said. "Raymond's parents will be here in the morning. I've got a couple of sleeping bags around here somewhere."

"He seems a sweet boy, actually," Helen said.

"You should spend a few months in a mental hospital with him," Harry said. "Craziness, up close, can get old pretty quick. It was a little like having a talking shadow. He'd read all my books, and I was his hero. When he learned I was writing another book, he couldn't wait to see it. I told him no. I was writing my black, venomous book. I wasn't about to let anyone see it. Raymond stole it, read it, burned it. He talked about it in group therapy. I didn't even know the book was missing; I'd put it in a dresser drawer. And here's Raymond, in group, and I'm only half listening because I've heard his crazy rants often enough, and I hear *Zod Wallop Zod Wallop* and I click into focus and there's Raymond going on about the River of Stone and how it's got to be stopped and how Lydia doesn't die, how that's a terrible lie.

"He looked right at me then. He'd been crying; his cheeks were wet with tears and his eyes were red. He smiled at me and he said, 'It's gone; I burned it.' And I ran out of the room with Dr. Moore shouting behind me, and I ran down the hall to my room and yanked open the bottom drawer and the book was gone all right, and I walked back to group, and sat down and apologized to the other members for being disruptive—that's good group therapy etiquette—and I caught my breath, calmed down. When I felt I was in control again, I made my move, came out of my chair fast, knocking it over, and got my hands around Raymond's throat and banged his head against the floor and did what I could to make it *clear* to him that it was a bad thing, a very bad thing, to destroy an author's only copy of his book. I think I might have got through to Raymond, or at least killed him, but Dr. Moore, a couple of orderlies, and a member of the group who had once played professional football intervened."

Harry stopped talking and continued to stare out the window. All that remained of the sun was a yellow residue on the pond's surface. Raymond and his friends were silhouetted against the water.

Helen spoke, "And then you wrote *Zod Wallop* as the world knows it?"

"Yes," Harry said. His voice creaked a little, as though from disuse.

Helen Kurtis did not say anything, but the weight of her silence was in the shape of a question, and Harry's answer to that question surprised him.

"I rewrote it because Raymond cried so," Harry said. "He cried like a child that has just lost his mother and father in some disaster. He cried like his heart was broken." Harry turned and looked at Helen. Harry shrugged. "It shook me up. I decided it wasn't worth it to tell the truth. *What the hell?* I thought. *Give the lunatic his fairy tale.*"

Harry got up and said, "Let's see if we can get these campers organized for the night. Raymond's mother tells me that that poor brain-damaged girl really is Raymond's wife. And Raymond tells me she's the Frozen Princess."

"Is she alive?" Lydia asked.

"She's the Frozen Princess," Lord Draining said, wiping the dead rat's blood from his mouth, "and the whole world is inside her. She can't talk, but we communicate. I know her thoughts. She wants me to pass them on to you, dear Lydia. She says she hates you, Lydia. She hates the way the blood jumps in your veins, and the way you laugh and clap your hands when Rolli does a somersault, and the way your heart beats like a bouncing ball. She says you are all wrong and don't even know it, and it makes her angry. She says you have stolen love that was rightfully hers, and she will take it back. She says that the Midnight Machine will open you up and get it, this love."

"I'm sorry she feels that way," Lydia said.

Lord Draining chuckled. "Oh, you don't know sorry yet," he said.

CHaPTeR SiX

✦ ✦ ✦ ✦ ✦ ✦ ✦ ✦ ✦ ✦ ✦ ✦ ✦

I WROTE IT because Raymond cried, Harry thought, walking back out into the cool of the evening. Was it really that simple? Those days at Harwood seemed like a bad dream.

As he walked back down toward the pond where Raymond and his friends now stood, a car's engine coughed and caught, the sound sharp and authoritative in the twilight. Harry turned to see the monkey, screaming, scramble from the open window of Raymond's car.

What? Harry thought.

The car began to move forward.

"Raymond," Harry said, turning back to Raymond Story and his friends. Raymond's voice was rising and falling in the near dark—the way it had so many times in group. A voice that ran after thoughts like a hyperactive child roaring through a room full of toys, breathless, dazzled by the wealth of treasures.

"Raymond!" Harry shouted. The car was coming faster

now, moving toward them, rocking and bouncing down the hill toward the pond. The monkey had leapt from the car and now shrieked in its wake.

Raymond saw it then, broke from his companions and ran toward the approaching vehicle, bellowing. "Emily! Emily!"

The girl, Harry thought. *The girl's in the car.*

Harry raced after Raymond who ran with his arms out and waving frantically, as though the air were underbrush, hindering his progress. It was a big man's awkward, lumbering gait, but it closed the distance quickly, too quickly, and Raymond was suddenly in front of the onrushing car and Harry shouted, "No!"

But the universe that heeds the injunctions of human voices was not in attendance, and indeed, the car seemed to turn, with a quick, animal awareness, as though sensing Raymond. Raymond stopped in mid-rush and leaned backward, arms still flaying the air, and he would have cleared the car's path but for its sudden, arbitrary lunge.

The car's fender caught Raymond, a glancing blow, and sent him hurtling backward into Harry. They fell together, rolling in the grass.

Harry was on his feet immediately, or so he thought, but there must have been some lapse of time, some jostled brain cells temporarily off-line. For when he looked, the car was already fifty feet away, accelerating as it approached the pond, and as he began to run, he heard himself shout, irrationally, "Wait!"

Regally, with the abstract precision of pure, ugly chance, the big car sped to the edge of the pond, rumbled unerringly onto the wood-planked pier—anyplace else and it would have foundered in the shoreline mud—banged down the runway of the pier and sailed, defiantly and leisurely, into the air. It hit the water in a great explosion, a dinosaur doing a belly flop, and was gone in a hiss, the water closing over it, a thousand startled frogs silenced in mid-song.

Harry ran to the end of the pier, kicked off his shoes, and dove. Instantly, the black water enfolded him, chilled his heart, and declared, "There is no hope; there never was."

The darkness was absolute, and full of the silence of a trapped scream. *No,* Harry thought. *Not this time.*

He clawed downward to the bottom of the pond.

You are not going to find her, the dark water said. *She's already dead. Best thing for the poor girl.*

This is not a deep pond, Harry thought, ignoring the water's voice. *And it's a big car.*

He touched bottom, feeling, for a moment, disoriented, as though a muddy ceiling loomed over him. He crouched on the bottom, shouted her name with his soul. *Emily!* Could the car have hit bottom, engine still roaring, and driven on into the center of the pond? It was not a deep pond but it was wide. The car—with poor, dead Emily lying on its floorboards— could be far away from this dirty patch of silt. A bubble of white panic bobbed to the top of Harry's brain.

Surely the water would have stopped the engine's heart; the gluelike mud would have embraced the massive automobile. The car had to be nearby.

Harry moved in what he hoped was an ever-widening circle. Sand roiled around him, an abrasive cloud of gnats. *I'll drown here too,* he thought. His lungs ached at their sudden poverty, and the thought of drowning was not entirely repugnant; it was a death that had its logic and symmetry.

The darkness was not complete. He saw his hand move in the water. Light. Harry saw the light and swam toward it. It seemed to recede as he swam—perhaps it was the cold light of his mind—and then, abruptly, he banged against the side of the car.

The driver's side door was partially opened, and the overhead light was on. There was also a dull whine in his ears, a sound that seemed to mirror the ache in his lungs. Only later did he identify that sound: it was the car's grating alarm.

Peering through the open window, Harry saw Emily. She had fallen to the floor, facedown, her hair drifting upward like seaweed, one of those harsh, flashed images in the aftermath of some newsworthy tragedy. *Dead,* the water said. *Way past alive. You've got just about half a minute before you join her.*

The driver's side door refused to open any farther. The bottom was buried in mud. The car was tilted toward Harry. Harry clambered over the car's roof. He found the passenger side door.

It's locked, of course, the water told him. *We couldn't have her falling out, could we?*

The door opened.

You don't know everything, Harry thought.

As he opened the door, the creature came for him. He staggered backward, falling, and he saw it above him, a black, writhing shape, and he saw the red glow of its eyes and the thrashing of its long, stalked neck and its hideous, undulating flatness. It rushed by—screaming, it was screaming—and was gone, and his mind instantly patched this crack in its rationality with the word *fish* and he caught Emily by the shoulders and dragged her out of the car and brought her to the surface where the giant Allan caught them and dragged them to the reedy bank.

Emily's lifeless eyes gazed at the vast, indifferent sky,

and Harry, vaguely aware of Raymond crying, said, "No," and he knelt beside the girl and tilted her head back. Dirty water spilled from her mouth; he leaned forward and began to breathe for her.

Harry did not doubt for a moment that she would breathe again. Suddenly her lungs would catch, the habits of life would reassert themselves, the heart would beat. He knew this would happen because he had visualized it all so precisely. He knew it would happen because, in a thousand replayed moments of excruciating remorse, he had brought Amy back to life in just this way.

Except he hadn't been there that time.

Breathe, damn it.

Raymond leaned over Harry. "It's my fault," Raymond said. "I shouldn't . . . it was not right . . ."

It's never anybody's fault, Harry thought, *because there is nothing you can ever do.* That was what the black water had been trying to tell him, and it was nothing but the truth.

Harry continued to breathe and count, mechanically filling and emptying the girl's lungs.

He breathed, watched her chest rise in phony life, saw in blurred, bug's eye perspective, the length of her body: yellow T-shirt rucked up to reveal her pale, mud-splattered stomach, blue jeans black with water, her feet encased in what must have been brand-new tennis shoes, New Balance, black with bright yellow *N*s.

Emily coughed, flipped on her side, and vomited.

"She's alive!" Raymond shouted.

The pretty girl whose name was Rene spoke. Her voice was loud in the surrounding silence. "Jeez. Of course she's alive."

Harry lifted the resurrected girl in his arms. "It's okay," he said.

Cradling the girl in his arms, surrounded by shadows, Harry started to walk to the house, but his knees disappeared, and he would have fallen if he hadn't been caught. Raymond took the girl and kept on toward the house while someone— the giant—helped Harry to follow.

Harry looked up and saw that the stars had come out. Like a thousand thousand cars at the bottom of an immense lake, tiny map lights flickering against inevitable night. Were their doors ajar, did they make a noise until their batteries ran down?

He was getting a little punchy, but that was all right. He would sleep in triumph, his fatigue a badge of honor. He had done it; he had saved her.

Harry was helped through the door of the cabin, and he watched as Emily, who had been divested of her wet clothes and wrapped in Helen's flannel nightgown, suddenly arched on the bed and began to die in earnest.

Harry ran to the side of the bed, pushed past Raymond and Helen, and pressed his ear to Emily's chest.

It was a sound he had never heard before, but he had *seen* the sound before. He had seen it on the monitor, there in the ER. Harry had heard the intern shout: "We got v-fib here!" That patient, an overweight, red-faced man who had come to the hospital from a restaurant when he had begun to experience sharp chest pains had been promptly hooked-up to the EKG monitor, had suffered another attack, and had died.

Emily's heart was beating wildly, like some lost sparrow trapped in a chimney. She'd failed to drown, but there were other ways to die. Her heart had gone into ventricular fibulation.

Four years working in an emergency room right after college would now pay off. Harry would be able to tell his companions just what it was that had killed Emily.

But he was powerless to prevent it.

If he had been in a hospital . . . if he just happened to have a crash cart handy . . . if—

They put the paddles on the big man's chest and his body jumped and Harry had been reminded of a documentary, seals being clubbed on a beach, skinned, white carcasses plundered.

Harry's eyes fell on the lamp he had been repairing. Well, why not? He had absolutely nothing to lose. Except this: He was no doctor. What if she was not dying? This first aid would kill her, surely it would kill her.

For a moment, he leaned over the girl, but there were no answers in the mask of her closed face, her blue lips, the mute, dark O of her mouth. Then Harry moved. Because he knew, beyond any logic except a sure knowledge of how life was for him, Harry Gainesborough, that if he did not act she would die, that the surest sort of murder would be to do nothing. This was the truth in his life, and since he was the person who was, well, *here,* then there was only one possible solution: Act.

"Raymond! Helen!" he shouted. "I want you to help me."

One wire here, above the right breast. "Raymond, take this wire and hold it here, down here on her left side. That's right." Harry looked into Raymond's eyes and saw fear, as though blue were the color of fear, and something even more troubling, a wild, absolute trust. Raymond would let Harry Gainesborough do what he pleased, because it was unfathomable to Raymond that the creator of *Zod Wallop* was capable of error.

Raymond stood holding the peeled-back lamp cord in hands sheathed in latex, disposable dishwashing gloves. *Budget doctors,* Harry thought, regarding his own gloved hands, his own spliced wire. *Hand me the brain, Igor.*

You'll kill her, the dark water said.

No, Harry thought, pulling away from that voice. *I don't have time for that.*

He spoke to Raymond, surprising himself with the steadiness of his voice. "When Helen pushes the plug in, Emily is going to jump. Keep the contact, Raymond. I'll be the one to break the contact. Okay?"

Raymond nodded.

"Are you ready, Helen?"

Helen looked up from where she was crouched by the sideboard. She looked like she might say something, but she simply nodded her head.

"Now," Harry said.

Emily twisted on the bed, tortured into momentary levitation, her pale bright body pitifully exposed as the robe fell back, her frail rib cage gleaming through the flesh like some sad icon of martyrdom. An electric whip crack, the ultimate bug zapper, sounded in Harry's ear, and a portion of the sheet was smoking. A red welt gleamed on Emily's chest—and no doubt a similar scar marked the site of Raymond's wire—while the air was charged with the blue, hot odor of overheated train sets.

Harry pressed his ear to the girl's chest. Her heart was out of control, spinning until it toppled. He had failed.

"Again," Harry shouted. And when Raymond hesitated, Harry shouted, "There's no time."

He nodded to Helen, crouched on the floor, and, with a knifelike thrust, she found the receptacle again.

This time they were spared the puppet agonies of the girl, for as the electricity crackled through her frame and began to animate her, the lights went out; the power died. The room fell into the waiting night. The hum of the refrigerator, unheard until that moment, died and silence fed on it.

Harry leaned forward, rested his head on the girl's chest with a sense of intense despair, rested there as though she might comfort him. He could hear no heart beat. And then he heard it, that sweet, slow cycle of a washing machine, that lub-dub, lub-dub that seemed as leisurely as the measured flight of some large bird. And more incredible than the sound of her heart were the words she spoke in his ear. "We don't have much time," she said, "They are coming."

CHaPTeR SeVeN

❧ ❧ ❧ ❧ ❧ ❧ ❧ ❧ ❧ ❧ ❧ ❧ ❧

THE EMERGENCY ROOM was harshly lit and smelled like stale cigarettes and disinfectant. Harry sat in a metal folding chair and watched a small, wizened woman in a white uniform type on what had to be one of the first typewriters ever made. She typed gingerly, while a cigarette smoked in her mouth. It was obvious that the typewriter was the source of much disappointment and grief in her life. "Ahhhhhh," she would say after hitting a key. "Bah." She would shake her head sadly.

The emergency room would have been empty were it not for Harry and his companions. Harry's companions, however, furnished the room with more than enough fidgety life.

Raymond Story loomed over Harry. "I think we should get Emily and leave," Raymond said.

Harry could see the girl, Rene, who had donned round dark glasses, now hunched owl-like on a bench on the other side of the room. She leaned forward as though preparing to take flight. The large, unhappy young man named Allan was looking out the plate-glass window at the lighted parking lot.

"Raymond," Harry said. "We have to see if Emily is really okay. I'm sure . . . "

"She's okay, she's okay," Raymond said, bouncing slightly on his toes. "She's okay for now. But they are coming. Didn't you hear her? They are coming. This was a bad idea coming to the hospital. We don't need a hospital. They will find us here."

"Who are they, Raymond?"

Raymond turned abruptly and marched to the receptionist's desk. "We've got to go," he said. "I need to get my wife and go."

The receptionist looked up at Raymond, crushed her cigarette in an ashtray, and said, "This ain't 7-Eleven. This is not easy come, easy go. This is a hospital, young man. You just sit down and wait. The doctor will see your wife just as soon as he can."

Harry got out of his chair—surprised by the pain in his legs—and joined Raymond at the desk.

"It has been two hours," Harry said. "Is there a problem of some sort? There don't seem to be any other patients."

"No problem, sir," the woman said. "It takes time to torture the truth from a stubborn child."

"I beg your pardon?" Harry stepped back, as though from a blow.

The receptionist was eyeing him with hard, bright eyes.

She sighed. "I said it takes time to get a resident down from the floors. They have other things to do, you know."

Harry turned. Raymond was gone.

*   *   *

It takes time to torture the truth from a stubborn child. Lord Draining had said that, had said it while apologizing to the Closet Police for certain delays.

Harry went back and sat down. He felt ill, overheated. The room was empty now, no Raymond, no Rene, no large, brooding giant. Where had they gone? He would have to find them. He felt an obligation here. He was the adult, the man in charge. The light in the room made a hissing noise, and as the receptionist bent over her typewriter again, she seemed, briefly, to undergo a transformation. Her flesh seemed mottled, iridescent, as though the light glittered on beaded scales, and her humped back seemed to sprout twin, knobby spines—for all the world like a feeding Swamp Grendel.

Oxygen deprivation, Harry thought. *I was underwater too long. It has done something to my brain. I need to . . . I need . . .*

"What do you need, Dearie?" the Gorelord asked, and he grinned, revealing his red company teeth. "Ask anything, and you can have it. But don't ask the price. That's bad manners. Don't ask what it costs." The Gorelord giggled, which is a sound that cannot be described but is as memorable as a root canal.

Harry got up and moved down the hall. There was a telephone in the hall, and he came upon it as a drowning man comes upon a floating spar, the last vestige of the ship that has gone down. He clung to it, feeling his legs liquify.

I need to call Helen, he thought. She had wanted to come but Harry had seen no reason for her presence. "We've got enough of a crowd," he had said. "Raymond's parents will be coming. Get some rest." Now he wished she had come. Unflappable, wonderfully skeptical Helen. Thank God for the practical people in this world, those whose minds remained intact, whose hearts were brave, whose manner in the face of the irrational was one of gruff impatience. Losing your mind. Bah. We'll have none of that.

Harry put a quarter in the phone and heard it make that satisfying, elaborate rattle that wakes the forces of technology. He dialed his number and listened to the phone ring. It rang once, twice, three times. It was ringing as Harry saw the receptionist get up and move toward him, coming around the desk.

Harry felt an impulse to bolt, to hang up the phone and run.

Helen answered the phone.

"Helen, it's me, Harry."

"Harry. Listen, the boy's mother is here with me. Not Raymond. The other boy, Allan." Harry heard Helen shouting, "Mrs. Tate! Mrs. Tate!" Then, "Well, she must have gone out for a breath of air. She has asthma, poor dear, and it's worse when she's upset."

The receptionist had come out from behind the desk. It was a curious uniform she wore, the skirt came to the floor and trailed behind her and seemed oddly wet at the hem, and you might—if you were imaginative, if you had just suffered some physical assault on your nervous system—you might think that she moved with too undulant a motion, not the proper sort of motion for a biped, and if you were really nuts, if you were inclined to hallucinate the contents of grim, terrifying children's books, you might think that she moved the way a Swamp Grendel moved, gliding on its plated belly, leaving a silver trail.

On the phone, Helen was speaking. " . . . came as quick

as she could." Again, the phone resonated as Helen put it down and shouted. "Mrs. Tate! Mrs. Tate!" Clatter of the phone being picked up again. "I'm sure she'll be right back. She's terribly upset. She's afraid her son may hurt someone. You don't think he really is dangerous, do you? I mean, be careful, Harry, these are people who have escaped from a mental institution, after all."

"Helen—" Harry said.

The receptionist had reached Harry.

"I've got to go," Harry told Helen, and he hung up the phone. He was losing his mind, no doubt about it. Where did this sense of suffocating menace come from? When, exactly, had his mind begun to crumble? It was . . .

It was when he had thought, in the dark, that poor Emily had spoken.

The receptionist reached out and touched Harry's shoulder. He did not look at her hand, but it did not feel like it had the requisite number of fingers. It would have three fingers, this hand, and a sucker on the palm, a sucker with rasping, lamprey teeth.

"Mr. Gainesborough," she said, "there is a call for you on my line."

Her voice was disapproving, but nothing more. She was a tired, querulous old woman with an exalted opinion of her office and its authority. Following her back to the desk, it was clear that she had legs. Nothing unusual there. Most receptionists have legs.

Harry took the receiver. "Hello," he said.

"I'm calling from the second floor!" Raymond's voice was an octave higher than usual. "We've got Emily. She is safe, praise Blodkin. We are taking the service elevator to the basement and we will rendezvous with you shortly. Go to the restroom. You will find that I have already prepared a means of exit. Once you are outside, follow the wall to your left, and if my reckoning is right, we will meet shortly. Blodkin willing."

The restroom floor glittered with shattered glass, and the metal chair that had no doubt shattered it now sat upright beneath the window, its aspect commanding and peremptory. "Hurry" it said.

Harry stood on the chair and hoisted himself through the hollowed window and into the night. Shards of glass, shaped like teeth, still edged the window and gave Harry the unsettling sensation of being swallowed. The blackness of the world he was entering did nothing to allay his fears, but he reassured himself that soon he would be safe in the company of his peers: escaped lunatics.

CHaPTeR eiGHT

❀ ❀ ❀ ❀ ❀ ❀ ❀ ❀ ❀ ❀ ❀ ❀ ❀

GABRIEL ALLAN-TATE STOOD in the humid, enfolding darkness, opened her mouth wide, and filled her lungs with the obstinate air. It was dark black out and any kind of horrid insect, or a bat, a rabid, shrieking bat, could bite her. A scorpion could rush out from under a cinder block and sting her. Her lungs felt as though they had been stapled flat, and any sort of venomous bite would activate her allergies and crush the last hope of a breath from her. This was all Allan's fault.

She adjusted her dress, tottered on her heels, wiped a hand over her forehead.

She leaned against the cabin's wall, supporting herself with one white-gloved hand.

What a day. What a day.

When she pushed open the door, the old woman was on the phone shouting, "Harry? Hello. Harry?"

The woman, whose name was Helen, turned and saw Gabriel and said, "He had to hang up."

Gabriel walked to the couch and sat down. She fished in her purse, found the inhaler, and brought it to her mouth.

With a sigh, Helen Kurtis hung up the phone and walked over to her visitor.

Gabriel replaced the inhaler in her purse and leaned her head back so that she stared for a moment at the ceiling. She sighed.

"Poor dear," Helen said.

Gabriel looked at her hostess and smiled wanly, thinking, *God, one of these good aunt types.* Gabriel hated their take-charge sympathy, as though the world were a pillow that you could fluff into shape. The world was a concrete pillow and you had better not fluff it if you had just done your nails.

"Feeling a little better?" Helen said. "Why don't I make us some tea." Without waiting for an answer, she went to the sink and began running water. "I did tell Harry that you were here. I'm sure they will all be along shortly."

"I hope," Gabriel said, "you cautioned him against telling Allan."

"I'm afraid I didn't have an opportunity. But I think Harry might come to that conclusion on his own. He's a very intuitive man, very sweet."

"I'm so glad to hear that," Gabriel said. "I wish I had more intuition myself. I have no idea what my own son thinks, you know. He's a complete mystery. Perhaps he communicates with that crazy boy who has him in thrall, but he certainly doesn't tell his own mother a thing. Not a thing." Shockingly, a sob escaped Gabriel's lips and she thrust her face into her hands as tears darted from her eyes.

Helen came around to the couch, sat down, and put an arm on Gabriel's shoulder.

"I'm sure it will be all right. You've had a hard day."

"I can't tell you," Gabriel said.

And that was the truth of it. It had been a harrowing day. The long drive down had been the final straw; she was no night driver and found the rush of those big, belligerent trucks a life-threatening, adrenaline-spilling ordeal. And of course, the morning had been no lark. While she could not call it the worst experience of her life—in fact, to be perfectly honest she had found it somewhat exhilarating—it had been stressful and, yes, frightening.

That morning she had killed her psychiatrist.

Dr. Theodore Lavin was an unpleasant, even a revolting man, and so, by Gabriel Allan-Tate's reasoning, he was the perfect man to confide in. You do not want to tell the grotesque and outlandish details of your personal life to someone you like. You do not want to repel a friend with disgusting—or, worse, boring—histories of aberrant behavior.

What Theo Lavin thought of Gabriel's obsessions was of no consequence to Gabriel. He was a pompous old fool, his great bulk squeezed into pathetic three-piece suits, his red face throbbing like a boil.

He had called her that morning.

"Gabriel," he said. "I've got to come over."

His call had awakened her, and as was often the case in the morning, she was confused. The big room was filled with sunlight, which splashed over the satin sheets and cut a wide, golden highway in the plush white carpet. Her eyes moved over the room wildly, and when she found the mirror and the image of the pretty, slim woman in the vast, canopied bed, she felt reassured.

She was a widow, a lovely, dark-haired widow as demure

as a Victorian heroine. She was, most importantly, alone. Marlin Tate was dead, self-murdered when, finally, it all spun away from him. She had almost followed.

The mirror showed her solitude, anchored her to the present, where she was visited by a throb of yearning for the only man she had ever loved, followed by a flash of rage. He had no right to kill himself.

Theo Lavin was telling her that her son had left the hospital again, an escape engineered by the infamous Raymond Story.

"Your incompetence might almost be called inspired," Gabriel told the man.

Theo explained why it was not his fault. Psychiatrists, Gabriel thought, were much like God, accepting none of the blame and all of the praise.

She interrupted him. "Find my son," she said, preparing to hang up.

He told her again that he had to come over.

And what, she wanted to know, would be accomplished by a visit?

He could show her the book.

What book?

The book her son had dropped in making good his escape.

And what book was that?

It had to be seen. It could not, really could not, be described.

She had agreed to see him.

And so he had come over, brought the horrid book with him, made her look at it.

"That's you," he had said, thumping the page till it

seemed to writhe. "And this, this is supposed to be a wicked likeness of me."

It was a good likeness, Gabriel thought. The artist had captured Harwood's director with photographic clarity, right down to the mottled teeth, the pendulous lower lip, and the sly, calculating gleam in the eyes. The artist had, however, taken liberties with Theo's attire. At no time in his life—to Gabriel's knowledge, in any event—had Theo ever worn a gray cloak made from what appeared to be entwined lizards (biting each other or, perhaps, goodness, copulating). In the book he was called Lord Lepskin.

"Well, it's a book, and a very nasty one, the product, obviously, of a diseased mind, but I don't think it warrants all this fuss," Gabriel said, with undisguised irritation. It didn't sit well with her, consoling her own psychiatrist. It felt—well, it felt very perverse.

Then Theo Lavin had said an odd thing. "It changes," he said.

"What?"

"The book," he said, "the book changes. The pictures change. Oh, not when you are looking at them but . . . " His voice lowered. He was obviously unhappy with this thought. "It's hard to stop looking at. I think it's . . . it's changing me."

Gabriel laughed, one sharp, brittle bark that made the man look up sharply.

"My son has run off, God knows where, and you are worried about a children's book that contains an unflattering portrait of you. I think you have lost track of your priorities, Theodore. Perhaps, subconsciously, you desire a different career. No telling what your subconscious is up to. I've never thought of it before, but a psychiatrist's subconscious must be quite a swamp, a sort of public restroom. Well, I don't care to think about that either. As long as you are here, I think a session is in order."

Gabriel walked swiftly across the thick carpet, threw herself with acrobatic grace onto a low white sofa that curved like drifted snow against a wide window. The window offered a vision of springtime industry, the long driveway filled with gardeners toiling over colored banks of flowers.

Gabriel was dressed casually, in old jeans and a gray sweatshirt, but she had turned the air on high, feeling a need to deny the season, and she had donned the voluminous white mink coat that Marlin Tate had given her on the first anniversary of their marriage.

Now she snuggled in the coat and regarded the crystal chandelier that dominated the room like some cold, transcendent spaceship.

"I was an unhappy child," Gabriel said. "My emotional needs were not met. I never had a real dog, you know. Only puppies my father borrowed from an uncle who owned a kennel. I'd cry and cry when they came for the puppies. 'Getting too big,' my father would say. 'Getting too big.' Do you think, Theodore, that I might have developed a fear of getting too big, of just being shuttled off one day?"

"I don't think it's a good day for a session," Dr. Lavin said.

"I'm upset," Gabriel said. "I need to talk. You don't even know what day it is, do you?"

She turned her head quickly, like a schoolteacher hoping to catch an inattentive child in some perfidious act, and Theo Lavin blinked. "What day?"

"Today is the day Marlin killed himself. Four years ago today," Gabriel said.

"Ahhh," Lavin said.

Gabriel turned her back to Lavin, pulled her knees to her chest, and retreated further into the warmth of her fur coat. She spoke to the window and its shimmering vista of renewal.

"I feel guilty, Theodore."

"You think you could have stopped him?"

Gabriel sat up and stared out the window. "No. Nobody could stop him. He thought the drug would make him a god."

"Delusions of grandiosity. These are symptoms of drug addiction," Theo said.

Gabriel slid around on the sofa so that she faced Dr. Lavin. "Oh, I believed him. It was just a matter of time. But he lost his nerve, you see. He killed himself, destroyed all the research. It was a failure of nerve."

"He was a brilliant man destroyed by drugs," Lavin said. "It is a sad story, but not an uncommon one, and you are not to blame."

"I should have been more supportive, should have been there to keep his courage up."

Gabriel stared at her psychiatrist as he shook his head, smiling that rueful, seen-it-all smile, and said, "Gabriel, Gabriel. You are saying that you should have encouraged him when, of course, that is precisely what—"

Gabriel interrupted. "And, of course," she said, "a court of law might find your involvement in the whole affair a little—well, unethical."

"I have done nothing unethical," Lavin said.

"You are such a hypocrite," Gabriel said. "I don't know how much money Marlin gave you, but I know the sum was a tidy one. You have too great a sense of your own dignity to go cheaply."

Lavin shook his head. "Really, Gabriel. Corwin-Smart is a perfectly reputable pharmaceutical house and my dealings with them have always been . . . "

Gabriel was no longer listening. She saw, as though it were just yesterday, her husband, the distinguished Dr. Marlin Tate, crouched naked on the bathroom floor. She peered in at her husband, and he looked up at her. His face always looked vulnerable and naked without his glasses. He clutched the toilet bowl with his hands, elbows crooked, as though he might lift the bowl, and he grinned as he spoke. "You want to be very careful of your companions," he said, his voice pontifical yet boyish, his child-prodigy history in every syllable. "You don't share Ecknazine with just anyone because it tends to confuse ego boundaries. It has no . . . no respect for the envelope of self and so—"

Her husband coughed, his shoulders rising, scapula flaring. "I . . . " He coughed again. And then he began to vomit.

Gabriel pulled back from the bathroom door as her husband opened his mouth and showered silver coins into the toilet bowl. Some of the coins pinged against the rim and spilled out onto the tiled floor.

They were silver dimes, a jackpot flood of silver dimes, and as Gabriel bent to pick one up, her husband's laughter filled her ears.

"I think," Dr. Lavin was saying, "I had better be going."

"Two days before my husband died," Gabriel said, "He vomited dimes, silver dimes. Quite a lot of them actually. Eighteen dollars and sixty cents worth. Or at least that's what I recovered. That's a lot of dimes." Gabriel paused, her hands folded primly in her lap. "Quite a lot of dimes."

"You understand, of course," Lavin said, "that your

husband was almost certainly administering the drug, this Ecknazine, to you during those last months. Since it was taken orally, there are any number of ways he could have given it to you without your knowledge. That explains the hallucinations you experienced."

"When your husband vomits dimes," Gabriel continued, "you ask him about it. If your marriage is not utterly dead, you try to keep the avenues of communication open. So I asked of course. You know what he told me?"

"No," Lavin said. "You have never described this incident to me before."

"Well, he was very pleased, very excited. He said that he had wanted a candy bar that afternoon, and he'd gone down to the vending machine but it wouldn't take his dollar. The machine required exact change; there was a little blinking message to that effect. And my husband had no change. Not a dime. He yearned, briefly but intensely, for a pocket full of dimes."

"Delusional systems are often elaborate and possess an internal logic," Lavin said.

Gabriel stretched to her full length on the sofa and again regarded the chandelier. "My husband is dead. My son is psychotic. And my psychiatrist is as indifferent as an old whore."

"I am not indifferent, Gabriel. I am trying to help you. I would not be here if I were not."

"You are here," Gabriel said, "because a children's book has frightened you, Theo. That's why you are here."

Theodore Lavin glanced nervously at the book that lay on the end table next to him.

"I thought you might be able to tell me something about it. Your son dropped it when he fled the grounds. I thought you might have seen it before, might know something of its history."

"No."

"It's not a published book," Lavin said. "It's a sort of mock-up. Actually, its author is famous, a writer named Harry Gainesborough who was a patient at Harwood. You must have met him. He has certainly seen you. This evil countess in the book is supposed to be you, Gabriel."

"I don't recall meeting anyone named Harry. I suppose I might have. Perhaps at one of those picnics."

"Your son never spoke of the book? It's called *Zod Wallop*, but it is not at all like the book in the stores. This is much different. This is not something any child should read, I can tell you that." Dr. Lavin's voice had grown louder, tremulous, modulated by anger—no fear, it was fear—and he reached out a hand toward the book, prepared, no doubt, to show Gabriel some proof of its vileness. But he stopped, pulled back his hand, as though remembering the serpent was poisonous. This seemed to require some act of will, and he closed his eyes and exhaled. His jowls quivered like a curdled pudding.

"What was this man doing at Harwood?" Gabriel asked.

"He had lost a daughter. She drowned in the ocean. He began drinking heavily, became suicidal. Dr. Moore was his doctor."

"When I was eight years old," Gabriel said, "I had a dread of swallowing my teeth. I thought I would probably swallow them in my sleep, and, consequently, I couldn't sleep. My mother knew I wasn't sleeping, but I refused to tell her why. Perhaps I was afraid she would have them removed."

The phone rang and Gabriel answered it. She handed it to Dr. Lavin.

"It's for you," she said.

Gabriel walked into the kitchen while Dr. Lavin spoke on the phone. He had adopted his official bullying voice.

When she came back, carrying a bottle of wine, Dr. Lavin was replacing the receiver and folding a piece of paper.

"We think we know where they are," Lavin said.

"You know where my son is?"

Lavin shrugged. "We think he is with Raymond Story, and it seems Raymond Story has gone off in pursuit of this writer of children's books, this Gainesborough fellow."

"Why?"

"Gainesborough somehow figures in the boy's delusional system. Apparently Story was almost drowned as a child, so he feels a bond to this man whose daughter drowned. Schizophrenic systems are not, by definition, rational, and since Story's problems are not amenable to interactional therapy, I've never been much interested in his case. I have very little time for any individual therapy these days—I make an exception in your case, Gabriel—and speaking of time, I've got to go."

Dr. Lavin stood up, swept the book from the table, and strode toward the door.

"I can remember my father licking my kneecap!" Gabriel screamed at her psychiatrist's retreating back. "I once grew sexually excited while fondling a kitten. When I was in the third grade, I bit a boy on the ankle, clean through his sock, made him bleed. I didn't even know him."

Dr. Lavin had his hand on the door.

"I am terrified of ants. I think, I think it is their smallness that frightens me. They shouldn't be so small, you see, and so busy at the same time. You understand me, Theo?" Gabriel shouted, coming quickly across the lush carpet. "I need some answers here!"

"Come to my office tomorrow morning," Lavin muttered. "We'll discuss it then."

He opened the door, intent on doing what males did best, abandoning her, and Gabriel screamed.

"You old whore!" she yelled, and she swung the full bottle of wine, clutching it by its thick neck, and it traveled proudly at the end of her arm, a heavy, aerodynamically confident instrument suddenly recognizing its purpose, and it struck the psychiatrist's head, the back of his skull, eliciting the sort of sound you might get by hitting a waterbed with a baseball bat. Dr. Lavin rocketed forward, colliding with the opening door that instantly slammed shut and then bounced open again as the psychiatrist tottered backward. The door swung wide as Dr. Lavin fell straight back, a stiff cartoon of a fall, something a stuntman might execute with impunity but hardly the sort of thing a man of Dr. Lavin's fifty-some years should have attempted. A cool, lilac-laden breeze tossed Gabriel's hair as she caught the front door and quickly shut it.

The next half hour was a fuzzy one. When it became clear that Dr. Lavin was dead, Gabriel called her hairdresser and canceled that day's appointment. Then she found a corkscrew and drank some of the contents of what was, she supposed, the murder weapon. Then she saw the book lying next to Lavin, and she took it into the living room and sitting on the sofa she opened it and began leafing through its pages. They were dark, murky drawings, but they did have a certain power.

The drawing of the woman named Lady Ermine did, Gabriel had to admit, seem a vicious caricature of Gabriel Allan-Tate herself.

"I can't catch my breath," Lady Ermine said. "My breath has outdistanced me. Ever since that beastly child tried to strangle me."

Lord Draining sighed. "There's a lesson to be learned," he said.

Lady Ermine raised an eyebrow.

"I mean," said Lord Draining, "one wants to be absolutely sure the child is tied down, quite secured, before getting too close."

"Children are treacherous," said Lady Ermine.

"Truer words were never uttered," said Lord Draining.

Stranger yet, and certainly a sign, she recognized another face. It was the face of Dr. Roald Peake.

She found Dr. Peake's number in the directory, and she called his office.

The secretary was disinclined to connect Gabriel.

Gabriel said, "I am the major stockholder in Corwin-Smart and Chairman of the Board. I am also a friend of Dr. Peake's." She was transferred.

"Gabriel," that large, hearty voice boomed. "How are you?"

"I'm in trouble," she said.

"I'm so glad you thought of me," he said.

"Well." Gabriel was always uncomfortable renewing an acquaintance with a request for a favor. But there was no way around it. "This is serious trouble, Roald. I'm afraid I've killed someone. In fact, he is lying here on my carpet, even as we speak."

"Anyone I know?"

"Theodore Lavin."

The phone exploded with laughter.

"I'm sorry, Gabriel," Peake said. "I just . . . if you were going to kill someone . . . well, you are just so consistent, Gabriel. Your taste is always impeccable."

"None of this is funny," Gabriel said, on the verge of tears.

"Of course it isn't," Peake said. "I'll be right along. I'll bring Karl; he's handy in a crisis."

"Wait," Gabriel said, afraid he would hang up. "I can't stay here another minute. I've got to go out. I'll leave the key in the mailbox."

"Of course. Of course."

One last distasteful task remained after she put down the receiver. She had to find Gainesborough's address in the psychiatrist's pocket. She had seen Lavin tuck the piece of paper away, and so she knew where to look. It could have been worse. But it was nonetheless a terrifying experience. What if he suddenly grabbed her. The way his head was pooched in like a punched milk carton, and the large, garish quantity of blood on the carpet were strong arguments that he was dead. But there was a long tradition of corpses coming alive, and although this tradition was a Hollywood one, Gabriel thought it might be based on careful observation, might really be a commonplace occurrence.

Lavin did not grab her however, and ten minutes later, in possession of Harry Gainesborough's address, Gabriel locked the door, dropped the key in the mailbox and marched down the drive to her Mercedes.

"What do you have in your tea?" Helen asked.

"I don't know," Gabriel said. "Anything will be fine."

CHaPTeR NiNe

DRIED BLOOD HAD glued the psychiatrist's face to the carpet.

Dr. Peake shook his head as he watched his assistant, Karl, peel Theodore Lavin from the floor, a task accompanied by an ugly, rasping sound.

"Theodore," Dr. Peake said, "I believe you may be on to something here. Quite an extraordinary therapy. The ultimate transference. You have allowed Gabriel to kill her father."

Karl, a large, broad-shouldered man, grunted as he wrestled the body onto the stretcher. He threw the plastic sheet over the body, covered it with a blanket, and began securing the straps.

"You've made a mess of the carpet, though," Peake said. Roald Peake pursed his lips in thought. His brow displayed distinct ripples, like corrugated cardboard, while he thought. He was the sort of man who was almost handsome, nature having embarked on good looks and overdone it, creating a caricature, the jaw a little too square, the cheekbones too wide, the mouth too full. He wore a dark suit, impeccably tailored to his tall, thin frame, and he held an unlit cigarette between the first and second fingers of his left hand.

Karl stood up, and Peake put an arm on his assistant's shoulder. "I can't see replacing the entire carpet," Peake said. "Let's improvise here, Karl. Why not a tiled area here, by the door? Black-and-white tiles, something tasteful and simple. If Gabriel doesn't approve . . . well beggars can't be choosers can they?"

Karl Bahden studied the room with a workman's eye. He was a square-faced man with clipped, white hair and a perpetual squint. He nodded his head. "Yeah, we could just take a six-foot square, lay down tile there. A design element. Good idea."

"Thank you. I'll leave it to you. But first let's remove the good doctor." Peake walked into the living room. "I'd better take a look around, see if Gabriel hasn't left any other bodies lying about."

Peake put the cigarette between his lips as he walked into the living room. He was trying to stop smoking—and having some success—but he still liked the feel of a cigarette in his mouth; it focused him somehow.

"What's this?" he said, picking the book up from the end table. He sat in an armchair and opened it.

He was unaware of Karl speaking his name, and it was not until his shoulder was touched that he looked up.

Karl's face seemed far away.

"Ah," Peake said, resurfacing from a welter of thoughts and emotions. "Karl." Peake closed the book and rested it in his lap.

"You okay?" Karl said.

"Karl," Peake said, "I have found something quite extraordinary." Peake stood up. He noticed that the cigarette was still between his lips, and he lit it and inhaled. Just the one. "You remember that unfortunate business with Gabriel's husband?"

Karl nodded. "Yeah. That's one of the things we don't talk about."

Peake nodded, beaming. He slapped Karl on the shoulder. "Well, it was too painful to talk about, of course. It was so full of frustration and failure. All that work destroyed. And the widow, dear Gabriel, she was no help at all, another dead end. Well, this just demonstrates the truth of my philosophy."

Karl blinked. "What's that?"

"Always be a friend."

"Ah," Karl said.

"Yes. Here we are, helping out Gabriel for no better reason than a desire to be of service, and perhaps, one day, acquire Corwin-Smart Pharmaceuticals, and because our hearts are in the right place, because we are doing the right thing, we are rewarded." Peake clasped the book to his chest. Suddenly he thrust it forward. "Do you know what this is?"

Karl squinted negatively.

Peake nodded. "Well, of course you don't. It's a book written—I'm sure of this—under the influence of Ecknazine. These drawings are of Harwood patients and staff." Peake paused, such a wealth of good feeling rising within him that he was suddenly mute with joy.

Karl grinned.

Peake nodded twice, shook off the paralysis of delight and said, "There's even a caricature of me. I am someone called Lord Draining. It's quite good, actually . . . although I could choose to be offended at the length of my nose and the way he's given me such an excessive number of sharp teeth, but all and all—" Peake stopped. "The point is this, Karl: Unless I am sadly mistaken—*and I'm not Karl, I'm not*—these are the subjects."

Karl smiled, but it was the smile of a man trying to share a joke that had eluded him.

Seeing his assistant's confusion, Peake spoke slowly. "These are the Ecknazine subjects. These are Marlin Tate's guinea pigs. We only have to find out who these faces belong to and—" Peake paused, shrugged. "Well, I don't know what exactly, but I think . . . I think we'll be back in business."

Peake held the book in front of him and gazed at it lovingly. He stood enraptured until Karl coughed.

Peake looked up. "Of course. We have pressing business. Let's get the good doctor out of here. Let's get him back to the lab and reduced to a more compact and elegant form."

They carried the stretcher out to the van, moving under a vast canopy of stars. Peake had waited until dark to visit Gabriel's mansion. If the body had been discovered in the interim that would have been too bad—there were limits to the risks he was willing to take in order to secure a better bargaining position with Gabriel.

Peake stood in the darkness under the stars, clasping the book to his chest. He heard the muffled sound of the rear doors slamming shut on the company van. He inhaled the rich, turned-earth air, fruit of the gardeners' industry.

"Mother," he said, looking heavenward, "don't let me be disappointed."

"I hope I'm not disappointed," Lord Draining said.

"Ah," said Lord Lepskin.

"I hope, for everyone's sake," Lord Draining said, studying the Frozen Princess as she lay on the table, "that I'm not disappointed. You remember the last time I was disappointed, don't you Lepskin?"

The Lord Lepskin nodded gravely. Oh, he remembered. The servants had been a week scrubbing the blood from the council room walls.

CHaPTeR TeN

THE YOUNG MAN, Allan, was driving Helen Kurtis's big, white Lincoln. He leaned forward, studying the road with that intensity characteristic of new drivers. The girl Rene sat next to him, her black hair alive in the night wind.

The side of her face was silhouetted against the pale headlight glare, and Harry, from his vantage point in the backseat, was struck again by her beauty. It was a rare beauty that could assert itself in shadow.

Raymond was speaking. "We must make haste. Things are happening too fast. I hadn't anticipated the princess awakening so soon. If we can find the Duke quickly, we've got a chance. But I won't sugarcoat a bitter pill, Lord Gainesborough. There is a possibility the Duke will be dead, or so immersed in spiritual matters that our interests will mean nothing to him."

Harry felt as though he were coming out of anesthesia.

The source of his immediate confusion crowded him on the car's seat. Raymond's blue eyes glowed with the off-kilter ardency of a nun who has gone over the edge. Those large, sky-blue eyes were less than a foot from Harry's face— Raymond was no respecter of personal space—and Harry slid back on the seat until his spine pressed painfully against the window crank.

"Raymond," Harry said, speaking slowly, "Don't call me Lord Gainesborough. Call me Harry." It seemed to Harry that he might wrest control by degrees. Fear had caused him to flee a hospital and fear had put him in a car full of maniacs, but he was all right now; he had his faculties in tow again.

"Call me Harry," he repeated.

"My station will not allow it," Raymond said.

"I demand that you call me Harry!" Harry clutched Raymond's coat, which was not a coat at all but a brown terry cloth bathrobe of ancient appearance, bald in spots. Harry looked past Raymond and saw the dark, muffled form of Emily. Her head was nodding slightly, perhaps to the sprung rhythm of the big car's motion, perhaps in time to some internal music. She was not, in any event, chatting up a blue streak. *Had she spoken at all?* The monkey lay sprawled in her lap, probably sleeping, although it had the aspect of something dead for several days. Is this the way most monkeys slept, arms akimbo, mouths wide open? This monkey seemed more dissolute, more unsavory, then did the monkeys of Harry's zoo-going days. Granted, Harry hadn't been to a zoo in a long time, not, in fact, since he took Amy, which had to have been . . . a long time ago, in another life.

"True hearts," Raymond said. "Evil always underestimates the strength of a true heart."

Raymond seemed to be offering some sort of consolation here, but Harry had missed its context.

"Stop the car," Harry said.

"I'm sorry. Every second is essential. We must move southward without impediment."

"I order you to stop the car."

Raymond sighed, leaned forward, and tapped the giant on the shoulder. "Pull over, Lord Allan."

When the car came to a full stop, Harry climbed out. His legs were untrustworthy, not shaky exactly but possessing more elasticity than was warranted. The sound of gravel crunching under his shoes was consoling, however, a stolid, physical voice. They were on a stretch of two-lane blacktop, telephone poles marching into the distance, the lights of a Texaco station illuminating the horizon's last hill. A field of pale, tall grass rolled out into darkness. Harry took a few deep breaths—the air had a damp, doughy consistency that was not at all bracing—and got back in the car.

"Raymond," he said, "what you do with your life is your affair. We met briefly under unpleasant circumstances, but there is no fate that binds us together, no special karmic bond or whatever. I'm sure all this will be clear to you as soon as you are properly medicated again. In the meantime, I am not available for pursuing the fancies of your fertile imagination. Let's go back to the cabin now. Your parents will be arriving in the morning, and we can sort everything out then. I am sure they are worried sick. And they aren't the only ones. Allan's mother is already at the cabin."

A door slammed open, and Raymond leaned forward. "Allan. Allan, wait!"

That young man was already charging across the field, a diminishing white shape sinking into the darkness. The pretty girl named Rene turned around and glared at Harry, her eyes lighted with passionate disgust.

"That was smart," she said. "Everyone knows the bitch scares him shitless."

Harry sat in the backseat with Emily while Raymond and Rene hunted for Allan. Harry could hear their shouts through the car's open window. He had watched them run across the field until the darkness had settled like ink in their clothing, blotting them out, and now he had only their voices to tell him they were out there. He could distinguish the girl's high, irritated holler from Raymond's robust boom, but both voices were growing fainter.

Harry was aware that there were things he was not thinking about, that he was keeping a kind of mental stillness, as though any sudden, psychic motion might cause him to fall. And if he fell, he would fall back into what he thought of as the time of the Great Tiredness. The Great Tiredness had come on him after Amy's death, it had settled like thick tar on a dinosaur's bones, and it had wrapped the outrage and the pain and the craziness in a blanket of fatigue. It was in the time of the Great Tiredness, when he was at Harwood Psychiatric, that he had written *Zod Wallop*.

A hand clutched Harry's wrist, and Harry jumped. "Ah!" Harry said.

Harry looked down at the grinning monkey. It looked like an evil mendicant in a bad dream. "Jesus," Harry said, feeling his heart twist like a willful child.

The monkey released Harry's wrist, leapt to Harry's shoulder, and darted out the window.

"Hey," Harry said, but the monkey was gone, scampering through the tall grass in pursuit of his master.

An hour passed and Raymond and his companions did not return. The night breeze carried the sound of crickets and a single, insistent frog. Harry closed his eyes and slept.

He woke abruptly to stillness. His heart was beating rapidly, and he felt the dank reek of the pond constricting his throat.

He shook himself upright. He glanced to his left, and froze.

Emily was staring at him. There was just enough light for her face to coalesce in a grainy, black-and-white image, a blurred, guesswork vision, but the look of supplication was so intense that she might as well have shouted.

"Emily," Harry said. "What is it?"

He moved forward and touched her hand, which lay like white, broken crockery in her lap. Her hand was surprisingly warm.

She was trying to speak, the words a buzz in her mouth, and Harry leaned forward. Lowering his ear to her mouth, Harry smelled the forgotten sweet, acrid smell of childhood fevers and unarticulated fears.

"Close," Emily said, the word coming out amid *s*'s, wrapped in sibilance and urgency. "Close . . ."

Harry felt her fear, and his own fear translated the single word. She wanted him to close the windows, to lock the car doors. Her instructions were entire in the single word, and it was only later, in the desperate business of rationalization, that Harry claimed the thought for his own.

He did as she asked, in a flurry of clumsy motion, banging a knee on a door handle, bumping his head on the map light.

"There," he said, settling back next to her and patting her shoulder, "it's done."

They sat then, close to each other, shoulders touching, the both of them waiting. Harry could not say what he waited for, but he could almost chart its approach, and so when something slammed into the car's roof, Harry did not cry out. He hugged Emily and held his breath.

It made a noise as it crawled over the roof. Two noises actually. The one noise was like sandpaper on slate, a noise made by the thousands of small, hooked claws on the underside of its wings. The other sound, more unsettling if you knew its nature, was a series of short screams, like sonar—if sonar were designed to bounce off fear. It was fear the creature sought.

I made this thing up, Harry thought. *There is no such thing.*

It was, of course, a Ralewing. Harry was surprised at how his reason sought no other explanation.

Now it would find him. It would find him and suck the flesh from his face.

It would dine on his eyes. A Ralewing could pluck an eye from its socket and swallow it as effortlessly as a rat snake scarfing a robin's egg. *Except there is no such thing as a Ralewing.*

And it is going to get me, he thought. *This no-thing.*

Unless, of course, he kept his fear at bay. It would be blind to him if he were fearless.

But there was no way not to fill with panic. Fear was the proper response to the terrible cry it uttered. Unless you went elsewhere. Unless you just stopped hanging on the edge, just sighed a long, low sigh of resignation and let those numbed psychic fingers go limp—and fell back. Fell back into the Great Tiredness.

They told him he had tried to kill himself, and they refused to believe that it was an accident, that the sleeping pills, the tranquilizers, the alcohol that almost shut his system down were merely the result of absentmindedness.

"Look," Harry told Dr. Moore. "I'm not the suicidal type. That's too melodramatic for me." Besides, Harry thought, the Great Tiredness was every bit as good as death. There was no color here, no pain, no emotional weather at all, just an occasional oddness that was the outside world trying to puff itself up into significance when, of course, the secret of the Great Tiredness, the truth of this realm, was that everything was arbitrary and meaningless.

"I've read all your books," the big, blue-eyed child-man said. "My name is Raymond Story, and I've read all your books. I have read every one of them hundreds of times."

"Well," Harry said. "Good for you." The man held a yellow, grinning rubber toy animal under his arm. Harry recognized the toy instantly—he was, after all, to blame for its existence—but he ignored it, refusing to let it engage his eyes or conjure up any memories of Amy.

"Are you writing another book?"

"No," Harry said.

"Why not?"

"I don't want to."

"Why don't you want to?"

Harry sat up in bed. Had he been dozing when Raymond came into the room? Perhaps. In the Great Tiredness, the transition from sleep to wakefulness was often blurred.

"Go away."

The big man leaned forward, his wide face filled with stupid concern, his unruly mustache animated by passionate conviction. Harry was afraid, for one moment, that the man might burst into tears.

"It's because your daughter drowned, and you just don't care. Isn't that so?"

"I don't want to talk about it."

"I almost drowned when I was eleven," Raymond said. "I jumped off the side of the pool and hit my head, and I was underwater a long time, and I died and went to a place of light and when I came back they had changed this world."

"I'm very tired. Please go away."

"I'm sorry. I'm sorry. I'm always being a nuisance. I know. I'm going. I'm out the door." The fat man moved toward the door. Harry was struck by two things. The fat man was wearing a rumpled suit and his feet were bare. In the grayness of the Great Tiredness, these were small things, but they were noteworthy. At the door, Raymond paused. His wide face seemed to quiver slightly, shaken by some bulldog conviction. "You have to write another book. I bet . . . I bet . . ." He licked his lips, rocked back on his heels. "I bet if you wrote a book you could change it back. The world. You could change it back."

Dr. Moore was delighted when, a week later, Harry requested the watercolors.

"It's not going to be a pretty book," Harry muttered, oddly diffident.

"No," Dr. Moore said, his plain, kind face noncommittal, his hands in his lap. "I don't suppose it will."

Dr. Moore left and Harry stared at the blank white surface of the art board and felt an anger rise in him like steam.

You never change anything that matters, he thought. And that was the book he wrote. *Zod Wallop.* About the end of things, the winding down, the world turning into stone. It was a rebuttal to a poor madman's delusion.

The book began with a rock, a rock that wanted to live, to move, to participate in life. A fatal mistake. Everything awful followed from that desire, that romantic and doomed notion that awareness was a good thing.

The heroine of this book was a little girl named Lydia. Lydia, like Amy, was a worrier. She was right to be worried.

I don't worry anymore, Harry thought. He was above that. Or below it. The precise geography of his indifference was unimportant.

In the morning, the pharmacist would bring him a tiny little paper cup filled with pills. The pills were brightly colored, as though designed for children.

Raymond came in one morning, saw the little cup of pills and peered down at them. "He gives me those little red ones, too," he said. "They are full of bad dreams. The man who brings them doesn't work here. He lives in the place where they make the bad dreams. It is a big factory and they hurt animals there, in order to force the bad dreams out."

It was true that the man who dispensed these morning medicines was seen at no other time, but then, he probably worked the night shift, his morning rounds being the last task of his day.

This man wore thick glasses and had a long, pale, unhappy face. He asked Harry questions, took blood. There were endless tests to take. There was a temptation to answer yes to all the delusional stuff. Craziness had a fine expansiveness to it. Yes, the President talks to me through the radio. Yes, aliens have the cure for cancer and are waiting until we say the magic word. Yes, I believe in God.

In group, Dr. Moore asked, "How is the book going?"

"Wow!" Raymond said. "I knew it."

Harry shrugged. "It's coming along," he said. He didn't look at Raymond.

The pharmacist asked if Harry experienced any bad dreams, and Harry said he didn't. The pharmacist confided that he *was* having nightmares, and then he laughed nervously. "Just who is the patient here, anyway?" He grinned. He had taken to wearing tinted glasses that emphasized the darkness under his eyes. Sometimes he was unshaven, his hair uncombed.

"Call me Marlin," he said. "We are all in this together, you know."

No, Harry didn't know that. He had no sense of being in anything with anyone, but he smiled nervously as the man paced around the room. This Marlin Tate had taken to uttering non sequiturs in the morning.

"I hate rain," he would tell Harry. It would be a sunny day. Harry would agree, cautiously, that rain could be unpleasant.

"I am being watched constantly," the man complained.

"Ah," Harry would say, as Marlin Tate prowled around the room. The man made Harry more nervous than any of Harwood's certified psychotics.

"I'm depressed," he told Harry, sitting on Harry's bed

and smoking a cigarette (which was against the rules, but Harry didn't mind). "I should be happy. I've got a lovely wife, enough money for a lifetime, and my work is coming along. I don't have any right to be depressed. I mean, you have legitimate cause . . . daughter drowned, that sort of thing . . . but why should I be in such a funk? I just want to transcend this"—he waved a hand around the room—"this clutter."

He paused, looked up at Harry and said, "Are you acquainted with your fellow patient Raymond Story?"

"Yes. We are in group together," Harry said.

"What do you make of him?"

"I don't know."

Marlin Tate nodded, as though this were a sharp character assessment. "Yes, well. He says you are his best friend."

Harry blinked, said nothing.

"Schizophrenics come up with some fascinating delusions. He believes he died when he was eleven, and that now he is living in another world."

"Yes, that's a common topic with Raymond."

"That's the bond with you, of course."

Harry raised his eyebrows. "Bond?"

Tate stood up. "Maybe I've just got the flu or something."

"What bond?" Harry asked.

The pharmacist looked at Harry. "He's convinced that you crossed over too. Your daughter drowned, and it's you that slipped into this alternate universe."

Harry nodded. Alternate universe. Raymond had that right. This was manifestly *not* the world Amy had inhabited.

"Have you experienced any numbness in your extremities?" Tate asked, changing the subject—or perhaps not.

"No," Harry said. "My extremities are fine."

"We want to keep an eye out for side effects. Some of these medications vary considerably in their effect on the individual. No all-purpose elixir, I'm afraid." He frowned. "No bad dreams?"

"No."

Unless, of course, the Botwobble business had been a dream. That was the rational explanation for what had happened the previous night. Unfortunately, Harry was fairly certain it wasn't a dream.

It figured that Raymond would own a Botwobble. The last thing Harry wanted to see was this miserable marketing spin-off from his book *The Bathtub Wars,* so it was almost a given that Raymond would own one.

Botwobbles were small, balloonlike animals that surfaced in bathtubs. They were cheerful, winsome creatures, as playful as otters, delighting small children whose parents would never have been able to get their progeny into a tub were it not for the prospect of playing with these good-natured water babies.

Botwobbles and humankind coexisted peacefully until a villainous entrepreneur discovered that a Botwobble, rubbed briskly all over the face, made wrinkles vanish. This rejuvenating process caused the poor Botwobble to dwindle to nothing, uttering a pathetic whimper all the while.

Hard-hearted dowagers were indifferent to the creatures' plight. Botwobbles were relentlessly pursued so that vain humankind could recapture youth.

The book had a happy ending. Children refused to bathe without their playmates. Civilization foundered as millions of dirty, bad-smelling children brought social commerce to a halt. The lesson was obvious: It was dangerous to fool with nature's delicate balance.

All well and good except for the miserable yellow rubber Botwobbles that Harry had, in a moment of weakness and financial need, allowed a toy company to license. They looked much like Harry's drawings of them, long, sausage-shaped critters with broad, goony smiles and bulbous eyes. But the noise this toy made when squeezed was a shrill, irritating whistle that sounded particularly plaintive when bathwater had been sucked into the thing. Amy had owned a Botwobble, and she had been skilled in making it elicit a dismal, asthmatic squeal that could disrupt the brain's ability to think any coherent thought.

Raymond owned one, and he carried it everywhere, squeezing it absentmindedly when he was agitated. He even took it to group, but it was quickly banned from that environment.

Harry had been working late on *Zod Wallop.* Usually, when he wrote and illustrated a book, the drawings propelled the words. Then the words would surprise new drawings. The process was magical and energizing.

Not so with *Zod Wallop,* which was powered by despair. It hurt to write it, creating real physical pain, migrainelike headaches that could distort his vision. The pain didn't stop him, but fighting it was exhausting.

When the drawing in front of him wavered, when the sepia-colored dungeon became a meaningless blur, he got out of bed and drifted into the rec room just in time to see Melanie Jensen hit Raymond in the face with a Ping-Pong paddle.

Melanie, a teenager as pretty as she was bad-tempered,

turned away from Raymond, who was sobbing in that help-less, sagging fashion that somehow fails to inspire compassion, producing, instead, contempt. Raymond's nose was bleeding copiously, darkening his mustache.

Melanie glared at Harry. "I told him not to turn the TV off," she said. "He's not the only person in the world and just because he doesn't like TV doesn't give him any right to turn it off." She flounced back to the sofa, grabbed up the remote, and snapped the television back on. David Letterman, bored and mean, blinked into lurid focus. He was insulting a guest, a celebrity who might, in fact, have been another talk-show host. A third person sat on the couch, a child dressed in a me-tallic jumpsuit and wearing what appeared to be a brassiere on his—her?—head.

Harry snatched the remote from the end table and clicked the television off.

"Hey!" Melanie growled. "What the fuck!"

Harry leaned toward her. "Raymond's right. That stuff will rot your brain and make your ears bleed." He turned away. Raymond had left.

"Hey, give me my remote."

"Sure." Harry handed her the remote. Melanie sat on the couch, punching the remote at the television which refused to revive. "Shit," she muttered. "Shit."

Harry left the room, the batteries in his pocket.

Back in his room, he lay on his bed and closed his eyes. He never undressed for bed, never crawled under the bedcovers, never turned the lights out. The staff was always on him about that, but they didn't understand. He had to take sleep by sur-prise. Preparing for bed simply alerted insomnia, brought all the busy thoughts, the renegade remorses and guilts and re-criminations. The trick was just to close his eyes. Sometimes he slept.

Not this time. This time, as soon as he closed his eyes, the hysterical, repetitive whimpers of a Botwobble accosted him. He closed his eyes tighter, and the noise increased. Finally, he got up and went down the hall to Raymond's room.

The door was open.

Raymond lay propped amid pillows on his back in a rumpled bed, the trashed warren of some animal that fed on bags of Cheetos and cream soda. He had stopped crying but his eyes were wet and there was dried blood in his mustache. He still wore his brown suit jacket, now rucked up behind his head like a cape. His blue dress shirt had worked out of his pants to reveal his smooth, white belly. His bare feet stuck out of his trouser cuffs with the starkness of true tragedy. Although, Harry reminded himself, nothing really tragic had happened here. One crazy person had gotten in the way of another crazy person, that's all.

The shriek of the Botwobble filled the room. It did not come from the bed, where Raymond lay as still as a drugged Buddha. The sound seemed to come from the far corner of the room, an unlighted corner beyond a small, snack-cluttered writing desk. Harry edged cautiously into the room and peered into the corner. There it was. The little yellow toy, Raymond's precious Botwobble, bounced on a folding chair, expanding and contracting hysterically, whistling its thin lament to an indifferent universe.

Harry stumbled backward, banging against the door.

Raymond blinked and sat up.

"Oh," Raymond said. "Gosh."

The Botwobble stopped squeaking, rolling off the chair and hitting the floor with a final *eek* before resuming its inanimate status.

"That Melanie is really mean," Raymond said, rubbing his eyes.

Harry said nothing. He stared at the Botwobble.

He closed his eyes, accosted by a sudden, vicious vertigo.

When he opened his eyes, he was in the darkness of the car.

Is it gone? he wondered.

The sky was beginning to lighten—*my God, was it dawn?*—and he could see Emily, her eyes closed, her breathing slow and regular. He reached out and touched her shoulder.

Her eyes opened instantly.

"It's okay," Harry said. "I think it's gone."

He patted her shoulder, then said, "I'm going to start the car. Let's see if we can find Raymond and the others."

Harry climbed into the front seat and slipped behind the steering wheel. He turned the key in the ignition and the engine caught immediately. He looked back over his shoulder and smiled at Emily. "Here we go," he said.

Helen's car was a big luxury cruiser. Accustomed to his own small, responsive Mazda, Harry found it took some getting used to. It was like driving a boat.

He turned right onto a dirt road and bounced over deep ruts and the prehistoric prints of tractor wheels. Harry looked in the rearview mirror to see if Emily was still upright. She was. Her eyes were wide and unreadable.

A busted fence jittered past on Harry's right, silver

planks brought down by neglect. A large black crow shouted from a leaning fence post before heaving itself into the air and flapping off across the field toward the trees.

Harry could see the sun as though it were burning fiercely behind gray cheesecloth. He could feel the heat there too, preparing to roll out another suffocating carpet of dust and burning chaff.

The field was empty. They came to the trees. Here the dirt road was reclaimed by weeds. A hundred yards into the forest, the road grew confused, opened onto a wide, grassy circle as though attempting to get its bearings, shot narrowly to the left, and ended abruptly in a snarl of dusty shrubs, scrub pine, dogwood, hackberry.

Harry turned the engine off and climbed out of the car. He listened. The only sound that came to his ears was the thin, two-note cry of some bored or feebleminded bird.

Harry could not help himself. He stood on tiptoe and leaned forward. The paint had been burned away from the car's roof, a black stain roughly two feet in circumference from which dark, twisting tentacles writhed (where the liquid acid had run across smooth metal, and trickled down the door panels).

"Oh, Jesus," Harry whispered.

It was precisely what he thought he might see, and it shocked him.

He heard the voices then, over the rising tide of panic, and he distinctly heard Raymond's laugh, and he looked up to see Raymond and the others coming down the road toward him. Raymond—with Arbus perched flamboyantly on his shoulder—had his arm around Allan's waist, and Rene clung to the boy's arm.

"Ho," Raymond shouted, "Lord Gainesborough! Thank Blodkin you are safe. We have convinced Allan that his private reservations must be overruled by common good. We are prepared to return to the black pond."

CHaPTeR eLeVeN

❂ ❂ ❂ ❂ ❂ ❂ ❂ ❂ ❂ ❂ ❂ ❂ ❂

"I SUPPOSE," JOHN Story said, "you know what you are doing." Ada Story could always tell when her husband was angry. He would become very formal in his manner, speak with elaborate care, as though she were mentally impaired. When he was especially angry, his hair would sprout wildly from the sides of his head, not from the anger itself, of course, but from a nervous and exasperated rubbing of his temples.

He crouched over the steering wheel, his jaw set determinedly, watching the empty interstate as though his life depended on his vigilance.

"Just what do you hope to accomplish by bringing it?" he asked.

Ada shrugged, realized that her husband was not looking at her, and spoke, "I don't know. I just thought it might be useful if someone else understood about Raymond."

"I suppose," her husband began, "you've forgotten all those experts, all those folk who were after understanding

Raymond, and the consequences of that."

"John," Ada said, stiffening a little as the inevitable conflict escalated, "I love you, but if you say 'I suppose' one more time, I won't be responsible for my actions. I haven't forgotten anything. And I don't know . . . I just put it in the trunk. I just wanted to have it along. It's that man Gainesborough's story, you know, that's where it came from, so I just thought. . . . Oh I don't know what I thought." Ada found tears blurring her vision.

"Ada," her husband said, "I only . . . "

"I probably won't mention it," Ada said. "We've just come to fetch our Raymond and his wife and his friends. Raymond is our affair and nobody else's."

"I do think that's best," her husband said.

Ada sighed. "Yes." A big truck rocketed by them, blue exhaust in its wake. Ada snapped open the glove compartment and took out the map. "Did we go through Henderson yet?"

"Good half an hour ago," her husband said.

"Land, I hope we haven't missed our turn."

John Story laughed. "We haven't. Aren't you supposed to be navigating?"

Ada laughed too. This was an old, long-married set piece. "It's this map. It's written upside down. And the colors are all wrong."

They drove south into the morning. Oh, Raymond. He was the best of boys, the sweetest, but he was so . . . so melodramatic. The doctors didn't understand that. They thought something was actually wrong with Raymond's mind. They diagnosed him as schizophrenic. They said it had nothing to do with the head injury at the swimming pool, and Ada was certain they were right there. Raymond had always been melodramatic. He just wanted the world to be bigger than it was, more fantastic. He wanted to believe in evil trolls and fairies and elves. Other children grew out of such fantasies. Raymond, alas, grew into them. They were very real for Raymond. Did that make him crazy? Doctors thought so, but they didn't live with Raymond. They didn't know about the source of her present argument with her husband. They had never seen what was in the trunk.

Cows grazed on a distant hill. Raymond had always been fascinated with cows. "*Cawow,*" Ada said out loud. She captured her son's youthful pronunciation but not his exuberance. He would shout the word like a bomb going off.

"What's that?" her husband said.

"Nothing," Ada said. "Look, isn't that our turn?"

When they arrived at the cabin, they were greeted by a large, broad-shouldered woman who said her name was Helen Kurtis and that she was Harry Gainesborough's agent.

Ada wondered if all authors lived with their agents, decided that probably only the famous ones did.

CHaPTeR TWeLVe

Harry squinted through the windshield. The sun was well up now, hanging over forested mountains. Sunlight had gotten into everything, pouring through the branches of pale green trees, dappling the two-lane blacktop, burnishing roadside goldenrod.

It was beautiful, Harry noted. Sweet, meaningless, stupid beauty.

In the backseat, Allan was grumbling. He was flanked by Raymond on his right, Emily on his left.

"Mother will just want to lock me up again," he said. "She'll want to lock us all up."

"Of course she will," Raymond said brightly. "That's her nature. Lady Ermine is a very controlling person."

"We should just go," Allan said. "We should go to Florida."

"I was of that opinion myself," Raymond said. "But I see now that Lord Gainesborough is right. We cannot begin our journey without the Duchess of Flatbend. We'll need her to petition the Duke."

Harry, listening, felt no desire for clarification. He was tired. So tired that he had imagined some extraordinary things and ascribed a supernatural cause to what was, of course, only a stain on the roof of a car, some fault in the original paint job. He sought to cheer himself up by thinking that soon he would be rid of this crew. But the thought did not cheer him, and he realized, with panicky dread, that he did not, in fact, believe it.

On the passenger seat next to Harry, Rene was holding the monkey. The monkey was sprawled in her lap. It had discovered a roll of breath mints in the glove compartment and was now placidly stuffing them into its mouth.

The girl leaned forward, kissed the top of the monkey's head, and said, "Don't believe what the TVs say, Lord Arbus. You can eat them things all day long, have breath as sweet as a pine tree full of angels, and you still won't get any pussy."

The monkey tilted his head back and grinned.

From the backseat, Raymond's voice rose. "The woman named Helen, Lord Gainesborough's agent in literary matters, is the Duchess of Flatbend, of course. I don't know how I missed it, even for a minute. She's probably the only one who can reach the Duke, who can enlist him in our cause. The Duke is living at the St. Petersburg Arms in Florida according to the address on the occasional written communication he sends Emily, and that is where we must all go as soon as we have persuaded the Duchess to join us."

"Mother—" Allan began.

"Please," Raymond said, "our course is set, Lord Allan. It is a hard path, and we might wish for a smoother one. But it is Blodkin's choice, not ours."

Blodkin, Harry thought. The great windbag god of *Zod Wallop,* a vain idiot obsessed with protocols and the precise arcana of his worship, always arguing with his high priests, urging ever more elaborate rituals. Not a terrifically supportive deity. Even in the later, happy version of the book, Blodkin had been an ineffectual ruler and it had been left to a small, impatient girl to rally him to a sense of duty.

The big car crested a hill, and Harry studied a billboard of cartoon camels smoking cigarettes with sleepy style. *Camels,* Harry thought, *would be more inclined to chew tobacco, being such accomplished spitters.* But advertising agencies and their media-besotted public cared nothing for aptness.

A gas station crouched beyond the sign, advertising FOOD and SOUVENIRS as well as fuel.

"I've got to pee," Rene said.

Harry was already pulling into the station, having glanced reflexively at the gas gauge. The needle lay flat on its back.

Harry pumped gas while his traveling companions went off to use the restrooms. He saw the undeniable staining of the car's rooftop, the sinister black rivulets that scarred the door, and quickly looked away. He saw Raymond pushing the wheelchair that contained poor crumpled Emily. Raymond was headed toward the side of the building. He moved through the sunlight and dust as though he were at the head of a parade.

Rene came out of the ladies' room and took the wheelchair from Raymond. While he held the door, she pulled Emily within. The door closed. Raymond clasped his hands behind his back, rocked on his heels, waited.

Harry leaned over the pump, the gasoline fumes rising

up like old ghosts, conjuring up other trips. He was assaulted by an image of his ex-wife, Jeanne, playful, unharried by circumstance, pre-Amy, pre-marriage.

Jeanne was wearing a black-and-white checkered bikini. Her flesh was pale—they had embarked that morning on their summer's first beach trip—and seemed faintly scandalous in the brash sunlight. She came up behind him and, giggling, mussed his hair while he pumped gas. Then she ducked past him, lifted herself on the bright red fender, and sat, legs straddling the inserted pump.

She smiled and leaned forward in woozy, exaggerated lust, reaching down with her hands to touch the pump's curved nozzle.

He leaned forward and kissed the top of her head, a thicket of black, short-cropped curls. She looked up into his eyes; her own were black, bright, surely the most alert and impetuous in the entire world (until her own daughter arrived). "I'm gonna razzle you," she said, undulating slowly, pursing her lips, sighing loudly.

Her parody of eroticism was profoundly arousing, and Harry was instantly hard as he leaned into her kiss. When he finally surfaced he was shocked to discover an elderly couple climbing out of a car not ten feet to his right. That other people should inhabit the world had seemed, for the moment, wildly improbable.

That night, in a big, wooden house on stilts, in Kitty Hawk, North Carolina, Harry Gainesborough and Jeanne Halifax had conceived Amy. Jeanne's pregnancy delighted them both—and neither was surprised.

The gas pump shut off with a thump, and Harry replaced the nozzle in its slot.

Inside the convenience store it was cool; an overhead fan stirred watery shadows. Harry walked to the register, fished a crumpled twenty from his pocket, and handed it to the cashier, a tanned teenager in a blue uniform.

"Eighteen fifteen. And eighty-five makes nineteen, and one makes twenty," the young man said.

Harry looked up, blinked into oddly familiar blue eyes, saw the tufts of sunbleached hair poking from the sides of the baseball cap.

I've seen you before, Harry thought, *I've—*

Some other part of his mind rudely fetched this thought, snatched it and jerked it offstage. Harry turned and headed back toward the screen door, certain of only one thing: he had to get out of this place.

As Harry approached the screen door, it opened and Raymond, pushing Emily, entered, followed by Allan and Rene. The monkey was cradled in Rene's arm, and a nimbus of golden light seemed, for a moment, to surround them all, as though, dipped in a soup of sunlight, they could not be instantly drained of brightness by the relative gloom of the store. They exuded a reckless, irreverent energy. Allan, who had struck Harry as a serious boy, was laughing loudly, his head thrown back, his mouth open wide.

Harry's fear, pricked by his companions' noisy entrance, dwindled and the need to flee dissolved.

Instead, he turned and moved down an aisle to his right, asking himself what it was that had panicked him so.

He moved past rows of suntan lotion, gaudy towels, a mound of rubber sandals, a rotating display of postcards (blue skies, blue seas, bright scrawls of sand). Idly, he turned the display to the accompaniment of a thin squeaking. He paused and snatched up a postcard of a huge pink hotel.

Before he could examine the card, the thought that had been nibbling at the edges of his consciousness bit through.

He knew what was wrong here. Oh yes, this was a generic roadside oasis, a tourist stop for gas and snacks and sodas and novelties that were only purchased in the impulsive delirium induced by long hours in a rolling automobile. It was an unremarkable store. But it was in the wrong place. This was the middle of North Carolina, and this store should have been somewhere where you could smell the salt in the air, where bare feet tracked sand across the gray-planked floor, where the cries of seagulls (spice for the ear) spiraled from the sky.

He turned the corner then, the postcard still clutched in his hand, and looked down another aisle. He blinked at a row of blue plastic beach buckets with red handles. Something bounced from a nearby shelf and rolled toward him. It was a beach ball, divided into green and blue and yellow pie slices of color. He backed away from it, recognizing it—just as he had recognized the beach buckets. The inflated ball came to rest in the middle of the aisle, silent and ominous.

Harry turned sharply down another aisle.

A cardboard cutout of his daughter, smiling coyly, arms folded to display her decorated bicep, greeted Harry under a display for temporary tattoos of butterflies and puppy dogs. Amy had loved these play tattoos, and Harry had wondered whether indulging her in her formative years might not lead to needle-etched flesh and body piercing in later life, but had decided, in a moment of rare acceptance, that Amy would steer her own life.

Now he stopped, stunned, in front of this cardboard Amy. She was wearing her green bathing suit . . . yes . . . there to his left was a full shelf of the bathing suits and a sign, a blue-

and-white unadorned sign whose block letters explained everything, made it clear why so many painful memories were lodged in this landlocked store: AMY SOUVENIRS the sign read.

Harry slowly turned, his eye now effortlessly recording the artifacts of his daughter's life: The fuzzy pillow that was shaped like a flounder with big crossed cartoon eyes, the yellow magic telescope that rendered all images in a shimmering, rainbow aura, the giant sunglasses with plastic diamonds embedded in their pink frames, the stuffed Hemingway doll (one of a line of dolls called Pen Pals and featuring Poe, Dickens, Tolstoy, Shakespeare, and Faulkner). Gingerly, Harry lifted the Hemingway doll, which flopped limply in his palm. Papa was about ten inches long, full of good, solid beans—a clout to the side of the head with a Pen Pal could stun a prize-fighter—and wore a plaid hunting shirt and khaki-colored pants. His cloth silk-screened face was half burned away, the result of a carelessly dangled cigarette. Amy had refused to relinquish the scorched Hem, carrying her disfigured doll everywhere as a reminder to her forgetful father that smoking was very, very bad and nasty. And Harry had stopped, a good, obedient father when it meant something.

Harry nodded slowly, as though agreeing with the doll. A good Amy Souvenir department would, of course, have the genuine article, the doll with the cigarette burn.

Harry returned the doll to the shelf, watched his hand float back to him, inserted his hand into his pocket and walked down the aisle past the cardboard image of Amy.

He was walking down memory lane. All the colorful childhood things that crowded at the corners of his vision were freighted with meaning. He wasn't going to look, although he might scream.

He saw Raymond at the end of the aisle. Alone and large, a bulky shadow with light splintering behind him like jets of water from a high-pressure hose.

"My Lord Gainesborough," Raymond said, "we must leave here at once."

"Yes," Harry said, although perhaps he did not actually speak the word out loud.

"The others are in the car," Raymond said. Raymond turned then, moving away.

Harry followed, turning back into the main aisle.

He watched Raymond march resolutely toward the screen door, banging it open, swallowed by light.

Harry hurried after him.

"Ah sir. Excuse me, sir." The voice came from behind Harry, and Harry turned.

The cashier was smiling from behind the counter. "That will be ninety-five cents, plus tax, of course."

Harry faltered, looked to see if there might be some other customer standing nearby, someone to whom the words would make sense.

The young man smiled. "The postcard," he said, as though reading Harry's mind. "It's ninety-five cents."

"Ah," Harry said, looking down at the shiny-surfaced rectangle still clutched in his left hand. "I'm sorry, I—" He was about to say that he really didn't want the card, had not, in fact, examined it.

And the clerk would say—or perhaps just think—*yeah, you don't want it if you have to pay for it, right buddy?*

Harry was paying for the postcard when he recognized the young man.

All the details of that day were etched in Harry's mind

and he couldn't be mistaken. For proof there was the blue, badly etched anchor on the kid's wrist.

"You all right, Mister?"

Harry blinked. "I—" He was mistaken, of course. This was someone else, another blond teenager with—

"I got to her real quick," the cashier said. "I had my arms around her and I was ready to turn and haul for shore. There was a nasty rip clawing at my legs, but I knew I could handle it. That's when old Momma Ocean sucker punched me. Something floating in that wave, maybe a two-by-four (a lot of rotten lumber was landing on the beach after the hurricane), something plowed into my skull and I was out of the game, shark food, shark shit by Sunday."

"Jim Lansdown. You're Jim Lansdown, the lifeguard. They said you'd been drinking."

The young man suddenly jerked forward and, spit flying from his mouth, shouted, "That's a goddamn lie! I quit all that six months earlier, went through a rehab for it, was going to an AA meeting every night, ask anyone, they said as much at my funeral. You're the one, aren't you? You're the fucker that's tied me up, set this big stinking investigation in motion. I can smell the guilt in you, all the dead-fish guilt. You son-of-a—"

An explosive crash of thunder pitched the store into thick darkness. The floor buckled under Harry and a high, shrieking wind erupted, filling the blackness above him with flying objects, a pitched battle of poltergeists.

Harry crawled toward the door, toward where, that is, the door had been; no rectangle of light existed to guide him. Something slapped his cheek; he tasted blood on his tongue.

Some sort of epilepsy, perhaps. Maybe this was the disorientation one felt on being shot through the head.

I've been killed by a dead lifeguard, Harry thought. *I've fouled up his afterlife, and he's killed me.* Fair enough.

Still, reflexively, he continued to crawl through a welter of airborne debris. Hunkered down, the top of his head came in contact with something pliant. He lifted a cautious hand, pressed against the hot, rusty grid of wire. He pushed the screen door open, hearing the little shop bell that announced the comings and goings of customers.

A glare as devoid of detail as the night he crawled from assailed his eyes.

He heard Raymond bellow through the hot white air: "Lord Gainesborough!"

He felt his shoulders clutched as he scudded forward and down wooden stairs; then he was being carried, unceremoniously, through the upside-down splendor of blinding light. Then he was dumped in the dust, a lifesize Pen Pal.

"I can't see," he said. "Everything's too bright."

"Here," someone—Rene—said, "put these on."

He felt the frames slide over his ears. The light turned grayish green and the long-necked silhouette of the girl made a reassuring shape in the light.

Someone fumbled in his pocket for the keys. "Allan, you'd better drive."

CHaPTeR THiRTeeN

HER HUSBAND HAD gone outside to smoke a cigar, and Ada sat on the sofa, cradling her second cup of tea on her lap. The elegant, angry woman who had introduced herself to Ada as Gabriel Allan-Tate and who had said, without preamble, "Your son has kidnapped my Allan," was striding back and forth behind the sofa, her heels clacking on the wooden floor.

The older woman, Helen Kurtis, had fallen asleep in an overstuffed chair and was snoring. She reminded Ada of her own aunt Clarice, who could doze in a straight-backed chair, maintaining a starched dignity, as though mummified and on display.

Before falling asleep, Helen Kurtis had given a matter-of-fact account of the night's harrowing events, assuring Ada that her son and daughter-in-law were fine—that everyone was fine—and that, no doubt, they would show up momentarily.

Ada jumped when Gabriel leaned over the sofa and spoke directly into her ear.

"It's time to call the police, I think. For all I know, your son, urged on by imaginary voices, could be murdering the others."

"Raymond," Ada responded, turning to regard the woman and somewhat shocked to find herself addressing an upside-down head and expanse of white throat, "is a gentle person and has never harmed anyone."

Gabriel somersaulted into the sofa, righted herself with languid grace, and smiled wickedly as she brushed her dress down over white thighs. "I believe you have just described the average mass murderer. It is the gentle types that are always coming unhinged. Surely the local police have a right to know that a psychotic who has abducted a poor, helpless wheelchair-bound girl, an unfortunate woman who, I understand, is quite hopelessly brain-dead . . . surely the police should be informed that such an individual is at large in the community. I do not know how Allan fell under his spell, but my son must be released before his life is ruined by the association. I've seen how these things work. If you are along for the ride on one of these killing sprees, your reputation is ruined for life. Guilt by association, you know. Blame it on the media, but that's the way it is."

Ada glared at this rude woman whose arrogance and sense of privilege were as overbearing as the dark scent she wore, one of those aggressive, expensive perfumes with a name like Ravish.

"Raymond is not, I assure you, embarked on a killing spree. And your son is certainly free to—"

The sound stirred them all. Gabriel looked up at the ceiling. Helen Kurtis woke, snorting. And John Story entered the cabin, opening the door and letting the *whup whup whup* noise in. "Looks like we have company," he said.

Ada, her husband, Gabriel, and Helen all stood on the porch and watched the big helicopter settle in the clearing by the lake. The sun's reflection in the water shivered.

Three men, all of them wearing suits, disembarked from the silver chopper and moved gingerly—displaying great distaste for the muddy ground that sucked at shiny shoes and tailored pants legs—toward the cabin.

"Jesus," Gabriel said, her voice off to Ada's right, "it's Peake."

Ada disliked the man instantly. His lips were too red, and his habit of leaning forward and speaking in a low just-between-you-and-me voice reminded her of a smarmy talk-show host trying to woo gullible viewers with a whisper. He also had the annoying habit of running his long fingers through his hair while tilting his head back, as though he were luxuriating under a hot shower, and if someone had told him that this mannerism would endear him to people . . . well, all Ada could say was: They had done him a great disservice.

He sprawled in the sofa with his head back and said his mission was one of great urgency, life and death, as it were. He told them his name was Dr. Roald Peake and that he was the head of a corporation involved in pharmaceutical research and that Mrs. Allan-Tate could corroborate that.

Everyone looked at Gabriel Allan-Tate as though she would do just this, perhaps with some precise, formal gesture, but she seemed disoriented, staring out the window with an expression that might have indicated poor digestion or the end of a love affair.

"Gabriel," Peake said, coming off the sofa with a serpentine glide and swooping an arm around the woman's shoulder.

He leaned toward her ear, bowing to do so. "If you are worried about that housekeeping unpleasantness, that nasty smell in the foyer, let me assure you that it is taken care of. I urge you to put it from your mind and never approach it again."

He steered Gabriel to a chair—as though he were the host and this his house—and resumed his position on the sofa.

"I have just recently learned that Mr. Harold Gainesborough and the people who are presently in his company are all participants in an unfortunate drug experiment, administered by Gabriel's late husband, Marlin Tate, a man of genius but poor judgment. These experiments were conducted while the people involved were patients at Harwood Psychiatric. That such a thing could happen is lamentable . . . but that milk is, as they say, spilled, and I am here to prevent some greater tragedy from occurring. There is every reason to believe that this drug, this Ecknazine, has powerful hallucinogenic properties which may be linked to certain aging processes . . . which is to say that one or more of Dr. Tate's subjects may experience something equivalent to an LSD flashback. Only . . . well, more dramatic. Dr. Tate destroyed all of his notes, unfortunately, but"—here Peake smiled in a manner that was intended, no doubt, to be ingratiating, but which made Ada shiver—"as a competitor I was aware of some properties of the drug."

"Spies," Gabriel said.

Peake shrugged, continued. "The drug established a sort of communal bond, a psychic link. Mind you, the subjects might never have met, might not be aware of the influence they exerted on each other. Dr. Tate spoke of a resonant effect. Ah." Peake regarded his listeners with what Ada took to be his first genuine expression: one of frustration and anger. "I don't know what he meant by this 'resonant' effect. Perhaps he didn't know himself. But, here they are, all these Ecknazine folks, all come together. It could be very volatile, could cause psychological damage to one or all of them. Not a flashback, exactly. More . . . ah . . . explosive. Or . . . " He ran his fingers through his hair again, closing his eyes. "Perhaps nothing. In any event, better safe than sorry, and so I am here."

And what, Ada wanted to know, did that exactly mean, his being here?

Observation. That was the word he used. He wanted the Ecknazine subjects under observation for a period of time. He wanted to run some psychological and physiological checks on them to determine that they were in no danger.

Ada shot a quick look at her husband, who was standing next to the overstuffed chair that housed the ample Helen Kurtis. His arms were folded and he was glowering with bull-dog truculence, and he saw his wife look at him and spoke back with his red-rimmed, seen-it-and-suffered eyes: We are not going that route again, his eyes said.

Ada nodded slowly. Her boy didn't like to be studied and had not taken kindly to the six weeks he'd been at the Simpec Center for the Study of Human Potential. It had been a great setback for Raymond. It had been something of a setback for Simpec, too, actually. The director of Simpec, a heavyset, excitable man, had accused poor Raymond—who had only been thirteen years old, for heaven's sake—of outlandish acts of sabotage and—really!—mind control.

CHaPTeR FouRTeeN

❖ ❖ ❖ ❖ ❖ ❖ ❖ ❖ ❖ ❖ ❖ ❖ ❖

HARRY WAS WORKING on it, working on putting his world to rights, restoring order. One mental baby step at a time. He sat next to the window in the backseat of the car. Emily was propped woodenly on his left. Occasionally she would lean against him as the car sped around a curve.

The window was down and the wind ran green, honeysuckle fingers through his hair. His sight was fully restored and he studied the Carolina countryside through the tinted glasses, speaking the sights silently, like a foreigner practicing his new tongue: farm, tractor, oak, dog, pond.

Cautiously, he reached up and took the sunglasses off. The world was less demure, brighter. Cows were revealed, loafing in the shadows cast by green willows.

He gathered strength from the scene. Nothing like cows to center and calm a man. Visual sedatives, cows. *The Sneeze That Destroyed New Jersey* had begun with a family outing whose sole purpose was to "see cows in their natural habitat."

Hay fever had subverted that purpose and taught everyone a lesson in acceptance and given birth to world peace (after the unfortunate but necessary destruction of New Jersey) and ...

A small explosion—that registered on Harry's ear as an *ooph!*—was immediately followed by a bouncing deceleration and a number of exclamations from his traveling companions, and an explanatory shout from Raymond that said it all: *Flat!*

They all climbed out of the car, and Raymond set about the business of replacing the tire. Fortunately, the trunk did contain a spare, fully inflated, and, after much searching, a jack was also discovered.

"Please, my Lord," Raymond said, holding up a hand, "Lord Allan and I have the situation well in hand. If you will attend to the ladies, perhaps entertain them with humorous anecdotes, Allan and I will set things to rights in no time."

"Raymond—" Harry began, but he wasn't sure what he intended to say. Indeed, Raymond Story was at his best when engineering the changing of a tire. He brought to the task an enthusiasm that was perhaps unwarranted, as though it were a moon launch he was supervising, but he did get the job done, with surprising efficiency considering the high rhetoric with which he surrounded the task. The monkey contributed positive energy by jumping up and down on the roof of the car.

"Voilà!" Raymond was saying in no time, waving them forward, and Harry was wheeling Emily back into the sunlight when two things occurred.

Something fluttered to the dust and weeds at his feet and he bent down to pick it up. It appeared to be a piece of white cardboard, bent in the middle, but as he rose with it, it turned over in his hand, opening to reveal the satiny finish of the photograph. It was the postcard he had purchased—*from a dead* ... let's move along briskly with this thought—the postcard of a large, pink hotel, perched gloriously close to the ocean, white sand and sea grass in the foreground, a confetti-like celebration of seagulls falling toward the earth, pulling the eye with them, drawn by the small, fearless girl in a green bathing suit, holding her hand high with bread crumbs for the winged multitudes.

Amy.

He looked closer. No mistake. Amy. The way she stood, all her weight on one foot, her body bowed forward as though she were a human sail . . . Amy. And why not? Hadn't he snatched this card from that rack, there, amid the AMY SOUVE-NIRS? It made perfect sense.

He turned the card over and read: *St. Petersburg Arms, St. Petersburg, Florida. This hotel, built in 1918 by millionaire playboy Andrew Mallon, is a landmark for* . . . Raymond had just been speaking of the St. Petersburg Arms. Yes. The mysterious Duke lived there.

Amy had never been to St. Petersburg, Florida. What did this mean?

A shadow darkened the blank surface of the postcard, as though mirroring Harry's own clouded thoughts.

"Look!" someone shouted, and Harry turned in the direction of the shout—it had been Rene—and followed her gaze upward.

The cloudless sky was infinity blue, and a great, black dropcloth flapped across it, a shape-changing hole in the sky that made Harry's soul cower before he even identified the monstrous form, before it lay, illogically but perfectly, over the image of the creature that did not exist, the dream he had dreamt at the bottom of despair: the Ralewing.

"It's a fucking monster," Rene said. "I didn't know they got that big."

They don't, Harry thought. But what did he know? He had never seen one the size of an eighteen-wheeler before—but then, outside of *Zod Wallop,* he'd never seen one at all.

He heard Raymond then, his voice commanding but not, oddly, panicked. "Better get back in the car," he said. "I wouldn't be surprised if its destination is the same as ours."

Ada stood, clutching her handbag as though preparing to wring it, a ritualized stance that all Story women assumed before doing battle with clerks, salesman, tax assessors, any sort of authoritarian impediment to their will. She was a woman who did not anger easily, but she had listened to this Peake long enough. Ada spoke. "When my Raymond returns, I am taking him home," she said. "I can tell you right now that he will not want to go into any institution. He doesn't like such places, and judging from what you've just told me I can see he has been right all along. I might also remind you that he is on his honeymoon. He and his bride are not going anywhere for observation. I don't know if you have ever been married, Dr. Peake, but I can tell you that the newly married are shy and shun close scrutiny. I'm sure Raymond will be glad, at some later date, to fill out any questionnaires you might find appropriate, but he will not be shuffling around in any more hospital gowns, not while my husband and I draw a breath." She extended a hand toward her husband, who moved quickly to her side and hugged her in a show of solidarity.

One of Peake's colleagues, standing by the door, snorted. "We wouldn't want to upset them newlyweds, would we?"

Ada glared at him as he rocked back on his heels. He was a grinning man with a crew cut and small teeth—*lizard teeth,* Ada thought.

Peake raised a hand. "Quiet, Karl. Mrs. Story does not understand the gravity of the situation. There are people, unscrupulous people, rivals of mine, who are interested in the Ecknazine research and its subjects. I'm afraid that the spies Gabriel alluded to do exist in this business, and despite the most rigorous security measures I have reason to believe that there may be other interested parties in the vicinity. If they find Raymond and his friends before we do . . . well, their desire for knowledge would no doubt outweigh any other considerations. Your son and his companions could get hurt."

"It is high time we called the police," Helen Kurtis said, pushing herself out of the armchair and marching to the phone.

A muffled explosion shook the cabin; the windowpane rattled in its frame.

The man called Karl turned and ran out the door. Everyone followed him.

They stood on the lawn and stared down at the lake, at what remained of the burning helicopter (black metal wrestling with yellow flames), at the black column of smoke that probed the blue sky like a leprous tentacle, at the man running up the hill, his leather jacket identifying him as the pilot.

Ada noticed—with no surprise—that Karl had produced a handgun. The other man who had accompanied Peake came around the corner of the cabin, a rifle cradled in his arms.

There was fire on the lake itself, lines of fire that stretched on across the muddy bank. It was as though a giant hand had raked the ground, each finger-carved furrow sprouting flames.

The paths of flames ran past the helicopter and up the far hill into the trees. The top of a pine tree emitted a dirty thread of smoke. Ada leaned into her husband's strong embrace. A smoldering-tar stink surrounded them, and she felt stained by a foulness in the air, impaled by a curious, wild panic that was unwarranted. Whatever had happened, she was witnessing its aftermath; nothing immediately threatening was to be seen.

"What?" she asked—more exclamation than interrogative—as her husband suddenly squeezed her sharply, and she saw the black shape unfold above the pines and sail, like a funereal kite, down from the mountains, toward them.

"Dear God!" she heard Helen Kurtis exclaim. The old woman's gravel voice broke. "It can't be."

Ah, Ada thought, no less frightened but suddenly certain of the phenomenon. *It can be.*

It came toward them, moving with an uncanny, sinister shimmer. It uttered a piercing cry that made her heart race. The long stalk of its neck unfurled, stretched, as though it were attempting to sniff them out, bird-dog fashion, and then it twisted violently in the air and plummeted earthward.

They screamed as one (Peake and his minions, Gabriel, Helen, Ada, John) and fled toward the cabin.

Its shadow fell over Ada, a shroud. The reek of terror filled her lungs, and she thought she might explode, but then the sunlight came again, and she fell, breaking her fall with her hands, and blinked at the running shadow on the ground before her and watched it climb the cabin porch and disappear.

She stood up in time to see it dwindle on the horizon, an undulating black shape gliding over the mountains, easily mistaken at this distance for a plastic trash bag dragged heavenward by hungry winds.

The day was still and cloudless, however, and Ada knew

what she'd seen. The Ralewing's spewed vomit still burned on the land—the flames were now gone from the lake—and the helicopter shimmered in near invisible fire, a skeletal mirage.

"I wonder if I could talk to you a minute," Ada said. Helen Kurtis turned and smiled tentatively.

Ada's husband whispered in her ear. "Ada," he said, loading her name with caution and doubt.

Ada looked at her husband. "I have to tell someone, John. I don't trust that Peake fellow. This woman is a close friend of Harry Gainesborough's, and she's no fool. She knows what she saw today. I hardly think she'll be shocked by what we have to show her."

Helen smiled tentatively. "Well, I hardly *do* know what I saw."

"You see," John said, looking hard at his wife.

Ada took a deep breath. "You saw one of those creatures from Mr. Gainesborough's book *Zod Wallop*. Nasty things. Raymond had an unholy fear of them."

"I don't know, *really*, just what I saw."

"Ada," John Story said, "I don't believe Mrs. Kurtis cares to hear about all this. We've all had a shock. We just need to find Raymond and—"

Ada inclined her head toward the cabin where Peake had gone to make telephone calls, accompanied by Gabriel and the others. "He knows. It's clear enough. He's so excited he's about to burst. He wants to get my Raymond and find out how it's done and cause all manner of trouble." Ada thought her anger would override her fear, her sense of helplessness, but suddenly the momentum failed her. She faltered, and then, like a hiccup, tears surprised and embarrassed her. She staggered, instantly wretched, and assaulted by tears, she fled down to the lake, her husband's shouts behind her.

Ada could not stop sobbing. She stared into the sun-smeared water, saw her own stout reflection, the fuzzy halo of her hair; saw then the shape loom up behind her, thought it was her husband and was prepared to be irritated with the hand upon her shoulder.

"It was a Ralewing," Helen said, and Ada turned and smiled through her tears. "A Ralewing the size of a house."

Ada nodded. "That's exactly what it was."

Ada took the proffered handkerchief and blew her nose. She looked up. "Would you come with me? I've got something to show you in the car."

"Certainly."

Ada had her husband drive them to the other side of the lake. With the cabin (and Dr. Peake) safely behind them, she had her husband unlock the trunk. Ada reached into the darkness of the rising trunk lid and retrieved the wooden box, rectangular, no bigger than a shoe box. She looked behind her furtively.

Her husband closed the trunk, and Ada placed the box on the trunk and unlocked the tiny padlock. She looked at Helen, who had climbed out of the car's backseat and lumbered slowly to join them.

"Bad back," she said, explaining her labored progress.

Ada made a face of sympathy. "I have some Excedrin if it would help," she said.

The older woman smiled wanly. "Thanks, but I've got better drugs, stuff that would make an elephant woozy. I'm looking forward to taking them when all this excitement dies down."

Ada nodded. "Well." They both looked at the box. Ada decided that some background was in order before the unveiling: "Raymond is a great student of Mr. Gainesborough's books. He has read those books to tatters. Before and after his accident. He almost drowned in a swimming pool, you know, and he has all sorts of ideas about that, and when he met Mr. Gainesborough at Harwood . . . well, I have been unable to follow my son's very elaborate and strongly felt explanations of what it all means, but it certainly is *fraught* with meaning because nothing, absolutely *nothing* in Raymond's world happens by accident. I'm told that this is a function of his schizophrenia, but I think I know better." Ada smiled. Then, realizing that she had imparted no actual information, shed no light on the darkness, she continued: "You are, of course, familiar with Mr. Gainesborough's book, *Biff Bertram and the Rudeness from the Rim of Space?*"

Helen nodded. "*Biff* is one of my favorites, although at the time I thought parts of it were a little raw for young ears."

Ada nodded. "Me too."

"Children consider it immensely funny."

"Yes. Well." Ada didn't know how to proceed. She sighed. "Oh, here, see for yourself." She opened the lid to the box, unwrapped tissue paper. "There."

Helen leaned forward. She leaned closer then, pushed tissue paper away. It was a small, doll-like creature, or rather the remains of such a creature. White bone and some bits of dried skin remained, as though it were some desert roadkill, sterilized by pounding sun and wind and rain and the scavenging of crows and beetles. It looked piglike, part armadillo perhaps, with a gourdlike head, great empty eye sockets, and small, human-child hands (but three-fingered, no thumb). It suggested a number of other animals, but there was really no need to shop around for comparisons since it looked exactly like what it was.

"Well?" Ada said.

Helen looked up. "Is it real?"

Ada nodded. "It cried and cried—like a lost kitten—and couldn't be comforted. Then it died." And then, seeing this creature he had conjured die, Raymond had a sort of breakdown—that was his first hospitalization—and the doctors came back to tell Ada and her husband that their son appeared to have certain abilities that he was having difficulty integrating and that there was a place that could help him: Simpec, in Baltimore. Ada and John didn't know what to do, so they let him go, but the Simpec people were like Dr. Peake, they just wanted to poke and pinch, they didn't want to help Raymond, and one day Raymond ran away. Simpec didn't try to get him back. He was, if Ada was reading properly between the lines, something of a disappointment to them. The wild talents that had attracted their notice were gone.

Ada stopped speaking, looked at the tiny ruined creature in its varnished coffin and shook off the past. "You recognize it, don't you?"

Helen nodded. "It's a Politer."

"He's dead," Biff said, stunned.

The small creature sighed, nodded its head, and said, "Yes dear sir, he is dead. If it is not too much inconvenience, I would like to move him out of the roadway. He would be deeply upset if his body were to hinder anyone's journey."

"Certainly," Biff said. He grabbed the Politer's feet and helped his companion carry him to the side of the road.

"What do you suppose was the cause of death?"

"Well, he's pink, sir. I think that can only mean one thing."

"Yes?"

"Well, rudeness, sir. There's no doubt of it, really. Rudeness did him in."

"I was just coming up the stairs when it started to run down them. I thought it was a rat or something, but then I knew, almost immediately, that it wasn't, and I did recognize it, I did know what it was, and I remember thinking in my head, 'There goes a Politer' because I'd read the books, and I *knew* what it was."

When Biff Bertram crashed on the planet, Decorum, he had immediately encountered a race of cheerful, self-effacing creatures called Politers whose entire life and philosophy was founded on a code of extreme Decency. And, as is so often the case in such precipitous landings, his timing had coincided with an attack by monstrous Gutwuzzards, a race dedicated to touring the known universe, photographing everything (a Gutwuzzard obscuring the foreground of every snap), and terrorizing the locals with loud, menacing laughter, derogatory comments on local customs, and ribald jokes that were offensive to every known form of sentient life, even the perverted Mud Shoats of Warmslime.

Gutwuzzards on any world were a nuisance. On the planet Decorum, where the gentle inhabitants could be murdered by rudeness, Gutwuzzards were disaster. And only Biff Bertram, with the help of his friend, Stinky Lester (a match for any Gutwuzzard), could save the day.

"We never showed this to anyone," Ada said, pushing the tissue paper back and replacing the box's lid. "We thought about showing it to the Simpec people, but we didn't. We were scared. And when Raymond ran away from Simpec, that settled it. We put this box in the attic, and it stayed there. There weren't any more . . . manifestations."

Raymond had obviously been traumatized by the creature's death. He felt responsible for bringing it into this world where it couldn't live, and Ada thought he did what he could to prevent that from happening again. He became very remote, and for a long time he was like a stranger, hardly talking at all. It was Ada's opinion that her son was watching himself, trying to hold his imagination in check for fear of what might happen.

"He got very good grades at school that year. I think it was his way of coping, throwing himself into his studies."

And then, that summer, he began to hear voices and the radio would address him directly, suggesting that he pull one of his teeth out with a pliers (the tooth, it seemed, was an alien transmitter). He had a small 35-mm camera that John had given him for his birthday, and he began taking pictures everywhere he went. He was convinced that dark forces were clouding his mind, and that the camera would reveal what his bewitched brain could not puzzle out. The developed photos were mundane, showed nothing, but when Ada tried to reason with her son, he said that the ordinariness of the photos showed only that the Watchers knew to keep their distance when he carried the camera. One day, he left the house early in the morning, and he didn't return, not that day, not the next.

John Story notified the authorities of his son's disappearance, and the description matched that of a young man who had been discovered nude at a local construction site, cradling a shattered camera in his hands, incapable of speech. The police had transported him to the state psychiatric hospital.

Raymond's parents saw to it that their son was transferred to Harwood Psychiatric Institute, where he was diagnosed as suffering from schizophrenia, medication was prescribed, and in less than two weeks he was released. While lucid and able to return to school in the fall, Raymond remained convinced that he had broken his camera in a tumble down a hill. Having lost his protection against the Watchers, he had been attacked, robbed of his clothes, molested mentally and physically. The details, of course, had been erased by his alien tormentors.

Raymond's association with Harwood was ongoing. With the proper medication and outpatient treatment, he would rally for three or four months, and then some new delusion would surface, and he would have to be admitted to the Institute again. Ada did not want to talk about the procession of strange fancies. She had come to accept each new mental aberration with growing stoicism. And then Raymond had traveled back to familiar country, back to the children's books of Harry Gainesborough, back to a convoluted world of fantasy and a book with the unlikely title of *Zod Wallop*.

"Lord Gainesborough is in my group," Raymond had said, and Ada Story, having come to discount her son's version of reality, had been amazed to discover that the sad, awkward man in need of a haircut, who smiled apologetically when Raymond introduced her to him, was indeed Harold Gainesborough. He looked older and less confident than the picture on his books, but he was unmistakably the same man.

Helen nodded. "I saw to it that he went to Harwood. He seemed in danger of hurting himself. I suppose there's no medicine for a daughter's death. If he and Jeanne could have stayed together, things might have been different. But they didn't.

"You should have seen Amy. She had a sweetness that could light up a room and a way of laughing, hugging herself, like she was surprised that so much good feeling could inhabit her body. Well—" Helen stopped abruptly and Ada reached out and touched her arm.

"We better get back," Ada said. "I'm sure they will be along shortly."

Helen nodded, fetching a handkerchief from her purse and dabbing at her eyes. "I'm not usually this emotional," she said.

"Such a tragedy," Ada said.

Ada handed the box back to her husband, and he locked it in the trunk.

Harry was aware of the dust before he realized that the car had come to a stop. Since the Ralewing, since the shock of the postcard of Amy in front of the St. Petersburg Arms, the world of his immediate surroundings had receded. A wild maelstrom of thoughts churned inside, stirred by a single phrase: *You could change it back.* Raymond had said that.

You learned, growing up, that death was the ultimate minnow trap, entered with almost casual ease, down the narrowing funnel. Your goldfish died and turned into a pale, hard crescent, bobbing to the aquarium's surface, later interred in a matchbox. Spanky the cat yawned, stretched, sauntered slowly across the highway, and had his entire nine lives slapped from him by a diesel that didn't even slow on its way to Ohio.

Dead is the end of the line. Forever.

In this world.

Go to another world then. Flip the channel and find a world where Amy fed seagulls on a beach in Florida—something she had never done in this world.

And what if the other world was simply madness? What then? An easy answer, although he'd been edging up on it coyly: Better a madness where his daughter lived than any cold reality that was robbed of her.

He would follow the faintest promise, go with Raymond, go . . . But the car was stopped, and fine orange dust, sour-smelling and full of over-ripe sunlight, poured in through the window. A construction worker wearing a hard-hat approached. Road repairs, no doubt.

Then it happened, all the doors of the car sprung open, large men in tan jumpsuits shouting, rough hands clamping his shoulders, lifting him. "Let's go!"

"Unhand me, blackguard!" Raymond's unmistakable bellow.

Harry was spun around, slammed against the side of the car. He heard Rene scream and Allan roar, felt a pinprick at the base of his neck, accompanied by a coppery thirst that flared in the back of his throat.

The world slowed, and Harry watched the monkey scramble out the window and onto the car's roof. It leapt to Harry's shoulder, launching itself again immediately. Harry heard someone scream, felt the arms around his chest fall away. Harry turned, found that his legs disobeyed him, and crumbled slowly to the ground where tiny, purple flowers, triumphant amid the dust, greeted him. Someone shouted, "Shoot the monkey!"

Harry's head lolled sideways, his eyes turned upward; he watched a rifle being raised by a thin, unshaven man wearing steel-rimmed glasses.

The man took aim, assuming a prissy, stiff-as-a-deacon stance. Harry watched Lord Arbus scampering toward a dusty hedge, beyond which a forest of oaks offered shelter.

The spider monkey's narrow shoulders and scruffy pelt already seemed to show the black-red hole of the bullet's entrance and Harry screamed, "No!"

The rifle jumped in the air, a low *crack* sending the bullet skyward as the man toppled, howling, Emily's head rising in the bulldozed rubble, her eyes unblinking over the trousered leg, her teeth firmly sunk in the marksman's calf.

"Good for you Emily," Harry said, his words a series of dry coughs that expelled the last of his consciousness as the drug took hold and carried him away.

CHaPTeR FiFTeeN

⚬ ⚬ ⚬ ⚬ ⚬ ⚬ ⚬ ⚬ ⚬ ⚬ ⚬ ⚬

HELEN KURTIS CLEANED the cabin with fierce energy and then lay on the made bed, her hair still bound in a rag, a faint odor of Clorox rising from her like mist from a swamp.

Everyone was gone now and there was no reason to stay. The police had returned her car, and it was parked in the front yard. The tank was almost full. A storm was coming, rolling in from the east according to the radio, but if she left now, drove north through the night, she could beat the rain. A good plan. She closed her eyes and slept.

When she awoke, evening was approaching, the twilight hastened by thunderclouds, and Helen rolled on her side and clicked on the small bedside lamp.

She ached. Her blouse had slipped out from the elastic of her slacks, and she felt that curious disarray that she associated with growing old. In youth, she'd been a single, seamless entity, but now she was a bloat of stomach, a swelling of ankles, a knot of shoulders.

She sighed and climbed out of bed. She went to the front door and opened it, flipping the porch light on. A cold exhalation of rain glittered in the yellow light. She saw the shadow shape of her car.

"Harry, where the hell are you?" she said.

The police had found the car by the side of a country road, three miles from the cabin. Harry and his comrades had disappeared, vanished as though beamed up to Jupiter by those ubiquitous tabloid aliens.

Helen suspected that Dr. Roald Peake knew where Harry was. He and his crew had left abruptly in another summoned helicopter, but not before he'd received a phone call that had incensed him. Helen was the only one who had seen his reaction to the call—everyone else was outside when she handed the phone to him—and he had regained control immediately. But for a moment, rage had made the skull beneath his flesh visible, and his voice had grown cold.

"Are you sure?" he had said, causing Helen to turn and look at him. The words had been measured and quiet, but they had been encased in ice, brittle with menace. And then Peake had roared, "Why didn't I know Blaine was here? Why wasn't I informed? I do not pay you people to tell me what *has* happened! I pay you to see that it *doesn't* happen!"

He had slammed the phone down, made another call. He had turned, seen Helen in the room then, conjured a smile with such suddenness that it startled her, and said, "Business. One headache after another."

Helen had not smiled back. "You know something you're not telling us."

He shook his head no. "My dear lady, I don't know where your friend Harold Gainesborough and his merry band are. I wish I did. I assure you I will do my utmost to find them."

The police, when they arrived, offered the same assurances. And finally, they had all left.

Helen closed the door on the rain. She went back to the bed and sat on the edge. If she left tonight, she need only drive for a few hours before finding a motel. The anonymity of a motel room would surely be preferable to Harry's abandoned cabin.

The phone cried fitfully and Helen answered it, dizzy with hope and fear.

"No, this is Helen," she said, when the voice on the other end asked for Harry.

"Helen Kurtis?"

"Why yes."

"Helen, this is Jeanne."

"Jeanne!"

Harry's ex had called for no particular reason. Just . . . well, she was worried, because she knew Harry had blown off the teaching job, stopped writing, withdrawn . . . and she just had a bad feeling that he was out there alone thinking . . . well, she knew how thinking could go, alone, and . . .

Helen had interrupted to tell her that Harry was missing and the police were investigating. Helen told the story, omitting the part where a giant Ralewing set a helicopter on fire (no one had mentioned the Ralewing to the police, either, sensing that it was an event that fell, most emphatically, in the you-had-to-be-there category; the smoldering helicopter had, in a simpler telling, crashed). Helen also omitted, for the sake of credibility, any mention of the corpse of an imaginary creature from the planet Decorum.

"Helen," Jeanne said. "Should I come down there?"

"No, honey. I'm leaving myself. The police will let us

know when they find them. Or Harry will call. And there's no point in sitting around here."

They had talked for another five minutes, and on a second reassurance from Helen that all would certainly turn out all right, they had said good-bye and hung up.

"So what was that about, Halifax?"

Jeanne Halifax regarded her boyfriend, Mark, with mild surprise, as though she had forgotten he was in her apartment. He was standing at the door to the bathroom, naked and tall, his chest mottled with hair, clumped thickets that, for a moment, suggested some sort of tenacious weed blackened by fire.

"Come on, Halifax. What's this 'Should I come down' shit? You got a sudden yearning to see your ex-spouse?"

She had changed her name back to Halifax in one more vain attempt to elude the past, and Mark had taken to calling her that despite—or perhaps because of—her objections.

"Harry's missing," she said.

Mark came up to her and hugged her. He was wet and the wetness soaked through her nightgown, a clammy embrace. Instantly her apartment's air-conditioner hummed on, as though poised to chill her. "Missing on all cylinders," Mark said.

She pushed him back. "Hey. Come on. It's not funny."

He shrugged, walked to the dresser and dried himself while watching her in the mirror. "So what happened?"

She told him.

"So what?" he said when she was finished. "Maybe he's been eaten by fucking mosquitoes. You know, you could pay a little more attention to the man who is in your life. I get a little sick of 'poor Harry' this, 'poor Harry' that. That guy fucking left you, remember? He walked out when you needed him most." He lifted a small green bottle and poured liquid into his hands, leaned forward to massage his face. He dropped his hands and smiled at his reflection. Then he turned and threw himself backward onto the bed, arms outspread. "I'm here."

"Mark," Jeanne said, turning to him, "just because I'm not married to Harry doesn't—"

He reached out and caught her by the arm, jerked her toward him. She toppled into his arms, into the sea of his eye-watering cologne. His hands, big, rough blocks, lifted her nightgown up; her arms rose reflexively and it was gone.

"Mark," she said, but her voice wasn't protest. Her voice sounded, she thought, like a woman trying to place a stranger's name.

"Yeh, babe. That's right, Halifax. Mark. Man-in-your-life Mark."

He had her panties down around her ankles and then his finger was in her, businesslike, as though holding his place in a book, and then he rolled on top of her.

Jeanne stared at the ceiling. *Harry's disappeared again,* she thought. She felt a twinge of envy.

After the phone call from Jeanne, Helen thought about Abe. God, how she missed him. Still. Always. He had been so crazy wild about her that she had come to think of herself as beautiful.

And even now, when she thought of him, she seemed somehow strengthened. Conjuring an image of his face, the fire of pride in his eyes, knowing that she was its inspiration, she could rally her self-esteem, she could go on.

She felt sadness for married couples who could not sustain each other. She saw them all the time, these men and women who had contracted to live together but took no joy in it, frightened that they were wasting their lives, hoarding love as though it were a commodity to be bargained.

Abe had taught her, that was the thing. He had taught her that the well was bottomless and that spending recklessly would not exhaust his affection.

Helen sighed and walked over to the kitchen cupboard. She found a can of soup, chicken and rice, and opened it. As she heated the soup, stirring slowly, she thought of Harry and Jeanne. They had been unreservedly in love, blessed. Amy had come into their lives like a benediction, and her death had been a brutal explosion, shattering their marriage.

What they did not understand, what Helen knew because she had lived with Abe, Grand Master of the Open Heart, was that the terrible blast of fate had not destroyed one scrap of their love. But dazed, full of recriminations and pain, they had decided that seeking consolation could only be a sin. There was no way to ease this monstrous ache, and to try was to demean the loss. Together they had agreed, in silence and withdrawal, that nothing survived their daughter's death. But Harry had been the greater offender. He should never have left that day.

Helen poured the hot soup into a cup. Outside, the storm was in full cry. The thunder seemed to run along the ground, shaking the floorboards. The rain was hard, raging inside the wind, the dismal hiss of the downpour accompanied by the waterfall slap of the cabin's emptying gutters.

Helen had taken the first sip of her soup when something thumped against the door. She looked up. Silence. Then an undeniable thump again.

Helen put the cup down and went to the door. As she

crossed the room, the noise became a rhythmic, muffled pounding.

She put her hand on the doorknob, paused. The noise seemed to come from the bottom portion of the door, and she doubted that it was inspired by any human agent. It wasn't the rap of knuckles.

Perhaps the storm had hurled something against the door, an uprooted bush, perhaps, and it now banged mindlessly, animated by the wind. Or perhaps it was some forest creature, seeking shelter. Helen did not fancy sharing the cabin with, for instance, a skunk.

She pressed her ear against the door. "Hello?" she shouted.

She heard a noise then, an answering *whoop,* and she flung the door open and the monkey named Arbus entered, head down, arms akimbo, dripping water and muttering to himself.

After Helen had toweled the monkey down and watched it noisily gorge itself on soup, she wrapped it in a blanket.

"Well," she said, expecting no answer, "where is Harry? Where is your Raymond? Where are they?"

The monkey's eyes had begun to droop. It opened them at the sound of Helen's voice but it looked, if the term can be applied to an animal, dumbfounded, and closed its eyes again, lost in exhausted slumber.

Helen placed her small monkey-bundle on the armchair's seat and moved to the bed, changing quickly into her nightgown and sliding under the covers. She turned off the bed lamp.

She was awakened from a dream in which the sky was filled with floating marigolds and some sort of a parade was in progress and she was on a gaudy float, waving at people with her free hand. Her other hand was clasped in the small hand of . . . she looked down and there was Amy, smiling up, her hair wet and glued to her forehead, her features intense. "Aunt Helen," Amy said. "Why is Heaven so stupid?"

Helen woke then, so suddenly that the dream refused to leave, at least entirely. The storm had passed, and the moon had returned to fill the room with pale light, and Helen looked down at the hand she still held, hairy and black, and saw the small, dark body of Arbus curled on his side. The monkey's body exhaled a musky, reassuring odor. As Helen watched, Arbus rolled on his back and absently scratched his belly.

Helen remembered then, with a powerful shiver as though the memory were a revelation, that Abe had often reached out for her as he slept; hand-in-hand they had dreamed.

You choose your omens, Helen thought. She squeezed the warm, sleep-offered hand and felt the nearness of her dead husband and his gentle vigilance.

We'll find them, she thought.

CHaPTeR SiXTeeN

✦ ✦ ✦ ✦ ✦ ✦ ✦ ✦ ✦ ✦ ✦ ✦

HERE HE WAS again, down in the Great Tiredness of Group. It was a little different, of course. At Harwood, he had never been in group therapy with Emily, Allan, or Rene—and they were definitely here in their catatonic, truculent, and volatile (respectively) selves. But Harry had been in group with Raymond, and it was Raymond who dominated this new, mandatory gathering, Raymond with his gaspy, mustache-fluttering fervor, his wild eyes and sweeping gestures.

Today, it was difficult to make out just what Raymond was saying. Harry felt oddly meaning impaired. He could not seem to get the sense of words. That is, he could recognize individual words (a word like *danger* would suddenly come up to him, as a curious fish might approach a scuba diver's mask) but these words refused to shake down into logical sentences.

That was probably the result of the drugs they had given

him. The drugs were, he assumed, designed to make him more receptive to his feelings.

When they asked, he said, "I'm tired. I'm really tired."

That, apparently, was not a legitimate feeling. They kept at him.

"Where am I?" he asked, but they said that he was trying to change the subject.

"Sad," he told them. "I feel sad."

They wanted him to elaborate. He said that he felt sad for everything. He saw the President on television and felt sad that a man could be so filled with need that he would become a politician. He then felt sad for the media pundits who came on after the President in order to savage him, leaning forward in their chairs as though something besides their balance was at stake, mean-spirited, unhappy people whose parents had never, not once, said, "You are important. We love you." He felt sad for the talk-show host and the talk-show audience and the desperate guests. He felt sad for the actors on sitcoms and the people who crouched in dark rooms and watched them zing their one-liners into the void, and he felt sad for himself because he was one of the watchers, and so he got up and walked to the window and saw the children laughing under the streetlamps, and he felt sad for them because the futures bearing down on them were heartless if not actively malign and mostly he felt sad that being a human being was such an embarrassment of fouled motives and excuses that weren't good enough and transient desires and cheap dodges against death's unwinding.

They nodded their heads, took notes.

They were after something, and it seemed to Harry that what they were after wasn't his mental well-being at all. Perhaps the drugs had awakened a deep, unlooked-for intuitive sense. Or maybe, like many crazy people, he was simply growing more paranoid.

Still, it seemed to Harry that these doctors believed that he and his companions shared some secret, some vital information, and that with careful and relentless prodding, the truth would be revealed.

"I don't know anything!" Harry wanted to shout. Certainly nothing that anyone would want to know.

Harry concentrated all his attention on Raymond's moving lips, red, wet, and quivering with urgency. Harry watched each word as it was formed, hoping that close attention would bring whole sentences into focus. Raymond was sitting upright with his hands on his knees, a strangely old-fashioned attitude of body suggesting sepia-toned photos of portly baseball players braced solemnly for time exposures.

"We have to leave here," Raymond said.

Ah. Attention was paying off. There was a statement: succinct, certain in its meaning, delivered emphatically.

"The Frozen Princess cannot wake up here, in confinement. She must be at the Ocean of Responsibility when she wakes. It is our only hope."

So much for sense. Harry felt quick, light lizard feet scramble in his chest, and he was frightened. Frightened by the dim, elusive acknowledgment that it would not, absolutely not, be a good thing if the Frozen Princess were to awake here, far from the Ocean of Responsibility, here in the Great Tiredness.

And that fear made the rational part of his mind panic, because there was no Frozen Princess, no Ocean of Responsibility, no doom brewing in the Gorelord's Domain.

Gorelord? Harry wondered. *And what makes you think this hospital is Blackwater Castle?*

Fear focused Harry's mind, and he was able to give his full attention to the counselor's words.

"Raymond," the counselor was saying, "I wonder if you could explain all this to me. I'm afraid I'm not following you very well."

"That's right," Raymond said, nodding his head rapidly. "You are just a soldier. You don't know anything. You are just instructed to torture us, extract information, hand it on to your superiors. It's nothing personal. I know that."

The counselor, a narrow-faced man with limp brown hair who had decided long ago to adopt a hearty, familiar style (although a silent, thoughtful approach would have been better suited to his temperament and countenance), grinned painfully and said, "I hardly think I would call group therapy torture, Raymond. It can be uncomfortable, of course, to bring up certain events and the emotions attached to those events, but the end results are positive and—"

"You are working for the Gorelord," Raymond said. "You have no doubt drunk the blood of the Rawn Worm and inhaled the bone dust of the Hunkering Spinespits. To expect you, a minion of He Who The Vile Venerate, to be anything more than a pawn would be wrong. You can't really help it. Your mind has been usurped by a stronger Will."

Harry did not realize he was nodding his head in agreement with this assessment until the counselor, Mitford, spoke: "Harry, you seem to know what Raymond is talking about. Perhaps, then, you would be willing to clarify this business. We have spent a few weeks circling in on this fantasy you all share, and I've taken notes and even availed myself of your children's book, *Zod Wallop,* and I confess I'm no closer to understanding what we have here."

"Well," Harry said, "I think Raymond is letting you off the hook, morally. He's saying you are a sort of moral zombie, in thrall to an Evil you are powerless to resist. He's speaking of the Gorelord here, one of the two great Vile Contenders in Zod Wallop, the other, of course, being Lord Draining."

"Do you believe any of this?" Mitford asked.

"Well, I wrote it," Harry said, smiling, feeling an odd sense of pride rise up in the fog.

"And when you write a thing, does that make it real?"

"No," Harry said, frightened again.

Meaning winked out then; Mitford's words became a series of shaped sounds, abstract noises with a vaguely interrogative quality.

Harry looked around the small room, which had suddenly grown smaller. The walls had turned to gray stone, mottled with lichen, sweating droplets of black water. The bulletin board, usually shingled with pieces of paper (inspirational poems, articles on depression, announcements of Ping-Pong tournaments and vocational rehabilitation programs)—all of it, Harry assumed, bogus, camouflage for the prison that bound them—was gone, replaced by a large, hanging pelt, the barbed hide of a Virotomus still showing the howling shadow-face of its last human repast etched in the image cells.

It was a striking trophy, and it held Harry's attention until someone screamed.

It was Emily, twisting forward, mouth open in a howl, her wheelchair tottering sideways—a wheelchair of gold, encrusted with jewels, the wheels not wheels at all but great silver ornate discs with the entwined lizards of Mal Ganvern sinking their steel teeth into each other—and then falling in a cymbal crash, echoed and re-echoed in the Room of Screams, and Emily crawling from the ruined throne and raising her hand and clutching at something in the air.

A hand. A white, translucent hand that gripped Emily's own hand and drew her upright. The whiteness seemed to bleed into Emily's own flesh, racing up her arm and into her face, routing the color in her cheeks, glazing her eyes with ice. Emily shouted, a bleat of pain, her breath a shot of wintry mist.

Her feet had left the ground. She floated in the room, the wheelchair/throne on its side, a wheel spinning so that the etched lizards seemed to chase one another in a silver frenzy. For a moment, the room and its inhabitants entered Harry's mind in a welter of image and sensation, filled with revelation, truths riding on the backs of truths.

Harry could smell the cold and the mud and the blood-smell of the black waters and the sour-milk smell of the Ralewings that dwelt in the underground river. He could smell hopelessness, like strong disinfectant in a charnel house.

Mitford, hands clasped in his lap, was wearing a black shroud, the uniform of the Gorelord's minions, and Harry saw the tattooed stitches on the man's lips, the symbol of obedience in those chosen to speak. Harry—granted this moment of supernatural awareness—sensed a dull hum flowing from the psychologist, and knew that a grueleach dwelt within the man, drugging him into holy service. Raymond, standing, wore a wizard's blue robes, emblazoned with constellations of stars, moons, and Happy Faces. His hair seemed to writhe, and Harry realized that small, mischievous Ember folk cavorted there.

Rene was screaming, her hands raised, the palms red—*blood*, Harry thought—and she turned to run, falling over the chair, tumbling softly in the folds of her blue silk dress, screaming.

Allan caught her as she fell, lifting her, graciously, solemnly. Black flames flickered from the seams in his gleaming armor. *Anger,* Harry thought, *bone-melting anger.* Ripe with certainties, Harry knew that this was the anger of Blodkin Himself, the force that had brought everything into being and that had not always been killing Rage but had, once, been the Tremor and the Kiss and the Assault of Desire.

And Emily, her feet floating above the ground, turned slowly, the royal medallions that adorned the hem of her golden robe emitting a sparkling flurry of musical notes.

Emily, like a wind-chime angel, rotated in a slow circle, her arm wrenched toward the ceiling by the disembodied hand. As her face returned to Harry's gaze, he saw that it was a mask of frost, her mouth a purple O.

She spoke then. Although her lips did not move, the voice was clear, feminine, filled with the easy authority of someone accustomed to being obeyed. "There are three gifts," Emily said.

Yes, Harry thought.

"There is the gift of ease, of life unfettered. There is the gift of knowledge, which shatters the gift of ease. And there is the gift of death, Blodkin's apology for the gift of knowledge."

Harry saw that one of Emily's slippers had fallen off, and that her bare white foot was descending again, the other, slippered foot, slightly raised, and he knew what would happen *for he had written it* and—no hiding now—that made it true.

The Frozen Princess floated in the air, the last incantation having sent her to the ceiling. Now the pale Lizards of the

Apocalypse barked in unison, the Wire Cat screamed and spit green sparks, and the Gorelord's wizard roared, "Descend."

Slowly, she floated toward the spectators, all of them enraptured, some by the spectacle, some by the drugs. A young boy—for boys will be boys at the end of the world—darted close to look up the Princess' dress and was snatched back by a vigilant aunt skilled in grabbing adolescent ears and bending them to her will.

Down she came. She was an ice dagger, descending. Her bare, frozen foot touched the stone floor and she balanced, like some cardboard cutout of a ballerina, poised and perfect, and the crowd was silent waiting for something to happen.

And, of course, something happened, because something always does.

And what happens isn't always a good thing. In this case what happened was a noise, a sort of pop sound accompanied by a hiss. The hiss was uttered by the Gorelord himself, and was an expression of shock and dismay.

The pop was uttered by the Frozen Princess' toe as it came into contact with the stone floor. Her icicle toe shattered, blown into a glitter of dust. *Pop, pop, pop.* The other toes went. *Pop.*

"Ahhhhh," the spectators murmured. It was a sound that rose toward hysteria as the Princess' legs exploded, one immediately after the other, two ear-clobbering slams. Then arms. Then, with a howl, her head. Her torso spun end over end, bouncing across the stone floor and coming to rest against the wall in a scandalous manner but remaining miraculously intact so that the same small, lewd boy, escaping his aunt, approached warily.

And then the last of the Frozen Princess blew, lifting the boy up and out a window, as though his exit had been choreographed, and creating a dark hole in the floor.

And everyone came and peered in the hole and could not see the bottom but felt dizzy and reckless, as though they might plunge into its upside-down night. Quickly, they backed away.

The Room of Screams was empty and night was upon the castle and everyone was saying that it was a shame about the Frozen Princess but that perhaps it was for the best (a common attitude toward the misfortune of others). This was the hour when sleep is so heavy and time so slow and the night so long that the drowsing heart ponders whether it should take another beat and finally thinks, *oh, why not?*, and it's always that close, just a shrug in the uncertain dark. It was then that something crawled out of the hole. If you had been there you would not have heard it coming. But you would have felt it. There is a part of the brain born to sense the approach of such things. This part of the brain is very old. It has always been there because it has always been acquainted with the thing that came out of the hole after the Frozen Princess went off. In the old days, this part of the brain contained a powerful, deadly poison, and, on sensing the presence of the Abyss Dweller, it flooded the body with oblivion.

If you had been there, turned away from the hole, just admiring a new rack or gouging tool, humming softly, glad that the Room of Screams wasn't something a man (or woman) of your class had to fear . . . that part of your brain would have sensed it.

"Die!" it would shout, and it would discover then, sad

appendix to intelligence, that this modern world had made a mistake. It was now an obsolete organ, and it had no lethal poison, no killing tricks.

You would realize, with acid panic, that you couldn't die. You would realize you were in Big Trouble.

Harry watched Emily descend. No one else in the room moved; even the Ember people had ceased their wanton play in Raymond's hair and were watching.

Something bad was going to happen, and it was inevitable.

Harry rose up, shouting, his whole body shaking.

He dove toward Emily and caught her in his arms and the chill that was within her entered him, like an Arctic sea, brutal and implacable. He fell backward, Emily following him to the floor.

And he saw her face, her glazed eyes, saw blood on her lips and saw, on her shoulder, the disembodied hand, resting like a glass spider. The flesh under the proprietary clasp of ice fingers was blue. Harry reached for the hand to pry it loose, and it leapt up and caught him by the throat, and his head was instantly severed, or so it seemed, perched on a marble pillar, and he could not breathe, and the room flickered in gray light. He saw the room's ceiling, its familiar acoustical tiles, and the face of Mitford floated into view, filled with concern. The psychologist was wearing a suit. His face seemed oddly naked, and Harry realized that the tattooed stitches that outlined his lips were gone.

Mitford was saying something, reaching for Harry. He was jostled from view by Raymond, who bent close to Harry and seemed to be shouting, although Harry could hear nothing. The Ember people had fled Raymond's hair, and

Raymond was wearing one of the hospital's gray sweatshirts. He was holding a Styrofoam cup, lurching forward with it, the black, steaming liquid spilling out, small pinpricks of pain splattering Harry's cheeks.

Harry's throat was suddenly released. His body came alive, his throat a smoldering column of pain. Sound rushed in: shouts, screams, a door slamming, glass breaking. Mitford was wrestling with Raymond. Allan clutched them both and brought them to the floor. Harry was jerked around by the pain, flopping like a fish, and he saw Emily, lying very still, her head sideways on the floor and she saw him and light bloomed in her eyes.

Her smile reassured him, and he drifted into the darkness without fear.

The brace they used to keep his head immobile during the healing sometimes seemed to contribute to the pain, as though his shoulders were in a vise. He floated in a lotus dream of drugs, and people came and went in the fogged window of his perception. He remembered Raymond standing at the foot of the bed, sobbing, saying he was sorry. And he remembered telling Raymond not to apologize. "You saved my life," Harry whispered. Harry was certain that this was the case, although he did not try to explain what that meant, certainly not to Mitford who interpreted what had transpired in mundane terms: Emily had had an epileptic fit and Raymond, in his zeal to be of assistance, had accidentally poured a scalding cup of coffee on Harry. This did not explain Emily's being dragged off the ground by a ghostly hand, nor did it address the matter of transformation (i.e. group therapy turning into Blackwater Castle's Room of Screams).

One explanation for the events might, Harry knew, be

hallucination, but if so, it was a communal delusion, obviously shared by Raymond, Emily, Rene, and Allan. Harry also suspected that Mitford had seen more than he would admit. . . .

"Tell me about *Zod Wallop*," Mitford said. He tossed a glossy copy of the book on the bedcovers.

Harry shrugged. "It's my most successful children's book."

"And your last."

"Yes."

"Why's that?"

"I didn't feel like writing any more books."

"Because your daughter died. And yet this book was written after your daughter died." The psychologist tapped the picture book and sat down on the edge of the bed. Harry, propped up by pillows in the bed, his head gripped by an intricate orthopedic device, felt trapped.

"I want to call Helen Kurtis," Harry said. "And I want to call my ex-wife."

Mitford nodded. "Yes, I understand. We have had this conversation before, Harry. As soon as your condition has stabilized, you can talk to whomever you wish. You can leave here, for that matter."

"Why can't I leave right now? You can't hold me prisoner," Harry said.

Mitford assumed a hurt, rueful expression. "Of course not. I'm not your enemy, Harry. We can keep you here, however, for your own good. You might think of yourself as a man who has been exposed to a deadly virus and is being quarantined. You and your companions at Harwood Psychiatric were exposed to a drug that seems to have certain communicable properties."

"Those are not my companions," Harry said. "I was in Harwood Psychiatric for depression, and at that time I met Raymond Story. I had never met Emily or Rene or Allan until Raymond showed up at my doorstep."

"Exactly," Mitford said, slapping his thighs. "That's what's so fascinating. You and your friends have established a sort of gestalt—I'm sure you know the word—which seems independent of physical contact. Emily and Rene and Allan all visited Harwood while you were there, though. And Raymond knew you all."

The psychologist seemed profoundly pleased with himself.

"So what?" Harry said.

"Marlin Tate administered Ecknazine to all of you, that's what."

"I'm afraid I'm still not following you. What does that have to do with anything? It seems to me that the only thing we have in common is legitimate grounds for a whopping big lawsuit."

Mitford waved his hand. "I'm sure Dr. Blaine would be willing to compensate you all beyond the dreams of the most litigious lawyer. It's not a lawsuit you have in common; it's *Zod Wallop.*"

"*Zod Wallop?*"

The psychologist nodded.

Harry sighed. "*Zod Wallop* is a children's book that Raymond has some odd notions about," he said, speaking slowly now, cautiously. "He seems to have convinced both Rene and Allan of the reality of his delusions, but I don't see what their gullibility—they are mental patients, after all—has to do with your so-called gestalt."

Mitford stood up and walked to the wall where he studied a painting of a barn that appeared to be under siege by swallows or bats. He turned, walked back to the bed and, leaning close enough for Harry to smell the alcohol on his breath, studied Harry's immobilized head with a sort of clinical madness burning in his eyes, a greedy look, a fat-child-eyeing-a-cookie jar look.

"There are two *Zod Wallops,* aren't there?"

A strange, irrational fear stilled Harry's heart. He found he was holding his breath; he exhaled slowly.

"Two *Zod Wallops,*" the psychologist continued. "And in the first of them, created while you were a resident of Harwood Psychiatric, the drawings are of hospital staff and patients. These caricatures are quite recognizable and include Rene and Emily and Allan, people you had not met at the time of the book's creation. We do not have the book itself, but we have obtained excellent photos of its contents, and there is no denying the likenesses. My own employer is a prominent character in the book."

The Gorelord, Harry thought.

"It could all be an elaborate hoax," Mitford continued. "But the question then is: to what purpose?"

Harry was silent. What purpose, indeed.

"It's an ugly book," Mitford said, causing Harry to slowly rotate his upper body to regard the shrink with new interest. Mitford was frowning, musing to himself. "Not something you'd want a child to see, at all. Not an uplifting message. I mean . . . " He turned and regarded Harry with bafflement. "What is it saying, after all? That it is better not to live? Really." He shrugged, turned, and walked toward the door. A hand on the doorknob, he muttered to himself. "I don't have children," he said. "But if I did, I can tell you I wouldn't read them *Zod Wallop.* Not that ugly first book with its relentless gore and despair, and not the second either. In some ways, the second is creepier, sicker . . . once one has read the first one. I mean, once you know . . . you can't help thinking the second's all sunny lies, now can you? You don't believe for a second that things will really work out. Lydia stopping the river of stone with a kiss . . . I don't buy it. You can't help thinking there's a missing page, something ugly like one of those pop-up corpses at the end of a horror movie. It's an uneasy feeling . . . " Mitford's voice died away and he looked up, smiled wanly (but at nothing in particular; he certainly wasn't seeing Harry), and left, closing the door softly as he went.

An uneasy feeling. Harry knew just what he meant.

Mitford smiled at the secretary, a succulent charmer named Rachel, who didn't return his smile, seemed to have to squint just to register his existence, and who said, "Go on in. He's waiting."

Mitford pushed the door open and entered the big, carpeted office. CEO Blaine sat behind the black desk in a brown sweater that looked like something dogs might have fought over. He smiled, showing his toothless gums. Blaine liked to go toothless in the office, and Mitford was used to the sight but he could never entirely shake a sense of unreality. It was as though some old wino had slipped into the plush intelligence center of GroMel. Surely the corpse of GroMel's true founder, some dapper, well-tailored Harvard prodigy, was stuffed under the desk or leaking its life's blood into the executive bedroom's jacuzzi.

But no, in fact this wizened derelict with the oddly sheeplike countenance, the deceptive blankness of eye and gaping red-lipped mouth, this feeble old codger in need of a shave and a haircut, this was the mastermind behind GroMel.

Blaine stood up. "Well Mitford, any progress?"

There was no chair to sit in, just miles of gray carpet and in the far corner some sort of green rubber plant. There were no windows. "Newark's not going anywhere," Blaine had told the architect. "I don't need to keep an eye on it."

Mitford turned as the door to the executive bedroom opened. Dr. Gloria Gill walked over to the desk and leaned against it. She was a stocky woman with a round face, short-cropped hair like a skullcap, and a wardrobe consisting entirely of black sweaters, black dresses, and black stockings. Mitford guessed that something sexual existed between Blaine and this woman, although Mitford didn't like to think about it. Given a choice between sex with Gloria Gill or the Pillsbury Doughboy, Mitford figured he would spend the morning after showering off flour.

"Well," Mitford said, "I think the videotape of Emily Engel floating in the air could be called progress. We have actual, physical evidence of psychokinetic phenomena."

"I was thinking," Blaine said, his voice deceptively sleepy, "more in terms of progress toward recovering the Ecknazine formula." He coughed then, inhaled with a thin whistling noise, and said, "Gloria, the oxygen." The woman came to his side, fiddled with something behind the desk, and then walked behind him. She fitted the transparent mask over his nose and mouth, patted his shoulder, and returned to the side of the desk.

Blaine closed his eyes, breathed deeply for a moment—his Adam's apple bobbing as though he were gulping air—and then removed the mask and smiled. "I smoked two packs of unfiltered cigarettes every day for forty-seven years," he said. "I don't recommend it if you plan on growing old."

Mitford nodded. "Are you all right?"

Blaine slapped his hands on the desk. "As right as acid rain!" he shouted. Dr. Gill, standing by the desk like an honor guard, laughed soundlessly, the only indications of her mirth being a rocking motion and closed eyes.

Blaine said, "The Ecknazine. If we can regain the formula, we can have subjects aplenty. It's the formula we want."

"Yes, of course," Mitford said. "Unfortunately, I haven't discovered anything about the chemical nature of the drug. What I am able to study is the group dynamic, the result. It's fascinating. Gainesborough's children's book, this *Zod Wallop*, seems to serve as a sort of fulcrum for the psychokinetic effects, and if—"

Gloria Gill snorted loudly. "Waste of time."

Mitford worked at a smile. He hated this Gill woman, one of those brain-dicing bitches who thought everything was synapses and serotonin levels.

Blaine looked at the woman and smiled. He said, "Dr. Gill believes the time for this therapy fishing is over. She's already run a battery of tests. More radical and intrusive procedures are now in order. Her early workup suggests that at least one of the subjects, the Engel girl, may, as a result perhaps of her impaired condition, still contain traces of the original drug. If that's the case, then extracting such trace elements would seem to be our best plan of attack. Dr. Gill suggests we start immediately. I'm inclined to agree with her."

Mitford had known it would come to this. "If we lose these subjects, we lose everything," Mitford said. "We lose any knowledge they might have that could lead us directly to a cache of the drug. I believe there may be several other subjects, and we will never find them if we submit this group to procedures that render them useless."

154

"We don't have all the time in the world," the woman said. "All traces of the drug may be lost if we don't act now."

"A month," Mitford said. "Give me another month."

"A week," Blaine said. "We'll give you a week."

"I can't—"

Blaine stood up. "You will excuse me now. I have to move my bowels." He strode quickly across the floor into the executive bedroom. It was clear that the conversation was at an end.

Gloria Gill smiled at Mitford. "Just tell them to talk fast," she said. "Tell them to feel the feelings while the feeling's good."

CHAPTER SEVENTEEN

✦ ◉ ◈ ◈ ◈ ◈ ◈ ◈ ◈ ◈ ◈ ◈ ◉

THIRTY-SEVEN DAYS HAD passed since Harry's disappearance. Helen Kurtis sat at her desk and pored over a legal pad, seeking Harry's trail in her notes. Arbus was asleep behind her on the bed. He was wearing pajamas with clowns (Helen had discovered an unlooked-for maternal side that manifested itself in purchasing these tiny outfits).

The monkey reassured her, somehow. He was alive and there was nothing in his manner or character—he was something of a pleasure-seeker, cheerful, unreflective—that indicated he had suffered any trauma. Surely, if the others were dead, he would show it somehow, the horror would look out of his eyes.

The logic of this was, she knew, threadbare. But it was strengthened by her own conviction that she would have felt the loss of Harry if he were dead.

As it was, she only felt confused, old, ineffectual.

She had hired a private investigator who had, she assumed, bribed someone at Harwood Psychiatric Institute and so produced the brief biographies of Harry's companions.

Paul Allan, son of the stunning Gabriel Allan-Tate, was a young man whose anger had set him at odds with authorities. Had his mother been poor, he probably would have been consigned to juvenile homes and jails, but his anger was identified as pathology thanks to his mother's wealth. Harwood Psychiatric was his frequent refuge after outbreaks of rage and physical violence.

Rene Gold was addicted to alcohol and drugs and, according to her father, sex. In the write-up that Helen perused, her father was quoted as saying, "She's the Devil's work. She'll put anything inside her, either end."

Translating between the case history social-speak lines, it was clear to Helen that Clyde Gold and his wife, Nadine, were trailer-park trash.

What was curious about Rene's situation was that she should be in a ritzy place like Harwood. Someone had been paying her way for several years, the funds administered by a Newark law firm, and her actual benefactor was a mystery. Rene herself did not know—or at least said she didn't—where the money for her treatment came from.

Emily Engel had always been as she was now. She had come into the world without much interest in it and had received a variety of diagnoses from sage physicians of the body and mind and none of it had meant a damn to Emily Engel. Her parents had died in an automobile accident when she was twelve, and she had been adopted by her uncle, a man named Robert Furman—Helen found the name vaguely familiar—who had cared for her privately before discovering that the task was no small one and so had sent her on to Harwood.

Helen pushed the legal pad away and got up and went

into the bathroom. She brushed her teeth slowly, methodically, a habit developed in childhood when a dental hygiene film frightened her into elaborate ablutions.

She thought about them. It was a strange and tragic crew that Harry had disappeared with. That, in itself, might not be wildly coincidental; after all, their meeting ground was a psychiatric hospital. But what they had in common was deeper than that. It was, Helen thought, a condition of isolation, of retreat. Emily had fled at birth, had never greeted the world. Rene had retreated into the dark closet of addiction. Paul Allan had hidden in a fog of red rage. Raymond Story was convinced that he had never properly returned from a watery death, that he was exiled to an alternate world. And Harry . . . Harry's retreat had been so abrupt, so cruel.

It had occurred the day of the funeral. Morganson's Funeral Home had been packed, for Harry and Jeanne were a gregarious couple and had many friends. Helen had been talking to Jeanne's mother, a woman ill-equipped for tragedy, who dealt with the horror by talking tirelessly about a host of inconsequential subjects.

When Helen had first arrived at the funeral home, she had found Harry alone, outside, smoking a cigarette. She had embraced him, offered condolences, and asked where Jeanne was. He said she was inside, with her parents. He added—and it was later that this seemed ominous—that he thought funerals were barbaric. He did not believe in religious ceremonies, he said, and while some people felt that rituals were a way of dealing with grief, he felt they simply showed the true futility of any attempt to "pretty-up" death.

It was a strangely intellectual speech, and Helen had studied Harry's pale, twisted countenance and thought that he would need to find professional help if he were to survive.

"A child's coffin is an awful thing," he had said. "Cremation is really the only civilized alternative, but Jeanne—"

He had stopped talking, crushed the cigarette in the grass, and walked into the funeral home.

And Helen had been talking to Jeanne's mother when Jeanne interrupted them. It was Helen that Jeanne wanted to talk to.

"Harry's left," she said.

"Left."

"Randall says he saw him walking down the street, heading toward town."

Helen suggested that he would be back, had simply needed a walk to calm himself, but, in her heart, Helen felt that Jeanne's fear was justified. Helen suspected that Harry would not return for any portion of the funeral, and when Helen held Jeanne in her arms as she wept by the graveside, Helen hated Harry for the selfishness of his despair and knew that the marriage was shattered.

Helen no longer hated Harry, knowing he had been beyond rationality or decency that day and now despised himself for the memory of his own desertion.

Helen Kurtis saw herself in the mirror and thought that there were probably few sights more dismal than an old woman brushing her teeth and weeping.

CHaPTeR eiGHTeeN

DR. ROALD PEAKE sat at his desk, smoking two cigarettes at once, lost in *Zod Wallop*. He no longer read the words. He knew them by heart. He stared at the drawings, watercolors that at first seemed crude roughs (this was, after all, a draft) but that, with careful study, yielded incredible detail. You could see the hairs on the Swamp Grendel's tongue, and, if you narrowed your eyes and lowered your head so that the page filled your entire field of vision, you could catch peripheral images that were not, in fact, on the page. You could see all of the Duke of Flatbend when the page itself showed only his polished boots, his heavily medallioned chest, and one thin hand reaching out to shake the hand of the newly arrived Lydia.

Roald Peake was presently studying an illustration of the Hall of Atrocities (Lydia was being led down it by the devious Lady Ermine), and Peake was certain that he could discern, beyond the window of the page, two apocalypse lizards fighting over a severed hand.

The intercom buzzed for perhaps the third time, and, reluctantly, Peake surfaced and reached his hand toward the button. "Yes?"

"Mr. Bahden's here, Dr. Peake."

"All right. Send him in."

Peake closed the book and dropped it into the top drawer of his desk. His office was small and white (white desk, white carpet, white walls), and for a moment he thought the walls were translucent, and that the frozen bodies of ill-behaved children were tumbled every which way in the ice. Angel wings were attached, most realistically, to the naked children. This was a decorative motif, and Lord Draining's peers were lavish in their praise of this brilliant concept that served as a warning to hyperactive children while gratifying the aesthetic sense with a vision of soaring cherubs.

Peake blinked and this vision was gone. He was used to such moments now, and, if they had briefly troubled him, they no longer were a source of any discomfort. Indeed, he was fascinated by these afterimages and wished they might stay longer so that he could study them and gain some insight into their meaning. The only thing that was the least bit troubling about this phenomenon was his nose. His nose actually seemed to have elongated, as in the caricature of Lord Draining, and this didn't appear to be a simple, lingering hallucination. His hands confirmed this lengthening. He thought of asking his secretary if she noticed anything unusual about his physiognomy, but the question itself might influence her answer and so, for the time being, he decided to say nothing. The effect wasn't, in any event, unflattering. He rather fancied it made him look more intelligent and debonair.

Karl Bahden entered the room smiling. He was polishing something with a handkerchief. Was that blood? Another afterimage?

"We've found where Blaine has stashed the group," he said.

"Ah," Peake said, standing up. "Wonderful."

"We would have found them sooner if our own security hadn't been compromised. You won't like this part."

Peake didn't. He listened with growing anger while Karl told how Blaine's people had found a leak at Peake Pharmaceuticals and so kept Blaine posted of the search.

"It looks like they even have photographs of this first book, the one you came across at Tate's mansion."

Peake felt his hands clutch the top drawer. "My God!"

Karl was still talking. "Turns out Blaine has Gainesborough and the rest on a floor at the main building in Newark. We looked there, sure, but they knew when we were looking, knew how to misdirect us. I figure—"

"Who?" Peake said.

"The leak?" Karl said, smiling.

Peake nodded. Karl stood up, walked briskly across the white carpet, and dropped the knife onto the white stone desktop. It spun brightly. He stuffed the handkerchief back into the pocket of his suit jacket and rubbed the back of his neck. "You'll be needing someone new to take dictation," he said.

The morning of the next day, the security guard in the lobby of GroMel's Newark office looked up to see a tall man in a suit smiling at her.

"May I help you?" the security guard asked. She had seen this man before—not smiling—in a photo, she thought. Instantly wary, her hand moved toward the console that would summon Akerman and the others.

"Don't," he said.

She nodded. "All right." She couldn't remember the man's name, but she knew him now. He was freelance, expensive.

"I do not approve of women security officers," he said, leaning forward, touching her silver teardrop earring. He caught her wrist before her hand reached the console.

With her free hand, she unsnapped the holster, touched the butt of the revolver.

"You have already been overrun," he said. "A very toxic gas has killed your entire team, with the exception of a certain Kellerman who is, I believe, on sick leave today. And Kellerman isn't to be trusted in any event, at least, that's my opinion."

She did not move.

"Oh, I'm telling the truth," he said. He leaned across the desk and flipped three switches. The monitors flickered, revealing new rooms. In one, a uniformed body was sprawled across a desk. The second monitor showed an empty room. The third showed two more inanimate bodies: a middle-aged woman slumped in a chair, a bald man draped across the chair's back and leaning toward his companion as though prepared to whisper something wanton in her ear.

"I would like you to dial this number," he said. He handed her the small slip of paper. "Think only of dialing this number," he said, "and you might yet escape my disapproval."

She lifted the receiver and dialed.

The man came out of the executive bedroom and smiled apologetically. "Too much coffee," he said. "That's some bathroom. You could put a mariachi band in there and it wouldn't be crowded."

Blaine wasn't in the mood for this. "You were going to tell me good news, about the Underwood litigation."

"Yes, of course." He was a young, boyish fellow, this lawyer. Why, Blaine wondered, hadn't Watson, Wilkons, and Ware sent old Ware, as usual? Ware knew how to be deferential. Years of toadying up to big-money accounts had made Ware the ultimate sycophant. Maybe Ware had died.

Blaine didn't care for this young, brash pup. He seemed too pleased with himself, too at ease. He was talking. A phone rang.

Blaine was momentarily confused. Where . . .

The young man opened his briefcase and took out the phone. He flipped it open, brought it to his ear, and said, "Yes."

He only spoke once more, saying "yes" again. He put the phone in the briefcase, snapped the case shut, and walked toward the desk.

The impertinence of the boy, Blaine thought. Taking a phone call here. Ware would hear of this. Watson, Wilkons, and Ware weren't the only lawyers in town.

Blaine looked up. The arrogant young lawyer was smiling, heading toward the door. Impertinence upon impertinence. "Something's come up," he said. "I'm very sorry, but there's an emergency. I'll get back to you."

"Young man!" Blaine roared. "What in hell—"

The door closed. Blaine came up out of his chair and raced across the carpet, quickly covering the distance. The door appeared to be stuck; he tugged on the handle with both hands, rocked back on his heels, rattled the door, howled.

Goddamn.

He turned back to the desk, the phone. He stopped then, saw the briefcase lying there on the carpet.

The briefcase exploded, transformed into a dirty white cloud that rose up, expanding.

Oh, shit. Blaine held his breath, turned. *Get to the bedroom, the phone in there . . .* A second explosion—and a roiling wall of mist obscured the open doorway.

Blaine closed his eyes and felt the hot, biting cloud caress his face. He knew something about this sort of thing, knowledge gleaned from a military project here, some covert CIA thing there. His lungs ached. And he knew what would happen if he tried to breathe.

Harry sat in group listening to the girl, Rene, shout denials. The counselor, that sadist Mitford, was grilling her about her father. "You wanted to have sex with him, didn't you?" Mitford was saying.

"No!" Rene was shouting back, lying, of course, because any therapist will tell you that everyone wants to have sex with everyone else and that the symptoms many adults exhibit (compulsive/obsessive behavior, depression, an inability to remember the names of presidents) are sure signs of forgotten sexual encounters—often with relatives or extraterrestrials.

Rene looked quite beautiful, her eyes glistening, her cheeks shiny with tears of anger, her lips bruised seductively by shame.

"What about the Cold One?" Mitford asked, leaning forward. "What exactly is this Cold One? You were saying you had bad dreams about him?"

"Yeah," Rene said. "Anyone has a dream about the Cold One, I don't guess it is going to be a good dream."

Allan laughed at this, and Mitford turned to him. "Allan, do you have dreams about the Cold One?"

"No." Allan looked away quickly.

"Harry, what exactly is the Cold One? He's a character in your children's book, *Zod Wallop*, isn't he?"

"Yes," Harry said, "He's the deadly ghost created when the Two Vile Contenders clash."

Mitford nodded. "Yes, I remember now. Pretty bleak, as I recall."

"Yes."

"How do you explain that all your friends here are so enamored of this *Zod Wallop*?"

Harry shrugged. "I don't know—"

"Excuse me," Mitford said, "We have a group in session here."

Harry was thrown off, until he realized that the counselor wasn't addressing him.

Two men in business suits had entered the room. The taller of the two men had his hands in his pockets.

"It's okay," he said. "Please continue. Sounds interesting."

Mitford stiffened. "I'm afraid I'll have to call Security," he said.

Security, Harry thought, should have kept these men from sauntering in here in the first place. Something was amiss.

"We really are—" Mitford said, and a dark hole appeared in the middle of his forehead, accompanied by a polite cough as though a librarian were trying to get one's attention.

Mitford leaned sideways and fell, chair clattering.

The man was already turning with the gun. "I don't want to shoot anyone else," he said. "I had a bad experience with a therapist once; I suppose I was acting out, just now. I apologize. I don't want to harm any of the rest of you. I just want you to come with me."

They walked down the hall. Harry was in the lead. Behind Harry, Raymond was pushing Emily. Allan and Rene walked side by side, with the gunmen following in the rear.

They were getting in the elevator when Allan screamed, turned and grabbed both of the men. "Go!"

"No!" Rene screamed back, but Raymond jerked her into the elevator and pressed the button to close the door.

Emily's wheelchair spun in a quick circle, and she would have toppled out had Harry not caught her. He looked up, holding the girl in his arms, and saw that Allan had fallen to the floor with both men, the three of them rolling and shouting.

"Jesus!" Rene shouted, "We've got to go back. We can't leave Allan."

"Lord Allan has chosen to aid us," Raymond said, shifting into his loftiest manner. "It would be poor manners to refuse the gift." Raymond punched the button that would take them to the top floor.

When the elevator stopped, Raymond said, "We need a key"—he tapped the keyhole—"in order to reach the roof. Does anyone have such a key?"

Rene looked disgusted. "What do you think, asshole?"

"You are forgetting that I am a wizard," Raymond said. "In *Zod Wallop,* I am the Wizard Mettle."

"Oh, that's great news," Rene said.

Mettle? Harry thought. The Wizard Mettle was a buffoon, inept and windy, a parody of New Age pomposity and fuzzy thinking. Harry hadn't had Raymond in mind, and he wondered what it was that made Raymond see himself in the role.

"I have a key," Raymond said. He took it from his pocket and inserted it in the lock. It turned. The elevator hummed, shook, and rose. Raymond bowed.

"*That old guy!*" Rene said. "That weird thousand-year-old janitor with the dirty hair and the crazy snow boots. That's why you were always talking to him. You swiped his fucking key! Hey, Raymond. You are sharper than you look."

"My Lady, your conclusion is cruel. I did not steal his key. A miracle has occurred," Raymond said.

"Yeah, a miracle," Rene said.

"I call it a miracle when a despised and much abused old man whose lot has inured him to the suffering of others suddenly shakes off his chains and strikes a blow for freedom and decency and with no incentive other than compassion *gives* us his key to freedom."

Raymond smiled grandly.

"Okay," Rene said. "Let's haul ass, Saint Story."

They came out on the roof, into sunlight, and Raymond lifted Emily from the wheelchair. "There is a fire escape—I've seen it from the rec room—that will take us within debarking distance of the roof of a building which, I believe, will furnish us egress to the street."

They followed Raymond to the side of the building and, at his urging, eased over the ledge and dropped to the stairs. Raymond lowered Emily to Harry. He must have seen some anxiety in Harry's eyes, for he paused and said, "Fear not, Lord Gainesborough. Blodkin watches over us. We shall navigate these stairs with ease, and yonder building's office workers will offer no hindrance to our progress."

Raymond was absolutely correct.

On the street, they hailed a cab.

Andrew Blaine sat on the carpet, his back propped against his desk, his eyes closed. He held the mouthpiece firmly over his nose and mouth, breathing the oxygen methodically, as though the action of his lungs had ceased to be an involuntary function. A devout man, he thanked God for his emphysema.

He could not judge how much time had passed, perhaps half an hour, perhaps longer. He had fumbled under the desk, found the red button, and pressed it. Help should have arrived immediately, and its absence suggested that things were very wrong at GroMel. Help would come, though, eventually. The button would summon off-site aid. He had only to wait. He was glad that Gloria Gill hadn't been with him during this attack. He was fond of her and would have been saddened by her death. He thought of her sweet roundness, the toothpaste whiteness of her flesh as he peeled the black garments from her, the pocked scars of other love bites, and he was amused at how desire could stir in the midst of danger.

Surely the gas was dispersed by now. He supposed he could open his eyes and remove the mouthpiece with impunity. He wasn't, however, 100 percent sure on this count, and it did no harm to simply wait. Patience, he had learned, was a great virtue.

He passed the time by imagining the slow, painful death he would inflict on the man responsible for this. There was no doubt in his mind as to the identity of this person.

When the door was finally opened and Blaine's rescuers

poured in, he was, for a moment, unaware of their arrival, so lost was he in reverie, so involved in his own powers of invention, so pleased by the imaginary screams of Dr. Roald Peake.

CHaPTeR NiNeTeeN

❧ ❧ ❧ ❧ ❧ ❧ ❧ ❧ ❧ ❧ ❧ ❧ ❧

HARRY CALLED FROM a pay phone. "Helen," he said when she answered, "I don't know if they have tapped your phone or not. I want you to meet me where we celebrated after *Sneeze* was sold."

"Harry, are you—"

"Leave right now, Helen. We'll talk then."

Harry watched her enter the restaurant, obviously disoriented by the interior's gloom, older and frailer in her confusion.

Raymond was outside, watching to see if anyone was following her. No clear plan had been formulated if Helen were, indeed, being followed, but Harry thought that such surveillance was unlikely.

Harry watched her enter from where he sat at a far table in the gloom of Benny's Continental Club with Emily and Rene. Emily was sleeping, her head back, her mouth open. Rene was in a sulk, having argued with Raymond over Allan who, she felt, was in need of immediate rescuing. Raymond had vetoed this.

"The Frozen Princess is waking!" he had shouted, causing the cabdriver to turn his head sharply and glare at Raymond.

"The Frozen Princess is waking," Raymond had repeated, with no discernible lessening of volume. "We must get the Duchess and head south immediately. I am sorry about Allan, but if we fail to find the Duke and our destination, Allan's sacrifice will have been for nothing. Our fortunes can only be decided at the Ocean of Responsibility, and if it all unravels too soon, it will be meaningless in this unmagical realm."

Rene was not satisfied with this reasoning, and took particular umbrage with the word *sacrifice*, which suggested that Allan had already been written off, abandoned as it were.

"Allan will be all right," Raymond said. Rene was not convinced.

Now Harry watched Helen turn myopically in the dark restaurant and move slowly toward them. Harry got up, went to her, and embraced her.

"Harry, are you all right?" she asked. Her eyes studied his own anxiously. She wore a tan suit, and the scent of roses that met him conjured images of their shared past (other celebrations, Jeanne with him, laughing, saying, "Call me Zelda.").

"I'm okay, Helen. I'm fine, actually. But we've got to go to Florida. I need you to come with me."

In the end, she agreed to go, but it was not the eloquence of his arguments that made her acquiesce. It was, he knew, concern, pity, a conviction that he had lost his mind and needed a caretaker.

And perhaps he did. Certainly, when he heard himself speak, he sounded less than rational. He sounded, in fact, crazy, and this was with some serious editing, without mentioning Gorelords, levitating princesses, or Ralewings.

"Raymond says we have to go to Florida. There is someone there we have to meet, and Raymond is convinced we'll need you when we do."

She had leaned forward then, caught his hand. "Harry, you said yourself that Raymond was . . . well, deluded. Why would you listen to him now?"

That had been hard to explain. He had refused to look at it straight on. Saying it might kill it, somehow. Nonetheless: "Helen, things are different." He produced the postcard of Amy on the beach, let Helen study it at length without speaking, then tapped the pink hotel with his forefinger and said, "This is the St. Petersburg Arms. It's where this Duke is. It's where Raymond says we must go."

Helen looked up, blinked without comprehension.

"Helen, Amy was never in St. Petersburg."

"I don't understand."

He had let it out then, showed her the hope. Raymond had told him that there might be a way to *change it back.*

"Change what back?"

"Amy," he had whispered, his daughter's name a small, pink rose in his mouth.

"Oh, Harry," Helen said, squeezing his hand. "Harry." He could not look at her face.

"She was never in Florida," Harry insisted, still looking away. "And things are happening that I can't explain, things . . . " It was a sickly thing, this hope, and Harry felt it dying in the air, unable to survive even his own poor scrutiny, and he pulled his arm away from Helen's hand and stood up.

"Of course I'll go with you," she said.

She had brought Arbus with her—he was waiting in the car—and when Raymond saw the monkey, he whooped loudly.

"This is a good omen, my Lord," he said, bouncing the monkey in his arms. "This reunion suggests that Blodkin smiles upon our cause."

"Just what is our cause?" Harry asked.

Raymond had raised his eyebrows. "Why Lord Gainesborough, you jest. Our cause is to Return the Light, of course. We are to stop the Freeze, overthrow the Encroaching Darkness, and Return the Light."

"That's a tall order," Harry said.

"We are tall-hearted," Raymond said, and Harry thought he saw the bright stars and happy faces of a wizard's robes.

They drove south into the night, stopping finally a little north of Richmond (the exit sign off 95 said Ashland) and getting two rooms in a red-brick motel called The Pines.

Harry and Raymond stayed in one room while Helen, Rene, and Emily occupied an adjacent room. The bedspreads were dark green, the walls only slightly lighter. In Harry and Raymond's room, a slowly rotating ceiling fan—Harry could find no way of disabling it—made the light in the room shimmer unpleasantly. Sitting on one of the twin beds, Harry felt as though he had been dropped into an immense neglected aquarium. Raymond, still dressed and already snoring on the other bed, seemed to rise and fall as though lifted by watery currents—an illusion produced, Harry was certain, by the choppy light, the long hours of driving, and whatever drugs still rode his bloodstream.

On the drive down, Harry had filled Helen in. He found that he could not tell this story without including its fantastic elements, and at first he hesitated. "Some of this will sound crazy," he said.

Helen said, "Maybe I should tell you that I have seen one of your Ralewings—the size of a house, it was—destroy a helicopter. And I saw the corpse of another impossible creature, a Politer, that Raymond's mother showed me. I'm . . . I'm acquiring some tolerance for the fantastic. Do you want the details?"

Harry did, so Helen talked first, speaking of the arrival of Gabriel, the Storys, and finally Roald Peake and his men. She spoke of Peake's phony concern for Harry and his companions who were, in Peake's words, "at grave risk" thanks to an unauthorized drug experiment. She spoke in great detail of the Ralewing, reliving her horror, the fear its black shape had engendered even before, consciously, she had identified it as an impossible creature, hideously magnified. She told how Ada Story produced the mummified Politer from the trunk of her car, and the story of Raymond's summoning it.

When she was done, Harry nodded. "You see," he said, "anything is possible."

"Amy's dead," she said.

For a moment, he hated her, this old woman with her own losses, resigned to every awful thing.

"I know that," he said. He let his anger go and talked, telling her everything, hallucinations included, not bothering with disclaimers.

When he finished, she was silent.

"Well?" he had finally asked. It was dark by then, and he could tell nothing from her profile in the passenger's seat.

"I don't know, Harry," she said. "I don't know what any of it means."

Who did? Every journey was a strange one. Hadn't Chesterton argued that strangeness suggested some comparison, something more normal and reassuring? Some alternate world.

Outside, Harry could hear the hiss of long-distance trucks, sporadic at this late hour, a sound that would have been soothing had he been less keyed up, less primed for sinister fancies. Now every sibilant passing brought with it the image of a monstrous Swamp Grendel, rubbing its scaled hide against the motel's brick, its gray-green eyes glowing faintly from the luminous microscopic organisms within.

Harry lay back on the pillow but found that closing his eyes brought with it instant panic, vertigo, nausea. He reached over to the end table and clicked on the bedside lamp. A steady circle of light appeared, comfortable, unwavering.

All comfy at the bottom of the aquarium, he thought. He smiled, thinking of *Scoundrel Flowers,* a children's book that had been singularly unsuccessful, perhaps because he had tackled a big theme, the nature of evil, and discovered that neither he nor his art had anything happy and certain to say. Happiness and certainty were essential qualities in a successful children's book.

Here in the underwater motel, *Scoundrel Flowers* had come to his mind naturally—for there was a scene in the book in which two goldfish, Ed and Alice, fight.

Alice says, "I'm out of here," and she proceeds to jump higher and higher until she has cleared the side of the aquarium and landed on the table where, of course, she begins to experience extreme discomfort.

"I can't breathe!" she screams. "I'm dying."

Ed rescues her by elaborate means and, repentant, she tells Ed that she has discovered she cannot live without him.

Ed, honest to a fault, tells her that it is the absence of water, and not his presence, that nearly did her in.

Alice, angry again, declares that Ed is the most unromantic lout she has ever known and again leaps out of the aquarium. This time Ed resolves to let her dry out and wither away—unless a small girl or boy, reading the story, feels that Alice is still worth saving. A list of Alice's good qualities follows, in which her beautiful orange coloring and large blue eyes are featured, and most little boys and girls (Amy, for instance) vote to give Alice another chance, and so the story continues with an even more elaborate rescue mission from the daring and passionate (if unromantic) Ed.

Harry had dedicated *Scoundrel Flowers* to Jeanne who had said, "It's about time I got a dedication. I mean, first your parents, then your sister, then I think it was your friend in North Carolina, and then even your agent, and I was about to say something . . . "

The dedication had read: This book is for Jeanne, who is air, water, and fire and who loved the *Scoundrel Flowers* into bloom.

Scoundrel Flowers was Jeanne's favorite book.

The impulse to call was instant, and he had given the operator his telephone credit number before looking at his watch. It was almost eleven.

She answered on the first ring.

"Jeanne," he said. "It's me, Harry."

"Harry! My God, Harry! Where have you been? Are you all right? We've all been crazy. Helen—"

"Helen's here too," Harry said.

Jeanne said something Harry couldn't make out.

"What's that?" Harry asked. Then he realized she was talking to someone else in the room with her. Harry could hear a man's voice. She was shouting at him. He shouted back. Then she was back on the line.

"Sorry. That was Mark. Where have you been, Harry?"

"It's a long story," he said. The man in the room had thrown Harry off.

"Where are you?"

"I'm in Virginia. I'm traveling with some friends. We're driving down to Florida. I've been in a hospital and—"

"You *are* all right, aren't you? You didn't—"

"I'm fine. I can't go into details now. I guess I just wanted to let you know I've been thinking about you . . . a lot. I wanted to call and let you know I was okay, see how you were doing too. How are you?"

"I'm good. Look, what were you in a hospital for?"

"Actually, it wasn't a real hospital. We were being held against our will. Fortunately—"

"Is Helen there? Can I speak to her?"

"Helen's in the other room with Emily and Rene and Arbus."

"Arbus?"

"Lord Arbus. Not a person, actually. A spider monkey."

"Oh."

"What I called for, what I wanted to say was I'm in the middle of something that could be very important, for both of us, something strange, fantastic, and I wanted to say . . . I don't know, . . . just to tell you I'm all right and that I'll keep you posted."

"You're sure you are all right?"

"Yes."

"You sound sort of weird."

"That's probably the residue of the drugs. They had us on lots of medication. And I've been driving for hours; you know how that will wind you up."

"Yes. I understand. Could you go and get Helen? I just want to talk to her for a minute."

"I expect she's sleeping right now. I could have her call you in the morning."

"Okay. Please. Don't forget, Harry."

"No, of course not—"

Harry heard the man's voice behind Jeanne. Harry could make out none of the words, but the tone was angry. "Just a minute," she said.

"I'd better go," Harry said. "I just wanted you to know I was okay."

"Harry—" The man was still talking behind her, a querulous rumble.

"I'll tell Helen to give you a ring."

"Give me a number where I can reach you and—"

"We're leaving in the morning," Harry said. "I'll get back to you later. I love you. Gotta go." He hung up.

The conversation had not gone as planned. He had, he realized, contracted some of Raymond's enthusiasm for the adventure, and he had wanted to communicate that to Jeanne, and all she had sensed was the craziness, her voice full of that exasperating walking-on-eggs concern.

"I might *not* be crazy," he sighed, newly aware of how very tired he was. He lay back on the pillow without turning the bedside lamp off. He closed his eyes and the panic didn't rush him. Instead, he fell instantly and dreamlessly into sleep.

As Jeanne hung up the phone, Mark came from behind, caught her other wrist and pulled it back. She heard the snap of the cuffs as the metal band encircled her wrist.

"Hey!" she said. "I'm not in the mood."

"No?" he said, leaning down and running his tongue up the side of her neck to her ear. "I figured your chat with the ex probably got you hot. Still got a thing for him, don't you?"

"Give me the key," she said. She leaned back and looked him in the eyes. He smiled down at her.

The handcuffs had been his idea. In a weak moment, when he had looked his most boyish, a playful imp, she'd agreed that it might be fun.

It hadn't been, actually. But she had learned something. She did not trust Mark, did not know him. When her hands were locked behind her, she felt fear. He could do anything. He might hurt her.

The handcuffs had brought this knowledge to the surface, but still she hadn't left him. To leave would have required energy she lacked.

Now he had slipped up behind her and hooked her wrist to the bedpost.

"Come on, give me the key," she said, ice in her tone.

He tossed the key on the bed, muttered something. She heard the door slam. He might be gone all night now. That would be fine. More likely he'd return at three or four, wake her up, tell her he loved her, try to peel her nightgown over her head as proof. She might let him—the easiest solution if she were muddled with sleep—or she might tell him to get lost and then how it went would depend on just how drunk he was.

Thinking about it made Jeanne weary. Whatever.

She got up and went into the bathroom and brushed her teeth. Harry's phone call troubled her. Was he going nuts again? It sounded that way. Maybe Helen was trying to get him back in some psych ward. God bless you, Helen.

Mark and Harry were two different species, and the way Jeanne felt about them was utterly different. In the comparison, she could admit that she was beginning to dislike Mark. He was not a man she would have chosen, and he had entered her life because she had been lax, had left the door open, indifferent to burglary.

Harry. She loved Harry and so, when he disappeared, when he withdrew into vagueness and alcohol, she had despised him passionately.

But he still seemed, to her willful heart, like her friend, her confidante, and when she heard his voice she still felt that quickening, that feeling that here was the one meant to receive the news of her life, her dreams, her fears.

Often when they had made love, she would talk, regaling him with the events of her day or some thought she had come upon and wanted to share, and her casual words would not destroy the erotic impulse but would ride upon it, and she'd see, in his eyes, an intensity of pure listening and delight.

It was a hard habit to shake.

If Mark hadn't been in the room, she would have told Harry about the postcard. Perhaps, tomorrow, she would tell him. When Helen called . . .

She walked to the dresser and took the postcard out from

under several folded white blouses. Was she hiding it from Mark? Perhaps, but why?

The postcard had arrived two days ago, and since then she had studied it at length. It was a photo of a large, pink hotel, flanked by palm trees, white cumulus clouds billowing in the distance, the emerald ocean tranquil in the foreground. A number of elegant, antique cars filled the parking lot. The back contained no typeset description of the hotel—no name, no location, nothing. The card was postmarked St. Petersburg, Florida, and someone had written, in a childish scrawl that could have been Amy's: "Mommy—Please don't let Daddy get lost. Don't be so mad at him. He is very sad and misses you." Who would send such a card—and why?

She sat down in an armchair, the card resting in her lap. She remembered what Harry had said on the phone: "We're driving down to Florida."

She tapped the postcard on her thigh. Coincidence? It seemed unlikely. If she had had Harry's number, she would have called him back. As soon as he answered, she would have said, "You're going to St. Petersburg, aren't you?"

She knew he would answer "Yes."

CHaPTeR TWeNTY

❀ ❀ ❀ ❀ ❀ ❀ ❀ ❀ ❀ ❀ ❀ ❀

"MY NAME'S ALLAN," he said.

"Well of course it is," the tall man said. "I know that." He tore the top from a pack of cigarettes and dumped the contents on the desktop.

"Then why do you keep calling me Henry?" Allan fidgeted in the chair. He did not like talking to this man, who looked just like Lord Draining in *Zod Wallop*—except that this guy was wearing a suit.

"I guess you remind me of someone else," the man said, staring at the loose cigarettes. "Some other young man with an authority problem." The man plucked a cigarette from the pile with a long forefinger and thumb. He put the cigarette between his lips, delicately pushed the cigarette back into his mouth until it disappeared from sight, and began to chew. His expression was pained. He turned and hawked the contents into a wastepaper basket next to the desk.

He smiled then. "A nasty habit," he said. "I'm trying to quit."

"Yeah."

"Your mother should be along shortly, Henry . . . ah, Allan. I still believe that a longer stay with us wouldn't do you a bit of harm, but your mother wants you by her side, and I always respect your mother's wishes. What really saddens me is your reluctance to tell us where your friends have gone."

"I don't know where they are."

"I think you know and just don't trust us. This saddens me."

Allan brought a hand up to his neck and massaged a cramped muscle. "Well," Allan said, "this counselor in group used to say it was good to feel your emotions. You know, like sadness is okay, nothing to be ashamed of."

The man laughed, nodding his head in acknowledgment of the joke. "Henry Bottle," he said. "That's who I have you confused with. There's a remarkable resemblance. Henry Bottle was the young man in that book your friends love, that *Zod Wallop*. You know what happened to Henry, don't you?"

Allan said nothing.

"The Midnight Machines killed him." The man picked up another cigarette, sniffed it. For a moment, Allan thought the man might shove it up a nostril, but instead he tossed it into the wastebasket.

"Henry's problem was the same as yours, Allan. Misplaced loyalty. He thought his friends were worthy of loyalty, but they weren't. That's true in your case too. They ran off without you, didn't look back. Is that any way for friends to behave? And worse than that . . . worse . . . I've got something for you, Allan. Take a look at this at your leisure. Think about it. Ask yourself if it's a betrayal or not. I say it is. I say it's not right. You have no allegiance to these people. I hope you'll agree with me and decide to give me a call."

Allan stared at the manila envelope that was being offered.

"Nothing to be scared of," the man said.

Allan took the envelope. He stood up. "I can go then?"

"Of course. And give my regards to your lovely mother."

When Allan came out of the elevator in the lobby, he saw her entering the revolving doors. She saw him too, waved, and then began to run. Her hat fell off, but she didn't pause for it (already a security guard, one of the many bit players in her drama, was moving to retrieve it). She was dressed in something tan and formal; her stockings appeared to be silver.

She hugged Allan fiercely, the top of her head coming to just below his chin.

"Oh my prodigal son!" she shouted. She slid to her knees, her arms still encircling him.

"Mother."

"I've been worried sick. I told myself I was going to practice detachment, but I could just as easily have been serene about a detached arm. When it comes down to it, you are all I have."

"Oh, Mother."

"If you run away again, I'll hire someone to find you and kill you."

"Oh, Mother."

They stopped the next night at a motel maybe fifty miles south of the Georgia state line. The motel squatted amid scrub pines on the edge of a marsh. Its parking lot contained a single pickup truck and the VACANCY sign seemed sadly redundant. An unshaven old man smiled mendaciously as he checked them in, saw Arbus and noted that monkeys were an extra seven-fifty and not, as some people tried to claim, free like children under five.

Harry had planned to drive straight through to St. Petersburg, but the urgency that had initiated their flight from New Jersey was gone now, and he was tired . . . and, in truth, he was afraid.

What if their destination revealed, starkly and implacably, the sad madness of his delusion? What if this group hallucination, this frenzy of purpose, halted abruptly and there was nothing at the end of the line? What if there was no mysterious Duke to guide them, no salvation, no revelation?

What, after all, did he expect? That Amy be returned to him? And what was this expectation based on? A strange postcard? A clinically diagnosed schizophrenic's belief that an alternate, happy-ending world could be discovered in some supernatural juxtaposition of a children's book?

Harry sat outside, in a swing that was part of a small, decaying children's playground. A rusty slide had fallen on its side and green, leafy vines climbed the jungle gym. The night sky was filled with stars and a warm breeze carried the brackish, ancient scent of marsh, a stew of tidal creatures and mud and sun-marinated vegetation.

Harry saw something moving through tall weeds and the diminutive Arbus, resplendent in a yellow jumpsuit, came into view. The monkey walked with a sailor's gait, clutching to his stomach a bag of popcorn purchased by Raymond at the last roadside stop. He sat down and began to eat the popcorn in earnest, stuffing handfuls of exploded kernels into his mouth.

Harry heard voices and turned to see Emily and Rene off to his left. Rene had wheeled Emily underneath a white gazebo and was combing Emily's unruly hair.

Harry smiled at the two women. They were framed by the white, vine-entwined lattice and seemed complete, an artist's rendition of sisterhood and its intimate rituals.

Rene's voice, oddly musical, was carried by the breeze. "I can't wait to get to the beach," she said. "I've got a thing for beaches."

Rene leaned forward, saying something into Emily's ear that Harry could not hear, and, like some optical illusion waiting slyly for just the right focus or frame of mind, the brooding mountain-sized silhouette of Castle Grimfast loomed up behind the two women.

Harry almost lost his balance as he stood, forgetting the tentative nature of swings. This vision of Lord Draining's dark kingdom was accompanied by an ominous roaring sound.

Then Harry heard a wild shriek and turned to see Arbus disappearing into a black pool. The monkey was clutching hysterically at the weeds. Popcorn kernels lay scattered on the ground like stuffing exploded from a ragdoll. The monkey's screams of panic filled Harry's mind and seemed to affect his vision. The world canted oddly as he ran toward the monkey.

Harry's feet caught in the soft, clinging mud, and he fell, hands sinking deep into foul goo. He righted himself, lumbered forward, and watched the top of Arbus's head disappear under black water.

He leaned down, thrust his hands into the tepid, evil-smelling waters, and he felt wet fabric brush his left hand, closed on it, a fist of slippery, synthetic cloth, and found the squirming, child-sized waist with his other hand.

He howled to call down strength, leaned back, heaved. The water erupted and a great, scaled tail shattered the pool's surface.

A Swamp Grendel, vile familiar of the Less-Than, poisonous stalker—and coward waiting for dark, preying on children!

"My Lord, we cannot go into that wood."

"Pray, why not?"

"It is infested with Swamp Grendels."

"I have heard of these beasts, my Duke. They are skulkers and carrion eaters and have an appetite for the defenseless. One brave heart should route them."

"Such hearts are rare."

"What? We have two here already."

"Sonofabitch!" Harry shouted.

Harry floundered backward, his knees skidding in the mud, no traction, nothing but a frenzy of determination and rage. He held the monkey, a firm grip now, hands locked under the animal's arms. Arbus was inert, shocked insensible—dead?—the rope in a tug of war. Harry dragged Arbus out of the water.

The creature's head surfaced, rising in the water like some miniature, grotesque submarine. The leathery flesh seemed fake; Hollywood's high-tech special effects had accustomed Harry to more realistic ogres.

One of Arbus's legs was half-lost in the long, ragged mouth. The creature's cat's-eye pupils caught the starlight, emotionless, stubborn, no flicker of intelligence. Grim appetite ruled the monster.

Harry saw what he needed and risked it, released his right hand from its grip on the monkey, grabbed the jagged rock and threw himself forward, swinging wide, striking his target, the baleful eye. Instantly the pool turned into writhing water; mud splattered Harry's forehead and hair.

And then it was gone. That easy.

Raymond came running, shouting, as Harry backed still farther from the sinister waters. Arbus was already stirring, chattering pathetically.

"It's okay," Harry said.

"My Lord, what happened?"

Harry laughed then. "It's okay, Raymond. I thought . . . oh, I let my imagination get the best of me."

Raymond was bending down now, studying the monkey's bleeding leg.

"I forgot we were in Georgia," Harry said. "I thought we were somewhere far worse." Saying that, he turned and looked behind him. Emily and Rene were no longer in the gazebo; they were coming quickly down the path toward the playground. And Castle Grimfast had resolved itself into clouds that threatened only rain.

"What happened?"

"Arbus had a little run-in with an alligator," Harry said. "That's all. Nothing but an alligator."

Later that night, lying in bed, Harry reflected on the fears that all men conjured, how powerful that darkness was, and thought that not everyone, perhaps, would find an encounter with an alligator reassuring. Perspective was everything in life.

Gabriel entered Peake's office and began coughing; the room was filled with smoke.

Peake smiled at her out of the smoke. His features seemed sharper since she had last seen him. There were three cigarettes in his mouth, two more burning in the ashtray.

"What can I do for you, Gabriel?" he said, indicating a chair.

"I thought you were quitting," she said, fanning the smoke from her face. Her eyes had begun to water.

Peake raised a hand to his mouth and captured all three cigarettes between his spread fingers—a curiously elegant feat—and smiled. His teeth seemed larger in his head.

"I *am* quitting," he said. "I am in the aversive stage, overindulging my vice. The theory, of course, is that once one sickens of a thing it is easier to leave it behind."

"I've come—"

Peake frowned. "Actually, I seem to be enjoying this excess so far. There is a perverse pleasure in pushing the limits, you now."

"I've come about Allan," Gabriel said.

"A delightful young man. Makes me wish I had children."

"Where is he?"

"Why, he's residing with you, isn't he?"

"No. He's run away. Do you know where he is?"

Peake shook his head, sadly. "I would love to help you, Gabriel. You know how happy I was to assist with that unpleasantness surrounding Dr. Lavin. But you give me too much credit. I am not clairvoyant. He could be anywhere."

Gabriel stood up. "He's gone to find them," she said. "I'm certain of that. I thought you might be able to tell me where they are."

Peake nodded. "No doubt you are right. By 'they' you refer, of course, to Harold Gainesborough, Raymond Story, and the others. I am afraid, however, that all my efforts to locate them have come to nothing. And I expect the case will be the same with your son's attempts and that he will tire of the search and return to you."

"No, Allan is not likely—"

A high-pitched electronic wail emanated from the outer office and Peake stood up and quickly moved past Gabriel.

"Smoke alarm," he said in passing. "You've got to keep this door closed or—"

He was out the door. She heard him speaking quickly to the receptionist.

Gabriel darted behind the desk and pulled open the drawer. The man was not candid; honesty was not a reflex with him. Perhaps there would be something, some clue . . .

The drawer was filled to the top with loose cigarettes. Gabriel heard Peake's voice in the other room, shouting above the escalating whine of the smoke alarm.

She thrust her hands into the white mass of cigarettes, felt something, brushed away cigarettes, saw revealed a painting of a long-haired little girl holding a very unpleasant-looking doll. The girl was facing away, looking toward sinister mountains. A yellow road wound across a barren plain, losing itself in the ragged horizon. It was this bright ribbon that seemed, irrationally, fraught with significance. It was, Gabriel thought, the road down which her son had fled.

Her hand grasped the illustration. She retrieved it, discovering that she held a book, remembering clearly then Theo Lavin's frightened delirium and this same book.

She shoved it into her handbag, closed the drawer, and was back in her seat before the alarm shut off and Roald Peake returned.

The truck driver dropped him at the on ramp. Allan watched the big diesel slowly accelerate, pulling away. The driver's arm appeared in the cab window, waved. Allan waved back.

"Some people," the driver had said, "might not be inclined to stop for a guy like you. I mean, you're a big sonofabitch. It's one thing to stop for some runty little hitchhiker, but it's another thing to stop for a goddamn giant. But the way I see it . . . Charlie Manson was a little guy, you know. I been in a lot of bars, and when a brawl breaks out it's generally some sawed-off twerp started it, took offense over nothing. It's those short ones that have the tempers."

Allan had nodded, glad that the rage within him didn't color his flesh red or make his hair stand up straight or show itself in any visible way or else the man wouldn't have picked him up and driven him the first three hundred miles of his journey.

The anger inside Allan was restless in its prison, wanted to come out and make itself known. He wanted to smash something, fight, hurt and be hurt.

He thought no articulate thought, however, and was aware only that he must keep the violence in until he found them, until he was within striking distance of Harry Gainesborough, until he had Rene's throat in his hands. His energies were directed at holding these forces at bay until then. His will kept his arms folded, kept reopening his hands when they turned to fists, kept directing his thoughts to his destination.

He thought, perhaps every seventh second, of the photograph that was folded in his back pocket. It was the photo he had pulled out of the manila envelope, and his first sight of it had hit him hard, as though someone had taken a baseball bat and slammed him in the gut with it.

He had been sitting on the bed in his room. He had decided to throw the envelope away without opening it, because, he reasoned, nothing good could come from the man who looked like Lord Draining. And then, that willfulness that was his enemy took control of his hands, bent the metal clasp back, opened the envelope, and stared at the eight-by-ten photograph of Rene Gold and Harry Gainesborough.

The two were sitting by the side of a swimming pool, Rene in a black-checkered bikini, Harry Gainesborough in nerdy red trunks that emphasized the whiteness of his flesh. They were sitting on a blanket, torsos twisted toward each other, embracing, sharing a shameless kiss so passionate that any guardian of morality would have summoned the police. The photo was overexposed, the colors faded by the glare of the sun, and Allan thought he could smell the chlorine and suntan oil rising from the glossy surface. The photo was painfully sharp, filled with headachy detail: a small, pale green cactus in a clay pot behind them against a cinder-block wall, black hairs on the back of Harry Gainesborough's hand (the one that lay flat against Rene's ribs), beads of water on Rene's bare shoulder.

Allan had stared at the photo until its impression was stamped on his soul. He continued to stare until his mother knocked on the door, pushed it open, and said, "Allan, Dr. Peake says he needs to speak to you."

Allan, still in shock, had lifted the hall phone's receiver. And the smooth, hateful voice had said, "They wanted you out of the way, Allan. The lovers wanted to be shed of you. You don't owe them anything. Tell me where they are."

And Allan had hung up, gone back to his room, folded the photograph, stuck it in his back pocket, and walked downstairs and out of the house.

The funny thing was, he hadn't known then where they were. He knew that Raymond had talked about going to find the Duke, but Allan could not remember where the Duke was supposed to be or even if Raymond had said where.

And then the rage welled up, and, as was often the case, it brought with it other powers. The rage faced his memory down, stormed the corridors of recall, and came back with the answer: St. Petersburg, Florida. Raymond Story had said they were going to St. Petersburg, Florida.

And that's where Allan was going, so that he could let the terrible dark thing out, the whirlwind born out of this revelation of betrayal.

It was almost dark when a car stopped. It was a long, black car and the overhead light went on when Allan opened the door, and a fat man with gray, stringy hair, a goatee, yellow teeth, and a black scar on the bridge of his nose studied him. "This car got a big-ass appetite," he said. "You reckon you can pitch in on the gas? You got any money for gas?"

Allan nodded, climbed in. "Where are you going?"

"Atlanta. I woke up with Georgia on my mind." He sang a few bars, doing a Ray Charles imitation that consisted of closing his eyes, shaking his head, and howling, breaking the word *Georgia* into long, wavering syllables.

He stopped, grinned at Allan. "My name's John Jackson," he said.

Two hours later, the car pulled over to the side of the road, sending gravel flying, and stopped. Allan got out and jumped the ditch and unzipped his fly and urinated, studying the stars and the flat, silent farmland.

He was finishing up when something pricked the base of his neck, and he heard the man speak behind him. "Don't go turning around," the man said. "I spend a lot of time sharpening this knife. It's a nervous habit, passes the time when things are slow. I decided I'd just as soon travel alone, but I'm gonna need that gas money. I'll be sliding your wallet out of your back pocket there, and my advice is you stay real still while I'm doing it."

Allan zipped his fly up. He could see a light in the farm house perhaps a mile away.

"I ain't gonna hurt you," the man said.

"It's okay," Allan said.

The man was drawing the wallet from Allan's pocket. "I'm glad you think it's okay," the man said. "I'm glad you're okay with this loan."

"No," Allan said. "It's okay if you hurt me." Allan would have liked to explain, just something brief about the effort it took to keep the rage in check—like being tormented by a thousand biting fleas and not allowed to scratch, and how pain could come as a welcome distraction.

The man laughed, spittle spraying Allan's neck. He didn't understand though, Allan was sure of that. "Like it, huh? Like having your butt whipped, boy? Like—"

The fat man was a gift, Allan thought, as though an angel had taken pity on his anguish and said, "Here's something to hold you until you get to Florida. Here's something to scratch."

Allan held the whirlwind for two more beats, wondered if the fat man could hear the hum of straining engines, and then brought his right hand up and back and caught the man's knife-wielding hand by the wrist. Allan's own hand had known—full of the power—that the fat man's wrist would be there, just so. Allan had even anticipated the feel of that wrist, rubbery and slick with sweat so that a firm, iron grasp was required.

The fat man's wrist broke as Allan turned. The man screamed and sunk to his knees.

Allan lifted the man and slammed him on the ground.

"*Oof*," the man said, saying the word precisely—as though reading a cartoon balloon out loud. The fat man got on his knees and tried to crawl away. His jeans were sliding down and Allan saw the crack of his ass and flesh like curdled milk.

Allan lifted the man again, turned him. The man was heavier now, which meant that the rage was subsiding. Allan leaned into the man and pistoned a half-dozen blows into the broad belly and the man lolled toward him, sour breath burning Allan's nostrils, dirty long hair licking Allan's ear like a spider web encountered in a dank cellar, the man's body thick and stupid now, nothing to rage at except dumb flesh.

Allan rolled the man into the ditch, made sure that he landed face up and wouldn't drown in the inch of mosquito-rich water, and turned away.

He found his wallet in the weeds. The keys were in the car. Allan started the car and pulled back onto the asphalt two-lane. He had no idea where he was. He assumed the road led somewhere and the dashboard compass assured him he was headed south. Time would reveal more. He felt a mild regret that the man had had so little fight. Something, a small cut, some blood, would have been soothing.

CHaPTeR TWeNTY-oNe

✧ ✧ ✧ ✧ ✧ ✧ ✧ ✧ ✧ ✧ ✧ ✧ ✧

THEY ATE AT a family restaurant called The Pink Seahorse. The decor was early American tourist, with plastic lobsters, lamps made from mollusks, and paintings of sailboats and lighthouses. The restaurant was crowded with old people who ate with hunched intensity, uncertain, perhaps, of future meals. Out the window, Harry could see a tiny glittering shard of the ocean between two buildings. They had arrived.

Including an eight-dollar tip, the meal came to fifty-eight twenty-two. Raymond had two dollars and sixteen cents; Rene had a single quarter. Emily and Arbus had no money at all. Harry had two twenties, a dime and a quarter, and Helen, who said she would pay with a credit card and then discovered that, in her haste to meet Harry, she had left her cards in what she called her "dress" purse, scavenged fifteen dollars and eleven cents in cash.

They paid for the meal and left the restaurant, exiting into a St. Petersburg sunset as effusively colored as any amateur oil painting, colors straight from the tube. Harry stood on the sidewalk as his companions bunched up around him. Their entire capital now consisted of five one dollar bills and change amounting to sixty-five cents.

The plan had been to locate the St. Petersburg Arms and register there for the night, but it seemed that they had miscalculated. While Harry was quite rich, he had no credit cards and was used to going to his local bank for cash as required. He could, perhaps, convince a bank of his identity, have funds wired. . . . It was late in the day for such activities, however, and Harry was, in any event, more than a little paranoid. They were fugitives, after all. It was possible that a call to his bank could reveal his present location.

"My Lord," Raymond interrupted. "We must press on. We must obtain shelter before the sky is filled with their eyes."

"I'm afraid we don't have money for lodging. We'll have to spend the night in the car, or on the beach, and in the morning—"

"That won't do at all," Raymond said.

Raymond, Harry thought, was that particular brand of crazy characterized by immense stubbornness, an inability to reconcile what was with what should be. Indeed, all craziness might have something to do with a childish refusal to let go of a privileged view of the universe and get down in the dirt with reality.

Refusing to believe that your daughter could die, a voice within Harry said. That sort of thing?

"Ho! There's what we want, my Lord." Raymond launched himself across the street. The traffic was light, and those few cars on the street moved slowly, silver and black and gold cars like big, regal fish. Raymond easily dodged them, moving toward an illuminated sign reading: ST. PETERSBURG FIRST NATIONAL SAVINGS AND LOAN. Rene pushed Emily across the street in Raymond's wake and Helen, with Arbus in her arms, followed.

"Dammit!" Harry shouted. "Wait!"

Nobody waited.

Grumbling, Harry ran into the street. A black Cadillac screeched to a halt and an old man wearing a suit and a hat leaned out the window and screamed, "Are you crazy?"

Harry ducked his head and kept running.

He found the others standing in front of an ATM. The computer screen's green letters announced that it was prepared to handle banking needs twenty-four hours a day.

Raymond was leaning forward, smiling at the message.

He stood up as Harry came up behind him. "My Lord," he said, "this drone will give us money. I have never availed myself of one of these machines, but I have seen them operated by others. You need only put your card in, push your secret code, four numbers I believe, and ask for a sum commensurate with your needs."

So delighted was Raymond, bouncing slightly on the balls of his feet, eyes bright, that Harry was reluctant to tell him that he had never used such a machine and did not have the faintest idea how to operate one and did not, in any event, have a card or a personal code to unlock its electronic mysteries.

He put an arm on Raymond's shoulder. He looked hard into Raymond's blue eyes and gave him all the sad news.

"They are very easy to use," Raymond insisted. "They have a menu. It tells you what to do, step by step."

Harry explained that this was all well and good, but that—to repeat himself—he did not possess the necessary automatic teller card.

Raymond turned and sat down on one of the cement steps. He pulled out his wallet, a brown, frayed object that resembled some sort of baked pastry.

"Ha ha!" Raymond said, dramatically producing a rectangular piece of yellow cardboard. He held it in the air at arm's length. "A card," he said.

It was, indeed, a card, a business card. It read: MADAME RAMONE'S PALM READING in some sort of 3-D type whose lines converged on a badly drawn open hand. Smaller type, to the right and left of the hand, noted various other arcane services offered by Ms. Ramone (including something called "Entrails Divining") and an address in Trenton, New Jersey.

"Raymond," Harry said, sitting down beside the younger man. "That isn't the sort of card this machine accepts."

Raymond studied the card. He turned it over. It was blank on the back.

Raymond fumbled in the pockets of his baggy pants, produced a pen, and began to write, printing slowly, his tongue slipping out to wet his mustache, invoking, Harry assumed, some deeper state of concentration.

When he was finished—the task was slow and arduous and caused sweat to erupt on Raymond's forehead—he handed the card to Harry.

The flair pen, executing a series of straight, blocky letters, had achieved the following message: PLEASE GIVE US $300 DOLLARS. WE HAVE URGENT NEED OF THE MONEY, AND WE WILL REPAY IT AFTER, BLODKIN WILLING, THIS CRISIS IS AVERTED. I WILL TYPE 1234 FOR A CODE. THANK YOU. RAYMOND STORY.

Harry handed the card back to Raymond with new respect for that man's insanity. It was a kind of pure saintly madness, beyond reproach, really, consistent in its other-worldliness.

Harry said nothing as Raymond stood up and approached the waiting computer screen. Raymond found the slot and gingerly inserted the card. He turned to Harry and smiled, a pleasant, faintly put-upon smile that said, Although you have all been doubters and impediments, I will never flaunt this triumph. I am not petty.

The machine spit out the card. Raymond took the card and inserted it again. Again the machine rejected it.

Harry didn't want to see the dim, sad dawning of something like resignation in Raymond's eyes. He didn't want to look at the others either because that defeat would be there too, mirrored in their eyes.

A potent mixture of embarrassment and guilt caused Harry to turn and move slowly away, a hands-in-pockets stroll, studying the weeds between the sidewalk's cracks. *No, never seen those folks. Yes, they do look as though they recently escaped from some mental institution.*

An old woman was walking a dachshund, and the dog stopped to sniff Harry's shoes. The woman was very small and frail, with wisps of white hair tucked under a gray knit cap. She wore a lavender dress and a pink, gossamer scarf. The woman smiled at Harry and said, "That's a lovely dog you have."

"It's your dog," he said, and instantly regretted saying this. Her eyes widened and then her face seemed to shrink with pain, fighting to keep the smile. "Oh," she said. "Of course it is."

She turned quickly, back the way she had come. The dog,

hurried away by his mistress, cast one last look back, a look—Harry was certain—of reproach.

Everyone seemed to be crazy. And the coin of the realm was disillusionment. Harry sighed.

He might as well face the music.

As he came back down the sidewalk, he saw Raymond lean forward and gather the bills from the machine, snapping the currency out like paper towels from a rest-room dispenser. Raymond punched a key and his card was returned to him.

He held the card up, as though he were a celebrity touting the virtues of some credit vendor, and said, "I put it in upside down at first. What was I thinking?"

Harry said nothing.

When Raymond suggested that they move along, Harry agreed.

By the time Harry was in the car and driving again, with Helen bending over a map of the city and complaining about the size of the type, he realized that he felt, all things considered, rather good, rather hopeful.

They had reached their destination. And the magic hadn't played out yet. Reality had not reasserted itself. Hope then. Hope for miracles.

Gabriel lay in bed under the covers, her head propped up by a half-dozen pillows. Harry Gainesborough's grim children's book rested on the incline of her thighs. She studied the illustration of her son. In the painting he wore a shirt that appeared to be chain mail but which, upon close scrutiny, was seen to be made from linked pop-tops of the sort that one peeled off soda and beer cans before the advent of a higher ecological consciousness and the end of aluminum, tadpolelike litter. The artist's skill in rendering this tremendous detail in a style that nonetheless suggested great spontaneity would have dazzled a student of illustration, but Gabriel's sole concern was the story itself. Her son, whose elongated features and jutting brow displayed an implausibly angelic expression, was in grave danger, standing in a stone room whose shadows glowed with steel highlights, the mercury glitter of needles and knives, and the claws of mechanical killing machines. Gabriel read this part repeatedly, hoping each time that it would end less cruelly. A foolish hope, perhaps, but one engendered by a sense that the story did change somewhat with each reading. Gabriel could not have explained this exactly. She knew only that Henry Bottle—for that was his name in *Zod Wallop*—seemed sometimes closer to salvation . . . and sometimes his doom seemed inevitable.

So Gabriel read:

Henry Bottle was guided by Love and Hate. Either will serve as a guide in Zod Wallop, and only the Duke of Flatbend had ever been able to sort them out, and then only for a moment, only long enough for a small girl named Lydia to walk, foolishly, through the door of that moment with a purity and innocence that changed the balance forever, sent the two Vile Contenders into final conflict, and awakened the Cold One and his terrible, inevitable companion, the Abyss Dweller.

Henry Bottle had come across the long Desert of Academics, across the burned-out flats of Elite Despond, through the Forest of Burning Trees and, finally, to the dying ocean where Lord Draining reigned at Grimfast. He had come to tell a lady of the court that he loved her and, for her sake, to perform great deeds. In the journey, a dark spell had fallen upon him, and he had come to hate the lady, and so he arrived just as quickly and just as passionately with a will to destroy anything at hand that might remind him of his folly.

He was in the underground labyrinth of Grimfast Castle and, as luck would have it, he had stumbled into the lair of the Midnight Machines . . .

Gabriel read with tears burning her eyes and when she came to the end, that terrible, bleak moment when the Midnight Machines engulf Henry, chopping him into small pieces that are snatched up by waiting lizards and dog-shaped creatures that haunt the lower regions of Grimfast, she read on, turning a page she had refused to turn before, and so she read of—and saw hellishly depicted—Lord Draining's arrival on the scene. Lord D. sauntered into the room of carnage and casually snatched up a severed ear and held it up to his own ear, tilting his head in a listening attitude. "You can hear the ocean," he said, and his courtiers laughed heartily and laughed again when he affixed the ear, carnationlike, beneath the ruffled collar of his silken shirt.

Gabriel flung the book across the room, knocking a vase from the dresser. The vase thumped softly against the thick carpet and rolled without breaking. Gabriel screamed, hurled herself from the bed, and grabbed the vase. *We'll see what shatters,* she thought, eyeing the closed window.

She stopped then, pressed the vase to her stomach, leaned forward as though sheltering an infant from hurricane gales.

She remembered Allan as a small child, how willful he had been even then, as though independence were everything, the only goal. She had only wanted to be close to him and it seemed, perversely, that distance was all he craved.

And now he had fled her. She rocked slowly back and

forth, head down. She squeezed her eyes tight shut, thought to will her son's thoughts into her mind.

Where are you Allan? Allan, come back.

No echo of Allan came to her. But something else did. Something Peake had said. He had said that her son and the others were psychically linked by the drug Ecknazine. That the drug created a sort of daisy chain of consciousness, reaching out from one to the other, causing Gainesborough himself to create perfect caricatures of people he had never even met.

Gabriel rose shakily to her feet. Clutching the neck of the vase in her hand she raced from the bedroom, dashed up the stairs to the third floor, and down the hall to the guest bathroom.

She blinked for a moment at her image in the medicine cabinet mirror. Her hair fell in wild ringlets over her forehead. Her eyes were wet from crying and her nightgown was torn, revealing the curve of her left breast. Her disarray was artful, a heroine in a movie, and she allowed herself one moment of admiration, licking a finger and wiping a smudge of mascara from her cheek.

Then she swung the vase and her image shattered and she swung the vase again and it too exploded, sharp-edged pieces of clay tumbling into the sink.

A drop of blood fell onto the white porcelain, and Gabriel reached up and touched her forehead which was bleeding. She smiled, licked her finger, and reached toward the mirror. The envelope was there, where Marlin Tate had hidden it, and Gabriel yanked it out, tore it open, and emptied its contents into her hand.

She filled a plastic tumbler with tap water and counted the pills. Ten. The last of the Ecknazine. She threw the lot of them into her mouth, washing them down with the water, and then returned to her bedroom where she lay down on the wide, canopied bed.

All right, she thought, closing her eyes. *Where is my son?*

Jeanne sat up in the bed and clicked the light on. Mark was leaning over her. He had the handcuffs again, and the playful smirk that accompanied these games. He was naked.

"Hey babe. You are under arrest," he said. "House arrest."

He had taken a shower and gargled something minty, but the primary effluvia was beer, and not the summer bouquet of a cold one being popped at a barbecue, but rather the dank, gut-puking reek of a cheap roadhouse.

Jeanne deftly slid out of bed. "Gotta go to the bathroom," she said.

He caught her ankle; she wasn't expecting it, and she fell forward instantly, the side of her face banging the bare carpet hard, her left hand coming up reflexively but not fast enough, twisting her wrist.

He helped her to her feet. "Sorry," he said, wobbling slightly, the handcuffs stupidly waving in his hand, his lips puffed out in an expression of remorse that never seemed genuine, something learned as a child and dragged into adulthood.

She stared at him, rubbed the flame of her wrist, said okay or was about to say okay or it's all right or any of the hundred things that came in the wake of Mark's drunken moments. She said nothing, walked quickly by him and into the bathroom.

She sat on the toilet, urinated, considered crying but didn't, discovered, indeed, that no profound emotion was under the surface of her disgust.

She went to the sink and splashed water in her face. There was a small thread of blood she could taste with her tongue, but she could detect no real damage. She thought that she might even have sex with Mark, sex being, after all, a pleasurable way of passing time. And time had to be passed.

Pass that time, please.

Her reflection in the mirror showed a pale woman with tightly curled dark hair and large eyes, a woman who looked like she had intended to say something but had decided to let it go, had decided, in fact, that words were worthless, really. This woman turned away now, casting a cold, sad eye on the bathroom as though biding it farewell forever. And before Jeanne could do more than jerk back, startled by her reflection's desertion, a hotel shimmered into being.

It was a large, pink hotel on the edge of the ocean, and she knew it immediately for the hotel of the enigmatic postcard. Jeanne watched as the doors to the hotel swung open and a tiny figure emerged. The figure paused for a moment and then skipped down the steps and ran across the dunes toward the water.

Amy. She was too far away for any feature to clearly identify her, but Jeanne knew it was Amy. She wore Amy's green bathing suit. She ran, barefoot and wild, through the tide with Amy's style, an off-balance, clownish run. Her flying hair was Amy's tangled summer mane.

Amy.

As Jeanne watched, the girl halted abruptly and looked up at the hotel. The stillness of her attitude suggested she was listening. The call must have come again. Amy turned and ran back toward the hotel, water exploding brightly under her feet.

Jeanne gasped. Amy, head down, racing full tilt, was rapidly closing the distance between herself and the hotel. Only the hotel had undergone a transformation.

The hotel was now bloodred and black, a mountain of sharp needle-spires and crenelated parapets and blind, ancient towers. The seagulls that had wheeled above the hotel had suffered a corresponding change, and now swooped through the air in batlike arcs, their long necks stretching and turning as they maintained their baleful scrutiny of the ground.

Jeanne recognized the world. She had never liked the book, perhaps because Harry had written it after Amy's death and she knew it lacked real joy, but she had read it through. She recognized the castle and these airborne, fire-spitting serpents.

The castle was more horrible, shimmering in the mirror, than it had ever been in the gaily drawn children's book. It was palpably evil, nothing whimsical here, the kind of nightmare that would strengthen a suicide's resolve to end it all.

Amy took the steps two at a time and ran toward the black, yawning doors.

"No!" Jeanne gasped.

Too late. Amy leapt into the darkness and the vast doors swung shut.

Jeanne touched the mirror. And it was empty, a silvery surface that reflected nothing, not even her hand, nothing, a mirror that had gone blind somehow.

Jeanne turned away and stumbled out into the bedroom. She marched to the dresser, opened a drawer, and found a blouse.

"Hey," Mark said. He grabbed her from behind. "It's the dead of night. What are you getting dressed for?"

Jeanne struggled out of his grip, turned, holding the

blouse. "I've got to get to the airport. I've—I can't explain it, but I've got to go. I'll call."

"Fuck that." His voice was suddenly cold, strange, something he'd been hiding. He hit her, a quick blow that caught the side of her face, sent her back against the dresser then tumbling forward. He caught her by the hair, dragged her to the bed.

He held her arms, pined under his knees.

She fought to get out from under him, considered sinking her teeth into his bare thigh. He spoke again. "I'm sorry, okay. I got a little out of control there, because"—she hated the way his voice shifted into a whine—"because there's just no making you happy. It was an accident, okay. I didn't mean to trip you, okay. But you never give, not even a little, you don't try to understand me."

The stale beer smell seemed the perfect olfactory accompaniment to self-pity.

"Okay," Jeanne said. "Let's just lie here for a little while, let's just rest." She realized he thought she had wanted to leave because she was mad at him for tripping her.

No, actually (she could say) I was inured to escalating violence. It was something else, a vision.

"Let's just lie here quietly for a moment, okay. A little time out, okay?"

"Okay. Sure."

He got off her arms and lay beside her. "I don't ever mean to hurt you, babe. You know that."

She lay quietly on her side, waiting, watching the bedside clock, listening to his breathing. Five after four. It took hours for the clock to read four-twenty.

The weight of the beer had pulled Mark down into sleep. She rolled away from his weight and softly left the bed.

She was tying her tennis shoes when she heard his voice. "Going somewhere, sweetheart? Thought you could cruise while I snooze?"

She looked up. "I've got to go, Mark. The phone's right there. If you get lonesome, you can call a friend."

"You're not going anywhere," he said and he started to come out of the bed in a rush and his left arm straightened and he screamed. He blinked stupidly at the silver bracelet around his wrist, its mate locked between rungs of the brass bed.

"I've got to run," she said, and she left the bedroom, walked quickly across the living room to the door, and let herself out.

She locked the door and then she did, indeed, run, feeling a heady exhilaration that stayed with her on the cab trip to the airport and caused her to shout "Wonderful!" when the airline reservationist informed her that there was an available flight to St. Petersburg at six-fifteen that morning.

CHaPTeR TWeNTY-TWo

❧ ❧ ❧ ❧ ❧ ❧ ❧ ❧ ❧ ❧ ❧ ❧

THE ST. PETERSBURG ARMS was large, pink, and in a state of genteel decay—as were its longtime inhabitants, elderly men and women who dressed rather formally and who sat, during the day, in folding chairs on the beach. Protected from the sun by large yellow umbrellas and layers of clothing, they regarded the ocean with weak but vigilant eyes, like the last of some religious sect, their faith failing with their memories, awaiting the fulfillment of some ancient prophecy.

Half a dozen of them were already turning away from the dying sun and dragging their long shadows back to the hotel, a journey of approximately fifty yards, when one of their members, a short, hunched man wearing a white suit jacket, baggy pants (both articles of apparel so wrinkled as to suggest some personal antipathy toward ironing), and a Panama hat, strode purposefully toward the ocean. His feet were bare, and his right arm was straight at his side (shoulder raised a bit, something military in his bearing) and in his right hand he held a small, dark revolver.

The ocean was rough, the Gulf taunted by gusts of wind, and now he held his arms out from his sides as if walking a tightrope. When the water reached his waist, a white-crested wave rocked him viciously so that he faltered and lost ground. He moved forward with new resolve, however, and stopped with the waters slapping his chest and raised the revolver, pointing it at his temple.

"Land," a woman onshore said, leaning over to shout in her companion's ear, "what on earth is he up to now?"

Years of watching television daytime soaps had created in the inhabitants of the St. Petersburg Arms a sense of themselves as passive observers, and not one of them thought of shouting out or acting upon what was happening. There was a sense of something unpleasant occurring, and were the scene in fact a television show it would have been summarily flipped, via the remote, to something nicer.

The man raised the gun and then the big brother to the wave that had rocked him came rushing up and swallowed him. The next wave spit the Panama hat into the air and that was the last of it. The ocean pretended that nothing had happened.

But someone had seen. Now someone shouted, and two young men, a lifeguard and a teenager who had been walking the beach with his dog, raced into the waves.

They were both fearless athletic swimmers, plunging headlong into waves and plowing the troughs with long, powerful strokes.

On the shore, the drama could be observed from a godlike vantage point that excluded the uglier elements of chaos and panic.

"Look there," a man in a lawn chair said, pointing a liver-spotted finger. "He's surfaced."

The man in the white suit had, indeed, surfaced, the floundering action of his arms indicating that he had not lost consciousness. The teenager reached him first, but the lifeguard was only a moment behind. Together they brought the man back to shore.

His white suit was now a translucent gray as he lay on his back on the sand. His face was very white with grainy black stubble surrounding his open mouth like silt that had failed to wash down a drain. His eyes were closed—tightly so that he appeared to be angry—and his beaklike nose pointed skyward imperiously, causing several of the onlookers to look up nervously.

"He had a gun," someone said.

"They are calling an ambulance," someone else said.

"Looks too late for that," a third party observed.

"What's this?" Raymond Story shouted, climbing out of the parked car and racing over the dunes toward the crowd on the beach.

Harry didn't bother shouting "Stop" this time, but simply followed at a reasonable pace.

The man lying on the sand was coming to when Harry arrived. The man was not coherent, however. He rolled on his side and vomited salt water.

Someone touched Harry's shoulder. "It's the Duke," Raymond said. Harry blinked at the old man, whose thinning hair was plastered to his pale skull, patches of wet sand adhering to wet flesh. Their hope: the Duke.

Then Helen was next to Harry, leaning forward. Harry

heard a siren in the distance, saw flashing lights coming down the darkened beach.

He heard Helen's voice in his ears. "My God," she said. "I know this man."

"Robert Furman," Helen said. "That was Robert Furman."

Harry recognized the name, one of the once-famous, but couldn't remember the who, what, or where of it.

Harry and Helen were sitting in the lounge of the St. Petersburg Arms. Helen was sipping a glass of hot tea, Harry a beer. Raymond, Emily, Rene, and Arbus were lodged in two adjoining suites on the third floor.

"You remember," Helen said, "Robert Furman wrote *Liar's Kisses,* that poetry collection that all the college kids were reading in the early seventies. It was actually pretty good too, which is not what you expect from best-selling poetry. I knew him. I mean, I met him. Once, at a party in the Hamptons. His agent was Lori Ives, and we were friends then—that was a long, long time ago—and she introduced us. He was very handsome and very drunk—but charming. Later, he ceased being charming, did the entire alcoholic deranged-author thing including that famous moment on Carson when he slugged that rock star."

It was coming back. Harry did have some recollection of the event, talk television's scandals being, sadly, more memorable than lines of metric poetry.

Robert Furman had taught poetry at a small, eastern college, refusing to be wooed away by larger, more prestigious institutions. The students had loved him and he had loved them back—literally on occasion (at least if rumor were based on fact)—and then, as his alcoholism increased, he had stopped teaching and disappeared from public view.

"And now he's trying to kill himself," Harry said. They had heard the story of the gun.

"Perhaps he was drunk," Helen said. "People will do strange, irrational, melodramatic things when they are drunk and repent them in the morning. That is, of course, if they are alive to repent."

Harry finished the beer and ordered another from a hovering waiter. He noticed Helen's look, interpreted it as one of censure, and said, "I'm not planning on getting drunk and shooting myself if that's what you're thinking."

"I wasn't thinking that at all. I wasn't—if you'll believe it—thinking of you. I was thinking of Emily. I was thinking that, if there is any meaning to all this, then Emily must be its center. Our arriving here now, today—surely that can't be a coincidence."

Harry sighed. The beer had made him groggy. "I'm not following this," he said.

"No. I'm not making myself clear, of course. I don't believe I ever told you—everything has been such a rush—but I know some of Emily's history. I went to great pains to discover it when I thought—" Helen waved a hand in the air. "Emily has always had to have a caretaker. Her condition, whatever diagnosis you accept, has been with her since birth. Her parents were killed in a car accident, and after their death, she was adopted by her uncle who cared for her until . . . well, until that task proved too much for him, I suppose. He then turned her over to the care of private institutions."

Harry waited, but Helen's eyes suggested she had drifted into another revery.

"And . . . " Harry said.

"Oh," Helen said. "Well, that's it, that's the story. Poor Emily shunted from one posh caretaker to another, an expensive china doll. But the uncle . . . Emily's uncle is Robert Furman."

Harry fell asleep as soon as he crawled under the covers of the big, old-fashioned four-poster. In the early hours of the morning, he woke, feeling feverish, his heart beating in his temples. Raymond's bed was empty, and the room was silent. The bathroom door was open on a dark rectangle. Harry was alone in the hotel room. A small night-light a foot above the baseboard cast pale shadows on the ceiling. Harry tugged on his pants and shirt. He found his tennis shoes, pulled them on over bare feet, and walked out into the hall. He took the elevator to the lobby.

Outside the ocean was lively under the moonlight. It didn't accuse him, as he thought it might, but seemed simply strange and alien, nothing to do with anything human.

Harry thought of Robert Furman walking into the ocean to kill himself. Didn't the man know that that wouldn't be the end of it? At least, not in that damnable kingdom of Zod Wallop. In Zod Wallop, the dead were thrown into the Ocean of Responsibility and they returned, the Less-Than, to swell the ghastly armies under Lord Draining's command.

Why did I write that book? Harry wondered. If writing it was supposed to rid him of despair and loss, it had failed. The wound was raw and incapable of healing. His daughter was still dead.

He saw Raymond's unmistakable silhouette then, in the distance, pushing the wheelchair along the beach.

Harry ran and caught up with Raymond.

"Well met, my Lord," Raymond said.

They walked in silence for awhile. Emily, bundled up against the night chill, showed no signs of life.

"So Raymond," Harry said. "What now?"

Raymond turned and opened his eyes wide. "I am not a Diviner, my Lord. I am a humble wizard."

"Is there something we must do? We have come here for a reason, certainly?"

"Reasons and more reasons, my Lord," Raymond said, nodding vigorously. "We must do what all men must do. We must do our Best."

Raymond and Harry, with Emily between them, stared out at the ocean until the wind rose and salt water flew at them and finally they turned and retraced their steps to the hotel.

"I don't know if I'm up to my best," Harry said. "I haven't felt tip-top for sometime."

CHaPTeR TWeNTY-THRee

❦ ❦ ❦ ❦ ❦ ❦ ❦ ❦ ❦ ❦ ❦ ❦ ❦

ALLAN DROVE ACROSS the long, high bridge, squinting at the dimpled sea. Sunlight sprawled everywhere, an overabundance of pure light that made Allan itch inside. He didn't want it; couldn't use it.

He was in St. Petersburg—the sign had told him as much—but he still had to find them. He hoped it wouldn't take long.

He came off the bridge and drove for another mile. He stopped at a gas station, filled the car up, and realized he was empty himself. He lost track of his body sometimes, and he was always surprised when it announced its demands.

He found a vending machine and shoved change into it. A couple of Snickers and he'd be all right for a while. The machine did nothing. He thumped it; hit the coin return. Nothing.

He went up to the man at the register and told him, "I lost sixty cents in the vending machine."

The man behind the counter was a longhair with bad teeth and a ferrety look. He grinned. "Don't tell me. Come around here next Tuesday and tell it to Walt. He comes in about ten to freshen up the machine, likely he would be sympathetic to your troubles."

Allan didn't say anything. He figured he would pop the guy in the mouth, one tight, from-the-shoulder fist into those bad teeth. That's all, just one quick one.

A big, dark man with a mustache and curly black hair stepped up next to Allan and said, "I guess this is yours. I saw you at the vending machine before me, so I guess this belongs to you." He handed Allan the candy bar.

"See there," the ferrety guy said, "your troubles are solved."

Allan paid for the gas and went back to his car. Sitting behind the wheel, he swallowed the Snickers in two bites, confused. He couldn't believe that he wasn't meant to hit that guy in the mouth, and he waited a moment to see if anything else might be revealed. But there was nothing and the photo in his back pocket flipped into his thoughts again and his true purpose was renewed.

The man with the mustache, Al Butts, got back into the car with his employer, Karl Bahden. Karl sat behind the wheel. They pulled out into traffic following the kid.

"You figure he knows where he's going?" Al asked.

"You got to have faith," Karl said. "You don't have faith you might as well kiss your butt good-bye, Butts."

"Don't kid with my name," Al said.

"What's that?" Karl turned and smiled at his employee.

"Nothing," Al said.

At noon the kid pulled into a ratty blue motel called the

Periwinkle (the drawing on the sign looked a little like a gigantic twat with teeth but Karl figured it was some kind of seashell), and Karl stopped the car down the street at a fast-food joint and said, "I gotta make some calls. Get me a double cheeseburger, a large fries, and a chocolate shake."

From the pay phone he called Dr. Roald Peake. "We are in St. Petersburg," he said. "I don't know. I think it's the end of the line. He's driving around like he's looking for something now. His buddies are in the city, but he don't know where, that's how I figure it. Okay."

Karl hung up and then called Blaine and gave him the news too. Karl didn't think of himself as a traitor or some fancy kind of double agent. It was just that his mother had always emphasized the virtues of enterprise. Even as a kid, he'd always held two jobs. If one paycheck was good, two were better. It wasn't an inclination for betrayal that motivated Karl; it was just a real strong Puritan work ethic. For a while it had looked like the one goose was going to kill the other—and it probably would shake down to a single employer in the long run—but for now business was booming. God bless capitalism and the spirit of competition.

Dr. Roald Peake put the phone down. He blinked at the wall of smoke and lit another cigarette. He felt both good and bad. Good because events were rising to a climax and, as he always said, "It is better to blow up than to peter out." Well, perhaps it was Lord Draining who had always said this, but it was a sentiment Peake shared with his Lordship.

Bad because someone, some vile interloper, some scurrilous agent of, no doubt, the Gorelord himself (Andrew Blaine, that is), had stolen the book, the precious book. Ha! If they thought they could rob Roald Peake of its knowledge by doing so, they were mistaken. The book was committed to the deepest recesses of his memory. In fact, it wasn't simply memorized, it was busy in his mind. All manner of stories and shapes were growing.

He punched the intercom. "Ms. Goddard," he said. "Tell Jordan I want everything ready within the hour. We are going to St. Petersburg, Florida."

Andrew Blaine and Gloria Gill had been preparing to make love when the phone call from Karl Bahden came.

Blaine had answered on the speaker phone.

"I'm sorry," Blaine told Gloria, untying her from the polished rack. Her pale, round body was shiny with honey. "We've got to fly down to Florida immediately. We'll have to continue this later."

Gloria pouted, sticking her lower lip out. "They could die in the meantime," she said, staring ruefully at the mason jar full of ants.

Blaine patted her sticky shoulder. "My dear, Florida is full of *fire* ants."

Gloria grinned then, turning and hastening to the shower. Blaine smiled after her.

My little bundle of screams, he thought. *My sweet mortification.*

The man next to Jeanne on the plane was nervous and wanted to talk. He was a fat man in a blue dress shirt about two sizes too small for him, and he was sweating powerfully. "I don't go for flying," he said, waving his hands over his stomach. "I don't like the idea of it, up here thousands of feet in the air listening to Neil Diamond on earphones. Pretending to be something we aren't. Jesus didn't fly in airplanes."

Jeanne agreed and suggested they talk of other things. He got off into sports, baseball, which seemed to calm him, and Jeanne was able to smile and let her thoughts run elsewhere.

She felt remarkably good. She felt up for whatever was going to happen, for whatever terror and wonder St. Petersburg had to offer. She felt a curious physical hum, as though she were floating in some clear, heated current, thicker than water, massaging, electrifying. Her mind seemed better informed of her body, as when, coming home, one sees things for the first time.

And she had been gone, that was it, of course, she had been absent from herself.

She would find the pink hotel and enter it. She would do this because the vision had seemed to demand it, but she would also do it because, in doing it, she was alive again.

"Mickey Mantle," the fat man said. "I always say, 'Mickey Mantle.' "

"Good for you," Jeanne said.

Gabriel leaned into the page, her nose an inch from the illustration that showed the Duke, asleep on a purple cushion, being bound by the Ice Spiders. She recognized the Duke now. He had been one of Marlin's friends, one of the loud, artsy ones and he had, in fact, once made a pass at her—or perhaps slept with her that winter when she was sleeping with everyone because she was pissed at Marlin—and Zod Wallop was one fucking strange country although—and this was probably the strangest part—it wasn't strange so that you had to stretch to believe it. Oh, you knew it was true and that was what was strange . . .

"What an odd children's book."

Gabriel looked up. Her own mind might have uttered

this. Her mind was doing some talking since the Ecknazine. She was also wobbling in and out of various realities (there was the room whose walls were dripping blood and another room in which the door seemed to be made of living, moving snakes). But no. There was a woman. This woman was middle-aged and in desperate need of fashion guidance. With a round face, you didn't wear those round glasses and the bangs might have worked with, say, a clown's outfit (red rubber nose, blue lips, that sort of thing) but here the effect was pathetic.

"I have three children of my own," the woman was saying. "They are grown now, but when I did read to them, I liked to stick to the classics: E. B. White, A. A. Milne, C. S. Lewis. Goodness, I hadn't thought of it, but children's authors seem to go in for initials, don't they?" The woman giggled. *Another bad idea,* Gabriel thought. This woman should go with solemnity, stay away from cute, youthful, that sort of thing. She was wearing a frilly blouse that would have been coveted at a gay rights masquerade ball.

The woman leaned over and gave the illustration a closer look. "Goodness. Those spiders are revolting, aren't they? Not the sort of book for the under-twelve crowd. I mean, it's true children like awfulness, they seem to thrive on—"

Gabriel turned away and gasped.

"We are in a plane," Gabriel said, clutching her companion's wrist.

"Ah, yes—"

"Where are we going?"

"Why, straight through. We're going to St. Petersburg."

"Russia?"

The woman laughed nervously. "No. Ha, ha. Florida, of course."

"Of course," Gabriel said, leaning back.

The woman leaned away from Gabriel then and became engrossed in her magazine.

That was fine with Gabriel. So Allan was in Florida. The Ecknazine had seen this and then, imperious drug, had not bothered to inform her mind. Fine.

The plane was packed. Across the aisle and five seats up, Gabriel saw something extraordinary. A fat man who had to use his hands to talk, was rattling on, hands flying. There was nothing exceptional about the man or his demeanor, but his audience was another matter entirely. She was a delicate-featured woman, her profile nearly perfect, her chin proud, her nose set for mischief, her hair a bouquet of black, Irish curls, her smile angelic. And, most wondrous and the result, no doubt, of Ecknazine's ability to pierce the mundane, the lovely woman was surrounded in a glowing, golden nimbus, a halo of shimmering angel breath.

Perhaps, Gabriel thought, *this* is *an angel.* An angel might weary of getting about on her own steam. An angel might find herself in need of an airplane ticket to some seaside resort. Surely Heaven could grow stale.

Satisfied with this logic, Gabriel returned to the Duke, last hope and only friend of the impossibly innocent Lydia. Gabriel assumed the girl was supposed to be the heroine and to engage the reader's sympathy, but Gabriel had no patience with the girl, who fretted too much and wanted to save the world which wasn't, as anyone knew, what the world itself wanted at all. The world wanted to be bad, evil with a flourish. Like Lord Draining said, "You know you are alive when you are doing someone dirty."

CHaPTeR TWeNTY-FouR

❂ ❂ ❂ ❂ ❂ ❂ ❂ ❂ ❂ ❂ ❂ ❂

THEY GOT TO the hospital early in the morning, but Robert Furman was already dressed.

Helen, the first to enter the room, watched a pretty young Asian nurse, hands on her hips, stamp her foot and glare at Furman. "Doctor will be much upset if you leave without his permission," the nurse said.

"Yes," Furman said, smiling wearily, "but he'll live to forget it. It may not seem like it now, but, in time, he'll learn to go on with his life." Furman looked, Helen thought, remarkably chipper for a man who had, the prior evening, been on the edge of suicide and suffered a near drowning. His suit was extremely wrinkled, but it was dry and he wore it with flair, one thin leg crossed over the other at the knee, a jaunty pose for a sickbed scene. His smile was wry, his chin argumentative. Perhaps the drowning had canceled out the despair that had prompted the suicide attempt; Helen had heard of such things, of the will to live being renewed by a brush with death.

"You are being humorful," the nurse said. "But if you leave against doctor's orders you must sign a statement. We will not be liable for what happens to you."

"I appreciate that, young lady. I know the drill. Bring on your papers and let me sign them. I have a cab waiting downstairs."

"Perhaps your family can repel you from this course of action," the woman said, turning and smiling at Helen.

"I've never seen these people before," Furman said, rising from the bed. "They got the wrong room. If you'll all excuse me—"

"I'm Helen Kurtis," Helen said, coming forward. "We met once, a long time ago, at a party given by Lori Ives—"

"A dreadful woman," Furman interjected.

"And this is Harold Gainesborough. He writes popular children books. Perhaps you've heard of him. He wrote *Zod Wallop*, which is why we are here, actually—"

"*Zod Wallop*," Furman said. He had gone pale. "I have a cab waiting." He pushed past Helen, moving toward the door.

Raymond entered, pushing the wheelchair with Emily in front of him. Arbus was perched on Raymond's shoulder. "My Duke!" Raymond bellowed. Arbus jumped to the wheelchair as his master fell to one knee, bowed his head, and clasped his hand in supplication. "By all that's honorable, we implore you: Help us."

Helen hastened to speak, "This is Raymond Story and this, of course, his wife, your—"

"Emily," Furman said. He took a step backward and then, catching his balance, he moved forward and touched her shoulder. The monkey uttered a short trill of disapproval and showed his teeth. Furman ignored this, as though the presence of small, hostile monkeys was commonplace. "Yes, this is

Emily," he said. "My niece. How are you Emily?"

Emily's eyes studied the ceiling. Her blue cotton shirt was buttoned wrong, bunched out in front, and—or so it seemed to Helen—she looked generally more rumpled and remote than usual.

"I can see you are the same as ever, Emily." He patted her shoulder absently. "Vacationing in Florida. Well, I don't want to spoil it for you, but I should warn you that it can be a very dull place. That's my experience of Florida. You've seen one seagull you've seen them all. You've seen one wave you've seen the lot. And, unless you fancy lengthy discussions of ailments and digestive systems, the residents won't challenge your conversational skills."

"Your niece has married Raymond Story," Helen said, indicating Raymond who was standing again. "And Raymond has insisted that we seek you out."

"Why?"

"Raymond is convinced that you can help us."

"Well, Raymond's a nutcase," Furman said, smiling. "Mind you, I don't mean that in any derogatory sense. I myself am a nutcase. There should be no stigma attached to being crazy. Indeed, some would say that it is the only realistic response to the times. Now that I've drawn the proper context, I can say, with some assurance, that we have a few nutcases here. I am, it would seem, acquainted with you all, and I apologize for failing to recognize you immediately. I know all about Marlin's sad experiment, and I was even, to my shame, involved in the selection process. Now I suspect you've all been having bad dreams, and Raymond, your bird-dog crazy, has managed—"

"Hey, Emily's choking!"

It was Rene who had shouted, coming up behind Emily

just as the girl doubled over and began shaking violently. She tumbled from the wheelchair, retching, writhing in torment on the floor, face down.

"Somebody do something!" Rene screamed.

They all converged on Emily; the nurse clutched Emily's shoulder and turned her over.

Emily turned and Helen gasped. The girl's face was bright red, not the flush of blood but like metal heated in some forge, and she was dressed in liquid armor, a shimmer of gold, and her face was contorted hideously, an animal fierceness that had no analog in the human world.

The nurse spun backward, colliding with Helen. Robert Furman shouted, "Emily!" and Raymond leaned forward to grasp his wife's bare arm.

Emily stood up.

"Don't touch me," she said. "It ravishes me. This room burns with It. No soothing here. No, do not—"

Raymond touched her elbow. And a yellow serpent of flame raced up his arm, up the dirty coat sleeve, and Raymond shouted and turned and flopped on the floor, screaming, and Harry yanked the blanket from the bed and fell with it onto Raymond, embracing him.

An alarm went off, orderlies came running, and Helen blinked at the empty wheelchair and stumbled out into the hall in time to see Emily, a glowing, ghostly figure pursued by a small, simian shape, bang through the exit door.

Helen turned and Robert Furman stood behind her. His mouth was open and he was shaking, about as frail and desperate as a Hope could be this side of death.

Raymond proved to be unharmed. The flames that had flared so savagely had burned his coat sleeve to smoldering ribbons but had not, miraculously, harmed his flesh. His suffering was psychic, not physical, and under protests from the nurse, they all left in search of Emily. When an on-foot search of the surrounding area failed to discover her, they took to the car and continued to look, guided by Furman's knowledge of the city.

As they drove, Furman talked. "I didn't want to burden anyone with the unpleasantness of discovering my body. I had determined that there was a strong undercurrent that would take my corpse out to sea. I was rather pleased with myself, which, of course, is just asking for some cosmic pie-in-the-face."

"Why did you want to kill yourself?" Helen asked.

"I have been diagnosed as having cancer. Actually, it is an operable, localized form, and the prognosis is good if I were willing to submit to surgery. I'm not. The truth is, I am uninterested in struggle and pain. When I sickened of poetry, that's when I should have had the grace to leave. And that was long ago. Would you like to hear the story of my life?" They had stopped at a red light.

"No!" This was Rene. Tears were running down her face. "I don't want to hear your stupid life story. Don't anybody talk. I'm sick of talk! Just look for Emily, look with all . . . first we run out on Allan, now we let Emily go. Fuck this old fart's story!"

Helen tried to soothe the girl. "We are just trying to establish—"

Rene threw open the car door. "Fuck it!" she shouted. She dashed out into traffic. A car swerved, honking. Raymond jumped out and ran after her, but he returned shortly, sighed, and flopped in the passenger seat. "My lady Rene is fleet of foot and determined, I fear. I am afraid she eluded me."

Robert Furman told his story. Helen would have edited

out some of the philosophical commentary and omitted the dramatic pauses, but the story matter was undeniably intriguing.

"Marlin Tate was, for a scientist, remarkably literate," Furman said. "I met him at a party, where he demonstrated his acumen by recognizing my name and praising *Liar's Kisses*. Except in extreme cases (vicious serial killers or students pursuing an MFA in Creative Writing) any fan is a friend."

And so they did become friends, and Marlin Tate talked about a drug he was developing that created a sort of psychic gestalt. He called the drug Ecknazine. "You'd have to be careful in your choice of subjects," Marlin said. "You'd want people with rich imaginative lives, people devoid of some of the normal imagining constraints."

Robert Furman's part in all this might have remained that of listener and philosophical cheerleader, but several things occurred that changed all that.

First, Robert Furman discovered that he hated poetry. In the midst of writing a poem, he suddenly realized that there was not a single pursuit he could think of that was so trivial, so superfluous to living. He was in an academic setting, of course, and that could have been part of the problem. Here poetry was published in slim, arch magazines and read by perhaps twenty-five people who published in the same journals. But it was not just this elitism that troubled Furman. He realized, in the midst of composition, that he could attach any adjective to any noun (the "arbitrary teapot" or the "truculent rose," for instance) and then cobble up some sort of meaning to suit the phrase. There seemed something despicable in this wordplay, a kind of intellectual self-abuse.

Perhaps, he thought, it was only his own poetry that he despised. But no, he discovered that he hated the poetry of all his peers, and, incredibly, all poetry ever written. Behind every poem there seemed to crouch an immensely self-involved ego, the sort of man or woman who would let the infant cry in its cradle while seeking just the right nuance of tone and cadence. The people who wrote poetry were to be avoided as were the poems that emanated from them like methane gas seeping from a swamp.

So he quit the university and filled in the additional time with more drinking. And then his sister and her husband were killed in an automobile accident and Robert Furman did what he had to and acquired custody of a catatonic, wheelchair-bound girl named Emily Engel. Emily was twelve at the time and she stayed with Furman for two years.

"I thought she was, in an odd way, the answer to my prayers," Furman said. "Of course, what happened to Jessica and Tom was horrible, but at least, well . . . I thought of her as my salvation."

Here was a task he could turn his heart to with a will. He could care for the crippled, absent girl.

But he couldn't. "I discovered I was no Mother Teresa," he said. "I wanted her to respond and she didn't. I wanted her to look at me, say, 'Robert, how are you today?' and, alas, it was all one long today for Em. I was not equipped for the kind of altruism that asks nothing in return. I wanted gratitude and love.

"I drank more. One night I left her room and when I came back smoke was pouring out the door. I had left a cigarette burning in the ashtray, and it had fallen over onto the bedspread. I almost asphyxiated my dear Emily. And I decided she would be better off with professional caretakers. It was, after all, of no concern to her who bathed and dressed her."

Helen interrupted. "You committed your niece to Harwood Psychiatric Institute and then you let this Marlin Tate give her an experimental drug?"

"Doesn't sound good, does it? Actually, I took the drug too. What convinced me to proceed was Harold Gainesborough's name on the list of Harwood patients."

Helen blinked. "Harry?"

"It wasn't an entirely rational decision. But I often read Harry's books to Emily, and I sometimes fancied there was a response, some brightness in the eyes denoting laughter, some poised and breathless moment when, for instance, the moon weasels are about to eat Bocky. So here was Marlin Tate with this list of possible candidates for an experiment that would link these people telepathically. Harry's name seemed a sign. I felt that Emily had some emotional bond with this writer of children's books. Marlin Tate had already decided on one candidate, Raymond Story. Story had a history of psychic experiences and had even been, for a while, a resident of the notorious Simpec Research Institute.

"At first, Marlin was disinclined to let me participate. Knowledge of the experiment might alter it, you see. I might see shadows that were merely shadows and interpret them as telepathic phenomenon. But I prevailed. I wanted to speak to my niece, and I couldn't reach her in this mute world."

Robert Furman was silent, staring out the car window at the passing streetlamps.

Helen leaned toward him. "And were you? Were you able to communicate with her?"

"I have had terrible dreams for years now. They grow increasingly grim," he said, sighing. "I often dream that this shabby old hotel is a dark, monstrous castle, and I hear the screams of people being tortured in the dungeons, and sometimes I see Lord Draining walking the halls, his hands covered with blood."

"Lord Draining?"

Furman turned and studied Harry. "Yes. I've read *Zod Wallop*. I recognize the Vile Contender. But my dreams are much darker than that happy little book."

"Yes," Harry said. "They would be."

Furman, so calm, so remote, suddenly spoke in anguish, "If I have sentenced Emily to eternal nightmares, then I have done an evil, unforgivable thing. I saw her get out of her wheelchair and run down a hall. At one time I would have been delighted. But I fear now that, with volition, she may seek to escape these nightmares. She may try to kill herself. I know the power of these delusions."

"They are not delusions," Harry said.

Furman did not contest this remark but said simply, "Worse then."

Emily woke and brushed pine needles and small, dead oak leaves from her shirt. What was this garb? she wondered. Some peasant disguise?

She crawled out from under the bush, and Arbus followed her, squeaking sullenly. His Lordship loved to sleep and always woke with grumbling.

"I am awake, my Lord," she said. "The powers move. I am vital and I hum with revenge. Let all Zod Wallop experience this entrapped death, this sleep that does not refresh."

She lifted the monkey in her arms and looked around. They were in a park and it was twilight.

"I can feel the Cold One in my veins," she said. "He has

not mounted his terrible steed. The Abyss Dweller still sleeps. We must find them and urge them on their way. Even the Dark Ones sometimes hesitate."

She walked slowly toward the lake. A ragged man in brown pants, shirtless, approached her with a limping gait.

"That's a cute monkey you got there," he said. His hair stuck out in filthy knots and appeared to be burned at the ends, perhaps some cure for lice.

"This is Lord Arbus," Emily said. "He does not fancy himself 'cute' and he is not a monkey, but a man transformed by enchantment. The spell was intended to harry him, but he found he liked this low-to-the-ground existence and so has remained in this form although Mettle could change him back in an instant."

"Ah," the man said, spitting on the ground, "fucking crazy." He moved on past her.

She shouted after him. "Which way the ocean?"

He turned, pointed. "Just keep walking that way and eventually your knickers will be soakin'." He moved away.

He is very impudent, Emily thought. *I should have turned him to stone.* She thought she might be up to that. Not the world, not yet. But a single, arrogant man. Yes.

She moved on though, seeking the ocean. It called to her now, a salty, green, kelpish harkening.

Allan woke, got off the bed, and left the motel. Sleep—a few fitful hours—had not cooled the anger. He got in his car and drove the streets. He followed the oceanfront signs to the beach.

"Why we gotta keep following this guy?" Al Butts asked. "He don't know any more than we do now."

Karl Bahden grinned. "We are following this guy because that's what we have been told to do. You ever hold a regular job, Butts? You do what the boss says."

Butts hunkered down in the passenger seat. "I ain't never retiring to Florida," he said.

"The Chamber of Commerce hear that they'll have a heart attack."

Andrew Blaine peered out the limo's window at the old folks moving slowly down the sidewalk. *Cafeteria sheep,* he thought. He liked that and turned to Gloria and smiled. "Cafeteria sheep," he said, waving his hand toward the geriatrics.

Gloria didn't smile back. Her round face was filled with ill-tempered anxiety. "I need a lab," she said. "We could already be too late. If we hadn't let that asshole Mitford chat these people up for weeks, we'd probably have the drug by now. I mean, what was the sense of that? It's the Engel girl that we need; she's our best hope. We need to grab her, analyze her, no lag time."

"Yes, yes," Blaine said. "Analyze. A sweet word, but what do you mean exactly, my little wolverine?"

Gloria studied the roof of the limo. Her mouth softened and grew circular, as though she were savoring a bonbon. "Well at first I thought, 'Just grind her and start sorting' but then I realized that some trace elements might be too diluted. So I thought, 'Get the blood first, all of it, and shake that down. Then go after specific organs that might filter the drug.'"

"You are a marvel," Blaine said.

"We need a lab. We need a place we can take her."

Blaine nodded. He turned in his seat and spoke to one of the three men who sat behind him.

"We got any subsidiaries in this happy zombie hole?"

"I don't know."

"Maybe you could find that out. Also, see if you can link up with Bahden. Maybe the kid has found them."

They had no subsidiaries in St. Petersburg, as it turned out, but they supplied 67 percent of Regal Labs income.

"I think that's good enough; I think they'll be willing to hustle for us."

"Bahden's on the line," another of the men said.

Blaine took the phone. "Where are you?"

"We are at the goddamn beach," Karl said. "There's this big hotel off to my left. He got out of the car."

"What's the name of this hotel?"

"I don't know."

"Find out."

"Yes, sir."

He called back in five minutes. Blaine's man reserved two adjoining suites at the St. Petersburg Arms. "You'll want to talk to the people at Regal," Blaine said, turning to Gloria. "You'll want to tell them what you want and where you want it delivered."

Jeanne Halifax, driving her rented car through the city, did not find the hotel until the world was shadows. When she saw the building, she gasped. *Grimfast,* she thought, but then it shimmered into quiet, mundane reality. She recognized it from the postcard, although that photo had been taken, obviously, in grander times. At the desk, she asked if a Harry Gainesborough was registered. He was. Jeanne wasn't surprised. She knew he would be here. She still felt a powerful humming current within her, a rightness that was protective. Harry was not in his room, however, and she walked back down to the desk and registered. As she was signing in, she saw movers bringing in crates and boxes. The desk clerk looked up. He motioned one of the movers over. "What's this?" he asked.

"Delivery for Dr. Andrew Blaine," he said.

"Oh, okay. Somebody called about that. Jeez, he said he had a lot of luggage. This is a lot."

The mover shrugged, that half-lidded doing-my-job look. "Yeah, well."

"Okay. Fine. Fine. Dr. Blaine is in rooms 316 and 317. Here are the keys. Don't forget to return them."

The mover nodded, turned away, and walked back toward the other men, standing by their boxes and crates.

"Not that elevator!" the desk clerk shouted. "There's a service elevator around the hall. Thank you."

Dr. Roald Peake chewed on a cigarette while smoking another. "Is the helicopter ready?"

"Yes, sir," the man said.

"Then let's not stand here gawking at the sunset. Let's go."

"Yes, sir."

Roald Peake and four of his men walked across the scruffy airplane field. In the distance, palm trees fluttered their fronds.

"A balmy night," the pilot said.

"I hate balmy," Peake said.

Peake found himself thinking of the Gorelord, that piece of grendel phlegm that has stolen the Book. He had failed to kill the man once, but he wouldn't fail twice. You want to do a job right, you do it yourself. The Gorelord was ancient. Peake flexed his hands, lean, strong hands—he could have been a concert pianist or a massage therapist—and thought of that reedy, fragile throat. The Gorelord's neck would snap like dry kindling.

He felt a rush of adrenaline. It was not, alas, accompanied by the proper nicotine zing. His blood cried out for more tobacco. "Excuse me, gentlemen," he said. "Is there a rest room on the premises?"

The pilot nodded. "Over there."

It was a small, dirty cubicle with a toilet that Peake would not have sat on for any amount of money. He studied himself in the mirror. His nose had ceased growing, but his cheeks were hollower and his lips fuller and, most noticeably, his hair had darkened and lay closer to his skull. He had a sleek and cunning aspect. "You are getting better in every way every day," he told himself, an affirmation that he remembered from his brief bout with self-improvement.

He grinned at himself and then pulled his pants down, bent over, and shoved a cigarette up his butt. He stood up and drew his pants back up, buckled his belt.

Got to stop smoking any day now, he thought. *I've just about reached my limit.*

Gabriel woke with the sound of the tide, unmistakable, in her ears. It was night, and the air was filled with the mysterious, dead-fish smell the ocean exhales. That was the thing about the ocean, it drew no fine lines between life and death. You came to the Ocean of Responsibility looking for answers, and the tide hissed *life, death, life, death, life, death,* and you chose, and the truth there was always some of the one clinging to the other.

She sat up and brushed sand from her cheek. She clutched her handbag. The Book was still there. All right, things weren't that bad—although she had no idea how she had gotten here, under this pier. She remembered some altercation with a cabdriver, but it was a clouded memory, whipped by sharp, hallucinatory images.

She stood up and brushed sand from her stockinged knees. Perhaps she should have worn something less formal for this excursion. She took her high heels off and tossed them away.

"Allan!" she cried out. "Allan!"

Her head ached. She pressed her palms to her eyes, exhaled slowly. She began to walk down the beach with no sense of purpose. She walked for perhaps an hour, with no sense of her son, no prompting from the Ecknazine. She watched her silver feet tread the sand. One foot in front of the other.

She heard the sound of an engine overhead and looked up and squinted at the lights that were descending.

The helicopter came down on the beach, tilting to this side then that as though manipulated by an inept puppeteer.

Gabriel brushed her hair back and waited.

A tall man jumped out of the cockpit and ran to her.

"Gabriel," he shouted. "I thought that was you. Fancy finding you here."

It was Peake.

"Where is my son?" she asked him.

He grinned wolfishly. "Not one for small talk, are you? Well, come along. He's nearby. Can't you feel it? I can smell it, you know."

Gabriel raised an eyebrow. "Smell what?"

"Why, Grimfast, of course. We're almost there."

He helped her climb in the helicopter. One of the men had to stay on the ground to make a place for her.

CHaPTeR TWeNTY-FiVe

"HEY! THAT'S HER," Karl Bahden said, pointing toward the beach.

"What? I thought we were looking for someone in a wheelchair?"

"Yeah, we were. But I'm telling you, that's her. I recognize the face, and that ratty hair."

"So what have we got here, a miracle?"

"I don't know. We got strange stuff, if you haven't noticed."

Butts peered out the windshield. "Our boy Allan is driving on. He ain't stopping."

"He's got other fish to fry." Karl had seen the faked photo. It was convincing; any lovesick fool would have swallowed it.

Karl pulled the car over to the side of the road, the tires grinding in the sand, and turned the ignition off. He got out, reached in the back and pulled the rifle out.

"You gonna kill her?"

"Nah. This ain't that kind of a gun. I'm just not gonna chase her down the beach. This line of work, you eat too many fries and burgers on the run. I got a high cholesterol. I can't overexert myself or I'll be studying the ceiling in some cardiac ward."

Emily walked along the tide. Strange little birds raced in and out of the retreating water, ducking down to suck some morsel from the sand, racing away from incoming waves, their little legs a frenzy of motion. Her gaudy shoes—another peasant fashion?—left odd, corrugated footprints behind her in the wet sand. Lord Arbus nuzzled in her arms, hugging her tightly. He did not care for the roar of the surf.

Emily was confused. Had not Blodkin promised her this boon for all the years of frozen darkness, the yearning that turned to cold rage? Where then were his servants?

She saw two men coming toward her on the beach, and she sensed, instantly, that they meant her harm. They were thralls of the Gorelord or Lord Draining. No matter. If they meant to hinder her, she would teach them manners.

Against his protests, she lowered Arbus to the sand.

She turned and faced the men, now fifty feet from her. "Come no farther," she said. "If you go on your way, no harm will come to you."

The taller of the two men, pale-haired and grinning, raised something to his shoulder and shouted, "Glad to hear that!"

Emily felt a hard, cold slap against her thigh. She looked down and saw a small, feathered bolt sticking through the rough fabric of her leggings. A heaviness entered her limbs, as though the Cold One himself had embraced her.

What enchantment is this? she wondered. She fell to her knees. No. Her time was now. She could not be Returned. This was an outrage. Blodkin would not tolerate it.

She rocked forward, toppling. She did not feel the slap of the sand against her face or the warm tide soaking her clothing, did not hear Arbus's screams as he fled.

Karl fired a shot at the monkey—just for the hell of it. He missed, and the monkey ran screaming over the dunes toward the road.

"Come on," Butts said. "Let's get the girl up in the car. I hear a chopper. I don't want the cops shining a searchlight in my eyes, not right about now."

Karl nodded. The sound of the helicopter was growing louder. They ran to the girl. Together they lifted her and scrambled up the sandy dunes. Karl opened the back door of the sedan, and Butts hauled her in. He climbed out past her and shut the door.

"Let's go," Karl said.

Neither of them noticed the small, dark monkey that leapt to the meager ledge of bumper and managed, incredibly, to stay there, hugging a taillight, as the car accelerated in a whiplash scream.

"Where we taking her?" Butts asked.

"Blaine's got a room for her. I got to say, Peake is behind on this one. He isn't showing me much. Blaine's been thinking all along, getting his ducks in a row."

"Where's this room?"

"Just down the block." Karl pointed to the hotel directly in front of them. "The classy but economical St. Petersburg Arms."

"How we gonna get her in without someone noticing she's conked out?"

Karl laughed. "Hell, half the people in this city are conked out. You think that's gonna raise an eyebrow? If this hotel's lobby doesn't have wheelchairs, then Detroit doesn't have automobiles. We wrap her up in a coat, she'll look like grandma-goes-on-a-trip. Trust me."

Rene was alone and discouraged. Maybe she shouldn't have jumped out of the car and run off like that. Her daddy always said, "It's your impulses that won't let you go," and he was right; she'd never been one to think things through.

Still, Rene thought, they weren't doing any good, driving in circles, and the sound of that old guy's voice, stuffy and pleased with himself—she'd had to bolt.

She let her legs go, flopping down on her butt, *bang*, like that, and glared at the headlights on the road above her.

Allan gone. Emily gone—up and ran off; Emily who you wouldn't have figured to have an impulse in her, not in a hundred million years—and Rene alone, the way it always shook down.

Maybe alone wasn't so bad for some people; they didn't need drugs or booze to forget being alone. Maybe they even liked being alone, cozy with all their private thoughts, amazed and delighted, fat and sassy.

Alone was being smashed and scattered and not even forgotten because what was there to remember?

Rene watched the headlights slow and stop on the road above her. The twin orbs died and the light inside the car came on as the door was opened and that wink of the light was all she needed because she was skilled in seeing him whole in a glance and then remembering at leisure.

"Allan!" she shouted, jumping on tiptoe. "Allan."

Her man ran toward her, like one of those corny-assed commercials, long, passionate strides because he had to get to his woman . . . so they could go have a beer or something . . . but this wasn't corny because it really was Allan and she wondered why she had never told him she loved him. Well, that was over now . . .

"Bitch!" Allan screamed, and he hit her. Her eyes widened just before his fist connected with her stomach. She bent over but did not fall, wobbling on bent legs, head down and holding up a hand as though to say, "Just a second. Be right with you."

Then she turned and ran. Allan hadn't been expecting that, but it was fine with him. He watched her run for a couple of beats and then screamed and raced after her.

She ran through the tide, arms crazy, water flaring in her footfalls.

He caught her and hurled her to the sand. "Run into the ocean!" he shouted. "All right, you can have your ocean!"

He grabbed her foot when she tried to kick him and flipped her and dragged her, belly down, into the water. She turned over, opened her mouth to scream, and he grabbed her shoulders and pushed her under the night-dark water. He watched her drown, as though it were a dream. Her hair fanned gracefully behind her head. She was frowning, a pinch of flesh between her perfect brows, but her expression was one of pale irritation more than pain. Her thin white blouse lost all its color revealing her perfect breasts, the pale flesh of her shoulders, the red-and-yellow rainbow.

The rainbow tattoo. "Because it's my name," she had

said. "Gold. Rene Gold. You know, the pot of *gold* at the end of the rainbow."

Allan stumbled backward and Rene, hands foaming the water as she yelled herself upright, fell forward, and clawed her way up the beach. She rolled over on her back and coughed.

Allan crawled to her. "Oh God, Jesus."

Rene launched herself at him, clawed his face, bit his ear, would have scratched his eyes out but realized, then, that he would have let her. He had gone limp. She rolled onto her back. "What the fuck is the matter with you?"

"I thought you were untrue to me," he said.

She rolled on her side to look at him. "Untrue? Where do you get off? We aren't even dating, you asshole."

Allan produced the photograph.

They both stared at it for a long time. Finally, Rene said, "You are a total moron. First of all, Harry's not my type; I mean, he's like a dentist or something, and second, that's not my body. Forget the missing tattoo, that body is just plain different. And third, how come this Harry has twice as much hair? Don't even try to figure that out. I'll tell you. This is no doubt a picture of him and his ex, taken way back in the good old days, and they stuck my head on his old lady. They probably said, 'Nobody's stupid enough to fall for this, but what's the harm in trying?' "

"Can they do that?" Allan felt a hole inside him bigger than the sky. He had hurt, almost killed, his beloved because he was a jealous fool, an angry, vicious monster.

"Can they do that?" Rene sighed. She flopped on her back again. "Fucker almost kills me and he wants to know, 'Can they do that?' Shit. You moron," she sighed. "I love you. Don't you know anything?"

"What?"

"I was going to tell you I love you."

Allan didn't know what to say to that. He lay silent. Finally, Rene spoke again. "Look, it's Arbus."

The monkey scampered up to Rene, clutched her hand and tugged.

"I think he wants us to come with him."

Jeanne sat on the edge of the bed. She picked up the phone and tried Harry's room again. Still no answer. She was right to come here, every energized cell said as much. But to what purpose?

Impatient, crazy for something to happen, Jeanne picked up the television remote and punched the power button. A cartoon was in progress, some poorly animated crap with a laugh track. She punched through the channels: a documentary on endangered owls, an infomercial, a Charlie Chan movie, people in small torpedolike cars (racing apparently), a jeans commercial, a sitcom about a nursing home—and there was Amy.

Her daughter's face was pressed close to the screen, and when the electric crackle ushered her in, her eyes widened and she backed away from the screen. "Mommy!" she shouted.

Jeanne stood up, dropping the remote.

"Amy?"

Her daughter leaned forward again. She pressed her hands and face against the glass and spoke. "Don't let Daddy change it back!" she said. "Dooooooon't . . ." Her mouth was a round howl, and her small fists began to thump the glass and the television began to rock on its stand.

"Honey," Jeanne said. "It will be all right. I'll tell—"

The television fell forward, yanking its cord from the

wall socket with an urgent *pock* and white sparks.

Jeanne ran to the television, turned it upright. The tube had not shattered. She fumbled for the cord. "Amy, Amy, Amy ... " she was saying. There were tears in her eyes and her hands were shaking as she pushed the plug back into the socket.

"Please."

No picture. She saw the round O of moisture where Amy's lips had pressed against the inside of the glass.

She stood up, found the door, and stumbled into the hall. She heard her name called and, looking up, she saw Harry running toward her.

CHaPTeR TWeNTY-SiX

❦ ❦ ❦ ❦ ❦ ❦ ❦ ❦ ❦ ❦ ❦ ❦

"THIS IS REALLY splendid," Gloria Gill said.

The hotel suite had been transformed into a laboratory. The arrangement, being temporary and established in mere hours, was not perfect. One had to be careful not to trip over the tangle of electrical cords or to step on the hoses bringing water from the bathroom, and there was a certain incongruity to all this porcelain and stainless steel amid the hotel's dowdy armchairs and faded rugs. Surely the St. Petersburg Arms had never seen a coffee table like the one that now resided in the center of the room and which could be used for serving drinks and snacks but was more commonly employed in the dissecting of cadavers.

Andrew Blaine smiled indulgently as Gloria, dressed in black tights and skirt and blouse, skipped to the gurney and spoke to the girl. "All this for you."

Emily Engel made no response. She lay, strapped firmly

on her back, her eyes closed. A faint trickle of saliva leaked from her mouth.

Gloria glared at Karl, who was sitting on the sofa next to Al Butts. "Really. A girl in a wheelchair and you have to bring her down with a tranquilizer gun. Two grown men."

"We keep telling you," Karl said, "she wasn't in any wheelchair. She was walking down the beach. Anyway, you're going to grind her up in a fine powder, what do you care if she's even alive?"

Gloria Gill rolled her eyes and turned to Blaine for moral support. "Andrew, I am glad there are men like you in the world or I would despair of the sex. I would say they had no soul at all, none." Gloria walked over to the laser scalpel and ran her hands over the polished machinery.

"Ms. Engel may not have the intellect to contribute to the body of scientific knowledge with her insights, but we all do her an injustice if we assume that she can't appreciate the very real contribution she will be making. I think she deserves to participate fully in the historic moment."

She plucked the laser scalpel from its clip and clicked it on. A small red beam of light speared the carpet. She clicked it off, instantly, and stared as a thread of gray smoke rose up from the floor. She giggled. "Andrew Blaine, come here and let me give you a hug. I ask you to do the impossible, and you trump it. This is just the thing. And Revel makes these! The gods have got to be smiling on us."

Andrew Blaine walked across the room and took her in his arms and hugged her. He bit her ear and she squealed in merriment and the scalpel leapt out of her hand, bobbing lazily in the air on its long, stalked neck like some indulgent serpent.

"Please," Gloria said, pushing him away, grabbing the scalpel, returning it to its clip, and brushing her dress demurely, "We aren't alone."

"You guys can go," Blaine said, turning to Karl and Al.

"No problem," Karl said, standing up. "You give us the money, we are on our way to the bank."

Blaine's eyes narrowed, sensing insubordination.

Karl kept grinning. "That was the understanding. I'm strictly contract. Me and Butts, we don't get benefits or nothing."

Gloria interrupted. "You all have to leave," she said. "I've got work to do now. You menfolks will just be in the way." She pointed imperiously at the door to the adjoining suite. "Adieu."

"Come on," Blaine said, returned to good humor by his paramour's saucy manner. "You gentlemen do have to get your money, and Dr. Gill does have business to attend to."

They walked through the door into the other room.

Gloria turned away and was pleasantly surprised to discover the girl staring at her. "Well, Emily Engel, you're awake," Gloria said. "About time, sleepyhead. I guess we can get started then."

On the other side of room 317, a man, a woman, and a monkey crouched, listening.

"This is the room," Rene whispered. "She just said Emily's name." Rene reached up and gripped the doorknob.

"It's locked," she said.

Allan stood up. "They'll have another key at the desk," he said.

Rene frowned. "They won't give it to you."

"Yes they will," Allan said.

Rene smiled at her champion. "Yeah. Maybe they will."

Gloria Gill approached the girl. "This won't hurt at all," she said. "First, I am going to drain your blood, which, of course, will be where we part company, as it were. It will be like falling asleep. I'm sorry, but I don't have time for torture." She giggled. "What's that?"

The girl was opening her mouth.

Dr. Gloria Gill leaned closer. "Are you trying to say something, dear? I wasn't aware that you spoke, but if you do, by all means share your thoughts with Dr. Gill."

Gloria Gill jerked back. "Goodness," she said. She laughed, a good sport. "I guess I asked for that. You nasty little cat." The girl had spit in Gloria's eye.

"I'll just have to be careful, I guess, just . . . dear me." She couldn't see out of her left eye. Well, perhaps . . . She darted into the bathroom, jerked the tap on, and splashed water into the blind eye. Then she looked up in the mirror.

Her left eye had turned gray, gray with small, blue-black flecks. She could still make out the etched lines of pupil and iris . . . it was remarkably like an eye carved from stone. She touched her eye: slightly gritty, cold. It weighted that side of her face, filled her with a queasy conviction that it could move, could roll . . . elsewhere.

No, the girl had tricked her mind. This was a trick of the mind, that's all, and when the girl was dead the trick would collapse like a tent without poles.

Gloria left the bathroom. Her eye didn't hurt, actually. She smiled at the girl whose ragamuffin head was turned to stare at her. *A prideful bitch,* Gloria thought. "I'm not impressed," she said. "Although I am a little upset. I do believe that this sort of disrespect for science cannot go unpunished." Gloria unhooked the scalpel. "No pain, no gain."

The door swung open and a giant entered the room. Someone ran toward the gurney where Emily Engel lay.

Gloria recognized the giant now. One of the Ecknazine set. She clicked the laser beam on and swung it in a wide arc. She'd disembowel the bastard; he'd trip over his own steaming guts. Just watch this baby work.

Some creature leapt up to meet the burning beam, howled as it flayed the air, and seemed to explode in blood and burning fur, tumbling into Gill, knocking her back. The scalpel slipped through her fingers, spun away.

The dead monkey embraced her chest, its grinning death mask savagely triumphant.

She thrust the corpse from her and turned to flee.

"Andrew!" she screamed. Where were they? Surely— she saw the girl Emily Engel, freed from the gurney, standing with her back against the door to the adjoining room, her arms raised like a kid's crossing guard, just a frail, teenage girl, her expression one of concentration, as might befit such an office, quietly holding the door against the hurled bodies of the men on the other side.

Then someone caught Dr. Gloria Gill by the arm and lifted her, and she looked down as she flowed smoothly through the air and saw herself plummeting headfirst toward the steel dissecting table.

Allan turned away from her crumpled body and saw Rene coming toward him.

"Allan," she said, "you are the—Allan!" She was screaming now, running toward him with her hands out. Allan saw it:

a red blur of neon, it drifted by once, twice, three times, mosquito bites. She came rushing at him and pushed him down, an easy task for his legs had turned to liquid and there was blood in his mouth and he was going to . . .

Rene grabbed the bobbing scalpel and shut it off. She dropped to her knees again. Allan's throat seemed a scarf of blood. There was a dreamy look in his eyes, as though he still didn't get it, didn't fucking get it. The moron.

Rene screamed at the ceiling.

Downstairs at the St. Petersburg Arms, the desk clerk looked up, not realizing that he was the last link between two very tentative realities. He was preparing to call the police. Some big jerk had leaned over the counter, grabbed the key to room 317, and said, "Emergency" like you could say "Emergency" and do something illegal, it was some magic password or something. The desk clerk had his hand on the phone when he saw the man and woman enter the lobby. The woman was expensively dressed but wore no shoes. The man was tall and moved with an odd, jointed gait that was disconcerting. He seemed to be wrapped in a cloud of smoke, and one hand did, in fact, hold three burning cigarettes.

They approached the desk.

"We are returned," the man said.

The desk clerk said his last words. "I'm sorry, but there is no smoking in this building."

Roald Peake picked up the letter opener that lay on just the other side of the counter, and stabbed the man through the eye, killing him instantly. The lobby of the St. Petersburg Arms disappeared and Castle Grimfast shivered into focus, apocalypse lizards skittering across the damp stone floor that stretched into gray shadows. In the distance, three of the Less-Than tortured a Wire Kitten with sharp sticks. Their laughter echoed hollowly through the moist air, the sound you'd get from beating a rusty oil drum.

"Oh, it's good to be home," Lord Draining said, inhaling the scent of Mal Ganvern.

Gabriel was not to be distracted. "Where is my son?" she demanded.

Castle Grimfast took possession upstairs too, and Rene watched the walls turn to dirty gray. Her beloved's blood now leaked into a faded rug of some ancient design. All the gleaming lab equipment was gone and Gloria Gill lay prone on the floor, garbed in layers of black—the dowager, of course, she was the Black Dowager—and in the tarlike shadows, steel, razor-clawed creatures rattled fitfully.

Emily Engel, with no reason to bar a door that no longer existed, moved away from the wall and looked at her surroundings with grim satisfaction.

"All the Believers are here," she said.

CHAPTER TWENTY-SEVEN

❀ ❀ ❀ ❀ ❀ ❀ ❀ ❀ ❀ ❀ ❀ ❀

HARRY HAD BEEN speaking to Robert Furman immediately before looking up and seeing Jeanne running toward him.

They had been coming up the wide, carpeted stairs that ascended from the lobby to the first floor, and Furman had been saying, "When you wrote this original *Zod Wallop* that you speak of, it must have been a group effort—a kind of *channeling,* to use a word in some disrepute, but one that seems to define the phenomenon. So it is colored by Raymond and Rene and Emily and Allan and—probably to its artistic misfortune—myself. And we all have our counterparts in the story, I suppose."

Harry nodded as he walked down the hall. "Oh, yes. Rene is the court beauty, Eve, and Raymond is a wizard named Mettle and Emily is the Frozen Princess and you are the Duke of Flatbend." Harry paused then, struck by a question so obvious that he wondered why he hadn't—and he *hadn't*—given it any thought. "Who am I?"

"Beg your pardon?" Furman said, stopping and looking at Harry.

"I mean, in *Zod Wallop*. If everyone else has a counterpart, then—"

"I should think that was quite clear," Furman said. "That is, I'm assuming the published version is a reworking of the original version. In both you are, after all, the author. You are Blodkin."

Blodkin! Mad, ineffectual deity, besotted with self-importance, obsessed with the rituals of his worship, self-involved on a cosmic level.

Harry had no time to reflect on the answer, for it was then that Jeanne burst from her room. Harry, looking away from Furman at the sound of the door banging open, turned, saw her, and ran to her. They held each other and Jeanne shouted in his ear—somehow she needed to shout for the hall was filled with a roaring wind. "I've seen Amy. She fears you want to change—"

A black thunder rolled over her words, and Harry looked up to see the walls of the St. Petersburg Arms shimmer into stone. The skulls of grotesque beasts with corkscrew tusks were bolted to the walls, retreating in a line down either side of the long hall. Balanced on each tusk was a glowing orb, the source of its light being, Harry knew, the blood of a Swamp Grendel.

I'm in Grimfast, Harry thought.

He turned and saw a man approaching him in a flowing robe. For a moment he did not recognize Raymond in the pointed hat, the ridiculous robe, and exaggerated mustache.

"The Contest is at hand, my Lord. I fear the Princess has awakened too early and may be ruled by her rage. Still, we must strive."

A scream of terrible sadness and loss arose and Raymond looked up to the floor above. "Quickly," he said, taking Harry's arm.

Harry saw the troubled faces of Jeanne and Helen and Furman. They looked to him for some answer, their eyes full of fear and confusion. "We are in Zod Wallop, in Grimfast, the castle of Lord Draining," he said. "I don't know why or how."

Harry saw that they wore the costumes of his imagination: Helen in her voluminous, green dress and jangle of turquoise jewelry, Furman in his parody of splendor and heaped honors, multicolored ribbons and large gold and silver medals, and Jeanne—Jeanne wore a dress of some golden metallic hue that had no place in Zod Wallop or anywhere else. Harry looked down at his own body and saw that he wore what he had been wearing before (jeans, a T-shirt) and thought, *Why not?* God shouldn't have to nod to fashion.

The mournful cry came again and Raymond shouted. "My Lord. All haste. Please!"

They ran up the stairs in the wake of the wizard.

Rene was aware that someone was touching her shoulder. She turned and looked up at Emily.

"He was always pissed off about something," Rene said. "Always angry. I would have been cool with it, though, just waited it out. It wasn't ever meanness, you know. There wasn't anything small about Allan, not anything small and mean like most people. We would have been all right, Allan and me, because—" Rene looked down at her beloved and pressed a hand to his forehead, as though checking for a fever. "Okay, he was a fuck-up. You meet some guy in a nut ward, he's maybe going to have some personal problems. But, you know what? My heart beat faster the first time I saw him. I think that counts for some goddamn something, don't you? I think—" Rene paused, coughed, looked up again into Emily's amazing eyes.

A strange compulsion caused Rene to lift her hand and touch Emily's pale, full lips. They were cold. Rene moved her hand to brush Emily's cheek, as a lover might, although her hand was not moved by desire but wonder. How, Rene wondered, could simply looking at this face hurt so fiercely? Emily's expression was calm, her eyes were the precise blue of that mouthwash Rene had drunk the day of her last suicide attempt . . . Rene put the thought away as a tear left the blue eye and moved slowly toward her finger and touched it.

The tear burned Rene's finger and she pulled her hand away.

"Sister," Emily said, moving closer. Her lips barely moved, but her voice was big, the biggest voice Rene had ever heard, bigger than her father when he was full of Jesus and Jim Beam. The voice filled Rene, like wind filling a sail.

"Sister," Emily said, reaching out her hand. "We have to leave this room. Soon everyone will be roaring. Everyone will be taking and killing and plundering. They will be full of their contest; the Vile Contenders will strive against each other. Warriors will war. They will make Great Enterprise. They will puff themselves up with false purpose."

Rene felt herself being lifted to her feet. She turned and looked at Allan, lying there still. She saw the monkey, curled at his feet, the way a cat might snuggle (cats always seeking to meld with the sleeping).

"Yes," Emily said. "Your champion is slain. But we have two more that will champion us. While all Zod Wallop is full of its importance and strife, we will find the Cold One and the Abyss Dweller and we will have our revenge."

Rene did not understand completely, but she believed completely. Together they left the room.

They were gone when Harry and the others followed Raymond into the room.

Now Raymond screamed, falling on his knees. "Allan! Lord Arbus!" He moaned. He lifted the bloody monkey in his arms. He began to sob inconsolably. His weeping was wild, his nose running, his breath coming in long, asthmatic wheezes. The walls of the room seemed to expand and contract in sympathy with his labored gasps.

"Dear God," Helen Kurtis said, kneeling beside Raymond. "Oh Raymond." She hugged him, the two of them on their knees in their great billowing inventions (his illuminated wizard's robes, her buttresses of starched fabric and oversized bracelets that Harry had spent hours illustrating). Jeanne stood silently behind the grieving pair. Her mouth was slightly open, as in some photo snapped at tragedy's first tick, before the realization of horror had settled to the heart, and Harry was rocked cruelly by a vision of that day, that beach.

Their lovemaking had just ended when the girl came to the door of the beach house and said hurry, hurry, and oh did they, and they ran down the beach and everyone (later) said it was not their fault—although no one knew they were making love; no one knew that—because the boy was after all a lifeguard and the girl, the baby-sitter, came recommended by everyone and if later people said he might have been drinking well maybe he hadn't been, others said that he had mended his ways and why speak ill of the dead because both were sadly dead and all you could say was what a tragedy and get on (why don't you get on?) with it.

Raymond's voice, full of new, booming authority, pulled Harry back into the room.

"Never," Raymond roared, still cradling the monkey, rocking on his knees, animated by grief, "have two such warriors lived more gloriously or died more righteously. Lord Arbus, how the days will dim without you, best of best men, apes, all creatures of light and freedom.

"Oh Allan, great knight, passionate-hearted soldier! Oh, you have left a king-sized hole, a hole all the angels could fall through. Robbed of your loyalty, your pride, your energy, I do not wish to rise up and continue. It is only your memory, your still echoing spirit, that will not let me rest, that urges me to the end of this enterprise. Until then, prince." Raymond leaned forward and kissed the dead boy's lips. Gently, he lowered the monkey to the floor and arranged it next to Allan. Raymond stood up.

Harry heard a sob and turned to see Robert Furman. The man was sagging badly, shaking. His mouth hung open; he looked like a man who had suffered several severe strokes and lost the efficient use of his faculties, and when he saw Harry staring at him, he said, "I brought this on, thinking I knew what Em needed." He looked at Harry apologetically. "I've got to find her."

He turned and wobbled out of the room. Harry thought of stopping him, but thought, *Why?* He had no better plan himself. Let Furman seek his niece and make what amends he needed to make. Harry knew who the real culprit was, where the true designer of so much evil lay. He did not have to look far to find him. Mad Blodkin: Harry Gainesborough.

Harry heard sounds of explosion far away, and screams,

and the thunder of hooves. Did they have guns in Zod Wallop? Did they have horses?

No, Harry thought. They had no guns, but they had explosive gases and fire and cutting and rending weapons and magics that could kill at short range, and as for horses—the Less-Than rode the hideously mutated creatures called Mires that had been created by Lord Draining's dreaded Splicers.

Harry had never actually drawn a Mire, so he had no idea how they would look. They would be ugly, of course, and move with a quick, lopsided gait, as though always stumbling.

Stop it, he told himself.

I'm strapped to some table somewhere, he thought. Out of my mind raving, pitied by nurses who are inured to my screams. A loony in a bin. None of this is real.

Someone pushed past Harry—a woman in a tight red dress that clung to her svelte form, her hair in black ringlets—and shouted, "I will not, I absolutely will not tolerate this, Allan! Get up this minute."

Allan would not get up—wretched boy—and Gabriel went to him and stared down at him. Dealing with him had made her very tired and so she lay down next to him.

"I can hardly breathe," she told him. "You've run me such a ragged race, with your escapades, one after another, and your tantrums and . . . oh, I'm just exhausted, Allan." She had a thought then, and she sat up and looked at her sullen, spiteful boy and brushed his hair back and said, "Suppose I read a story. I've got it here somewhere." And she pulled the book from her silken bag and read:

Rock yawned. "Gotta get moving," Rock said. A couple of hundred million years went by. A rock is always slow to take action. A rock watches an oak grow from a sapling to a towering tree, and it's a flash and a dazzle in the mind of a rock. *What was that?* Rock thinks. Or maybe, *Huh?*

Harry listened. And remembered how Amy had giggled. "Daddy, a tree doesn't grow in a flash," she had said.

He had read the beginning of this book to her. He remembered now. He had been writing it before Dr. Moore had urged him to write. Yes. He had been telling the story and he had stopped when Amy died.

Harry ran out of the room. The grim hallway was littered with bodies. Some dark, furred thing the size of a large dog snuffled amid the corpses. It heard Harry's approach and turned, regarding Harry with three small, red eyes. Harry snatched one of the glowing orbs that lighted the hall and threw it at the wall above the creature. The ball exploded with a cascade of arcing light and the creature grunted and lumbered away.

"Harry, wait!"

He turned and saw Jeanne coming toward him, golden, wending her way through the gore of shattered bodies.

"Go back!" Harry shouted.

"No."

He waited then. She took his arm. "You're going down to the ocean, aren't you?"

"I have to," Harry said.

Jeanne turned him and looked in his eyes. He saw them as he had never seen them before, not fearless—fear was certainly there—but filled with conviction, clear, dark, as luminous and mysterious as the universe itself.

"*We* have to," Jeanne said. "We."

CHaPTeR TWeNTY-eiGHT

❦ ❦ ❦ ❦ ❦ ❦ ❦ ❦ ❦ ❦ ❦ ❦ ❦

THE VAST HALL of Grimfast was littered with dead bodies. More of the furred beasts moved among the dead, and apocalypse lizards scrambled up tapestries, carrying choice morsels of human flesh.

Neither beast nor human hindered Harry and Jeanne, and they moved gingerly through the carnage and came out of the castle and into the night and the salt wind.

This beach smelled of death and acid. Harry looked up and saw that the pale night sky contained multitudes of black, sailing shapes, a malevolent swarm of Ralewings.

Harry turned and saw Lord Draining come from the side of Castle Grimfast where the stables were lodged. He was mounted on a Mire—*so that's what they look like*, Harry thought, with a shudder, like creatures made imperfectly from clay by some slow and stupid god—and a hundred of the Less-Than crowded behind the Vile Contender.

He held a long pike in one hand, and thrust upon its

spiked end, one on top of the other, were two heads, one pale, grinning and sporting a crew cut, the other dark complected with a black mustache.

"Traitors," Draining said, casting the pike to the ground. "Bahden and Butts. I do not condemn them for enterprise. I do not condemn them at all. May they make a good meal for Rawnworms."

"And now," Draining said, "for the end of the games. My dear adversary." The hooded Less-Than parted in a wave, and a man stumbled through.

"The Gorelord himself," Draining said, pointing. An old man stood up and began to run. He limped as he ran, already maimed, his forces destroyed. Draining laughed. "What poor sport," he roared. "Without his legions, what poor sport."

Andrew Blaine ran blindly down the beach. His reason was almost gone. Somehow he had been drugged, he knew that much. This could not be real. He had been in a suite at the St. Petersburg Arms. And suddenly—and this was when the needle must have touched his throat—it turned to a dank, stinking room of stone and rotting wood and mold and a hallway filled with dead bodies, hardly human, and beasts and he had watched as Karl Bahden and Al Butts had been killed by strange, boneless men wielding swords that were wider at the end than at the hilt.

Now he ran and he wondered what drug was so powerful, who owned it, and—something pierced his back as though, in truth, the hallucination of Peake that sat upon a strange beast and leaned forward with a killing lance were real.

Impossible. But the simulation elicited a scream and a mind-destroying applause of pain.

*   *   *

Harry turned away from the gruesome spectacle. "Run." They fled toward the beach.

"Wait, my friends!" Lord Draining bellowed. "Don't abandon us." And he urged his mount forward and the Less-Than surged after him.

Jeanne and Harry ran into the surf. It was rougher than it had been before, perhaps because Zod Wallop's Ocean of Responsibility was just naturally more turbulent than the Gulf of Mexico or perhaps because Harry's beating heart churned it.

Lord Draining paused at the edge of the water and dismounted. "Where do you intend to go?" he bellowed. "There is no domain that is not mine." He drew a small crossbow—his skill was legend—and marched into the water, his cape of desiccated hands fanning out as he made long strides toward deeper water.

"Your pretty wife first," he said, and Harry turned to see him slip a short arrow into the crossbow. Harry looked for Jeanne and saw that she was twenty feet behind him in the waves.

"Leave them be!" a voice roared, and Harry saw Raymond, standing at the edge of the water.

Lord Draining turned. "Well," he said. "Come in. The water's fine."

"I cannot go in the water," Raymond said, sounding querulous and young. "I'm sorry, but my mother says I am never, never ever to go in the water again."

"Well, how sad. If you can't come in the water, you can't play."

Raymond, in his foolish wizard's clothes, looked dismayed, bested in an argument by a smarter child.

A new voice boomed across the water: "Raymond cannot play, but we can."

Three figures approached from farther up the beach. The Less-Than moved away quickly, for although they would have attacked the women with impunity, they feared the Cold One more than death.

"Princess," Lord Draining said. "I see you are fully recovered. Go with my blessings. I'll give you your own kingdom to the east."

"Of kingdoms there will be none," Emily said. "Of love and hate and triumph and despair there will be none. There will only be Blodkin's vouchsafed gift. There will be the stone. And the stone will not hear the stone and it will be all a silence that the wind will rule and the Ocean of Responsibility will be for no one to charter and the Abyss Dweller will carry the Cold One across all known habitations until the silence is complete."

"You must think about this," Lord Draining said. Harry heard fear in that smooth, predatory voice. "This is no revenge, this nothingness. There are powers you could have, and pleasures. Surely you have pined for pleasure in your trance? You must reconsider."

Emily turned to Rene and said, "Sister, what think you?"

"Fuck em," Rene said.

They held the hands of the Cold One and entered the water. As they marched forward, Harry heard a sound that seemed—he could think of nothing closer in his experience— like elephants trumpeting.

He watched a wave roll toward him. He watched it slow with a rumbling sound then stop, the last outstretched fleck of foam snapping off a white, dime-sized pebble that struck Harry's cheek with painful force and bounced across the now frozen surface of the ocean.

Harry could not move. He was lodged to the waist in the stone sea.

The Less-Than had turned and were fleeing the beach.

"You are not being reasonable," Lord Draining said. He too was captured by the viselike grip of the ocean. He pointed the crossbow at Emily. "I could kill you."

The Frozen Princess laughed. "Oh, death. You threaten death? Really. Look who is coming." On the beach the sand was spinning, thrown into a thousand whirlwinds by the beating wings of Ralewings. The creatures, thousands of them, spiraled into a sudden, yawning blackness.

"No," Lord Draining said. "You don't mean to bring the Abyss Dweller."

"I mean to ride him across all the lands," Emily said.

Gabriel was reading to her son when the little girl tugged her sleeve. "Excuse me," the girl said.

"Yes?"

"I'm Lydia."

"Oh, yes," Gabriel said. She recognized this girl now. She hadn't ever warmed to this Lydia.

"I'm sorry your son is dead," the girl said. She was dressed in a white, lacy dress. *A little too cute,* Gabriel thought. Children, even girls, should be dressed more practically. There was no denying there was dirt in the world.

"Oh, he's not dead at all," Gabriel said. "He often sleeps so soundly you can't wake him."

"He's dead," Lydia said.

"Well, that's rude. I'm sure—"

"It's rude and I'm sorry and"—here the girl suddenly

shouted at the top of her lungs, her hands small fists—"he's *dead!*"

The shout made tears jump to Gabriel's eyes. "He is," Gabriel said. "He is dead, I suppose."

"We have to go," the girl said, and she took Gabriel's hand. "We have to go talk to my daddy."

Gabriel allowed herself to be led from the room.

Helen Kurtis had left the room because she could not abide listening to the crazy woman read to her dead son from a book that was now a reality. It was all sad but Helen was also tired and sick of so much strangeness—strangeness was not a diet she could stomach—and when she found old Robert Furman stumbling around in the hall and muttering that he needed to speak to his niece she shook him and said, "Well, you can see she's not here," and brought him along. She had been disgusted and tired, and as she watched the Ralewings pour into a great black hole in the sand and saw her friends stuck like sticks in an ocean that had simply stopped, she felt her terror had been usurped by a cosmic, godlike irritation with the impossible. She sat in the sand next to where Robert Furman slumped, and sobbed bitterly.

CHaPTeR TWeNTY-NiNe

HARRY HAD NEVER drawn the Abyss Dweller either, but he had no interest in seeing what form it had taken. He *would* see it though. Another of its names was The Thing You Had To Look Upon. The last of the Ralewings had descended into the pit, which was silent and black and curiously geometrical, smooth-sided, almost a rectangle.

A woman and a girl moved around the black expanse and walked toward the ocean.

Harry felt something hot in his throat. He knew. "Amy!" he shouted.

The girl broke free of the woman's hand and ran quickly across the sand and came running and jumping across the frozen ocean.

Harry reached to touch her as she ran to him, but she stopped before coming within his arms. "I can't hug you," she said.

"You are my daughter," Harry said, "Amy."

"No, I'm Lydia. And Amy can't go back and you know that. Wanting her back is a poofum wish."

A poofum wish, of course, was any impossible wish that could cause great mischief—as anyone who had ever read *The Everything Wish* knew.

"Amy, I love you."

Lydia looked up at the sky. "It's all your fault. Just because of a single bad thing, you want to hurt everything with a hurt so bad that there will be a big nothing forever and forever and forever. I hate you!"

"No, darling, I just—" He managed to grab her arm and so he dragged her to him, hugging her. "I want you safe, I want this nightmare—"

She turned and screamed in his face, spittle flying. "You can have anything you want. You are Blodkin, aren't you? And you just want bad things."

Harry looked up as several drops of water thudded his head. The sky was full of clouds, a storm was approaching.

"Let me go," Lydia said.

"I just want—"

"Let her go."

Harry turned. It was Jeanne. Jeanne was shouting at him. The rain opened up then, like that, and threw a curtain between them.

"She is our daughter!" Harry shouted.

"She is dead!" Jeanne shouted.

Harry hated her then.

The rain made the stone waves slippery and treacherous, but Gabriel came on. She knew her course and she held to it. Rain hid her advance, and she came up behind him. He was peering off in the other direction, but he turned at the last moment.

"My son is dead!" she screamed. She carried the shattered tip of a wave, a cold, deadly pyramid the size of her palm, and as Lord Draining turned, she brought it down. The first blow punched a hole in his forehead, and she hit again, smashing his vile nose, and then he was raising something—a man of cruel sinew and bone, hard as a scorpion to kill—and her jaw exploded in pain and she was gone—

Lord Draining pushed her away. He had fired the crossbow upward. Bitch. Show her. He felt weak though, woozy. . . . Not like him to let a couple of blows tire him so. Still, there was blood everywhere. And he was blind with rain. He could see lightning dancing on the surface of the stone sea. He coughed. He shouldn't have done that. He pitched forward.

And died. Two feet from him, Gabriel lay dead, sprawled on her back.

"Let me go!" Lydia shouted. The ocean began to move. Harry felt his legs move slightly in their stone leggings. He hugged Amy to him. He could not let her go . . . not again.

Emily felt the Cold One release her hand. "Wait," Emily shouted, but her champion had turned and was wading toward the shore. Emily turned and reached for Rene. They embraced. "I sense a loss," Emily said. "Two Believers are dead."

Rene said nothing and Emily hugged her close and spoke in her ear, "But fear not, Sister, we have the strongest of them still, we have the Engine of it All and he will see us to our reward."

* * *

"I have to go!" Lydia screamed. "I have to close the hole. It is my job to close the hole. You better let me do it, Daddy. You better!"

"No," Harry said, "I have you. We must get to shore."

The animate world was asserting itself in the Cold One's absence. Its transformation was not perfect or complete, and pebbles savagely pummeled Harry's shoulders as he hugged his daughter protectively and staggered toward shore. He saw Jeanne ahead of him, already being helped to shore by Helen and Robert Furman.

He had reached the shore himself when he stumbled and Lydia broke free. She was on her feet immediately and running, and Harry ran after her.

He knew what she intended to do. Wasn't he a god? Wasn't he Blodkin, designer of Zod Wallop? Yes, he knew what she was going to do. She was going to do her job. She was going to dive into the hole and be gone forever and ever because it would close behind her leaving nothing but a lovely, sun-licked stretch of sand for bikini-clad beauties to tan their tummies on.

Only Harry Gainesborough wasn't going to let that happen.

He ran after her, gaining. The rain had slowed, and he could see her, see the distance she had to the hole, and he knew that he could catch her in time.

"Harry!" his wife screamed behind him. "Let her go. Can't you see?"

See what? he wondered. See the hopelessness, the pain, the death that had come between Jeanne—he loved her then, he loved her now—and himself, see . . .

"Harry," Jeanne shouted, "if you stop her, It will come

272

out and there will be nothing! Nothing!"

And Harry knew that that was true too—it was the sort of thing a god would know—and he knew, maker of symbols, that the Abyss Dweller was nothing but death, resignation, apathy.

So what? Maker of symbols, there were none that could save him. He could not let his daughter die.

Through the rain, he saw the hole. He was within ten feet of his daughter's perfect shoulders. A few long strides and he would be able to snag a bare foot.

He saw the black rectangle, the Abyss Dweller's entrance to this world, and he recognized the way it widened, and he stopped. He stopped and let his daughter run on. He stopped and turned away, not caring to watch her fly away forever.

He had seen the coffin shape and understood.

CHaPTeR THiRTY

HE RACED TOWARD Jeanne, standing there in the slow rain, and he caught her in his arms, this time, and this time he did not leave before the coffin lid was closed but stayed, holding his bride, his companion on the earth, the one he was born to champion despite all evils, even the senseless and terrifying death of a daughter.

Behind them Grimfast Castle shivered and melted and the sun blazed and it was the minister who came to them and, touching Harry's arm, escorted them out of the church and into the waiting hearse.

He would have to watch the tiny coffin lowered into the ground. He had not done that before; he did not think he could bear to do such a thing. He knew now that he could.

And he knew that, tomorrow, he would continue work on *Zod Wallop* and that Jeanne might find that strange, so shattered would she be.

"Work, the day after her funeral?" she would ask.

Jeanne would be resistant to therapy too, and perhaps she would always resist that. She was a private person.

But she would understand his seeking help.

He would seek out a group at Harwood Psychiatric Institute. He would pay whatever money it took to participate. He had money and he wasn't above using it to put a little pressure in the proper place.

He would seek out the others. In particular, he would seek out a fan of his, a rather wide-eyed young man with a mustache named Raymond Story.

E P i L o G u e

⚘ ⚘ ⚘ ⚘ ⚘ ⚘ ⚘ ⚘ ⚘ ⚘ ⚘ ⚘ ⚘

ALLAN GOT MAD and walked out of group, but Rene ran after him and brought him back.

"Would you like to talk about it?" the counselor asked.

Allan glared at the man.

Rene spoke. "Allan wants to know where Raymond is. Nobody around here ever tells us anything. You say we should support each other, be a goddamn family, and then Raymond's gone and nobody says anything, like he was never here, like this is fucking Russia or something and people can just disappear."

"Ah." The counselor sighed, sucked on his unlit pipe. "You are right Rene, Allan. I apologize. We just hoped . . . well, we don't know where they are, either."

"They?"

"Emily Engel is gone too. We think—excuse me, Harry, but you seem to find all this very amusing."

Harry, caught smiling, nodded his head. "I guess I do. I

have been in touch with the two fugitives. In fact, they are staying with Jeanne and me."

The counselor blinked. "Staying with you?"

"Emily and Raymond are my greatest fans, you know. A writer likes to have such fans close at hand when moments of doubt strike. In any event, I have two announcements to make, both fairly momentous, I think. Yesterday, Emily spoke to me."

"Spoke?" The counselor leaned forward. "What did she say?"

"*Zod Wallop.*"

The counselor leaned back and frowned. "And what is that supposed to mean?"

"It was a request, actually, that I continue reading to her from a book I am in the process of writing. I was quite flattered, of course, that her first attempt at communication would be prompted by this desire."

"And what does Zod Wallop mean?"

"Well, that's not precisely the question. It doesn't *mean* so much as *act* on the heart. It is an act of love."

"You are not communicating clearly, Harry."

Harry shrugged. "Perhaps. Anyway, my second announcement is perfectly straightforward, is, in fact, in the form of an invitation. I have them here." He opened the briefcase on his lap and handed the envelopes around.

Rene ripped hers open while Allan simply blinked at his. She gasped, smiled.

She ran her finger over the raised type.

Mr. Robert Furman wishes
to announce the
marriage of his neice
Emily Engel
to
Mr. Raymond Story
on

———

She looked up and saw Allan still glowering at the unopened envelope in his hands.

"Go on, open it," she said. "It's not the end of the world."